T0149207

A killer's Instinct

IN THE NAME OF LOVE AND LOSS.

SOPHIA ALEXANDRA

iUniverse®

A KILLER'S INSTINCT
IN THE NAME OF LOVE AND LOSS.

iUniverse books may be ordered through booksellers or by contacting:

iUniverse
1663 Liberty Drive
Bloomington, IN 47403
www.iuniverse.com
1-800-Authors (1-800-288-4677)

ISBN: 978-1-4917-9437-1 (sc)
ISBN: 978-1-4917-9438-8 (e)

Library of Congress Control Number: 2016905752

Print information available on the last page.

iUniverse rev. date: 05/13/2016

BOOK 1

A Killers Instinct:
Fifty-Six and Tara's story part 1

CHAPTER 1 prologue

"White suits...

Soaked in blood...

I wanted him to know how I felt.

But love is a silent killer.

And I didn't want to cry anymore than I already had."

~ Tara Jones

CHAPTER 1

I'm here now.

In God's loving arms, I tell him I'm sorry for all the things I did wrong.

Then I wake up.

And I remember where I am.

I'm tied to a chair, kidnapped, beaten and scared. I don't know who they are or what they want from me. All I know is that I am going to die.

Love and loss.

Love and loss.

Love and loss.

To live and let live. To die and let die.

I think that in retrospect, I would've liked to belong to something before I went. I would've liked to know I had saved a life or left behind some great momentum that taught us that love is real and good and right. But I didn't get a chance to do any of those things. Instead, I was a lonely girl, who lived a long lonely life and hadn't had anything at all to do with anything at all. Nothing of importance anyway. Nothing that could make a difference.

I'm thinking my murderer does not in fact believe in love or good or rightness. He probably thinks IQ is love and love is some kind of earnable credit in intellect. But that's not the case in my heart. I feel like love may be more like an anti-IQ or in other words a defiance of IQ. When the IQ softens and shades and soft focuses and turns from 2D to 3D it starts to hold elements of both love and maybe even a negative shadow of hatred. But this man knew neither love nor hate nor nothing of soft and fuzziness, not even the shadow of such. All he knew was precise math, fact, IQ and precision and smartness that told him to kill if it would benefit his world somehow. And his somehow was based on a covet for money and money was his world and in order to propel robotically this world, he would kill me just to earn a little bit of money. That was who they were. Murderers in the truest sense possible.

My body is bruised and broken and tied to a chair. The room I'm locked in is dark and silent. The bottoms of my shoes stick to the grimed red floor.

I feel sorry for all the not nice things I had ever thought in my life and regretful for any feelings I may have hurt.

I try to move but I can't. My wrists are bound behind me and hold me fast.

A scream echoes from the hallway and through the closed door to my room, and I feel frightened again. I'm ridiculous. I know that now. A ridiculous soul to think that in the scheme of things, I mattered more than a microscopic organism in space.

When they killed me, I knew I'd become dirt and dirt becomes trees which bear fruit and feed deer and expecting mothers and people like the President, so at least I could leave something behind when I was gone other than nothing. My wasteful life would become a wholesome death of me giving back for once instead of just taking.

Who am I?

I am no one.

That was what I learned.

I learned that I am no one and they are everyone.

Who are they?

Everyone other than me. Not so much on an individual level but as a whole.

And to me, that meant, that artistically speaking, there's no such thing as you or me or I in this world of greed. Just THEY. THEY desire money. THEY desire respect. THEY desire fancy things. THEY desire your virginity for example. THEY are the takers and we are the ones who are taken from. We don't even get the chance to try to give to THEY because it is so soon stolen from us, whether it be our lives or our sex or our money, that we simply perish only and never evolve. And as a matter of fact, I kinda think, that in another world, I would've liked to have given my life up for THEY instead of having it taken from me. A perfect circle of sacrifice for once. Instead of a chain reaction of theft and evil from theft.

I reek of fear and chilled skin and yet a quiet resolution has fallen upon me and I am prepared to die.

There is a creak as the door to my cell opens. I'm scared.

I'm so scared

Fear.

Scared.

I can't stop shaking and I realize I'm screaming.

God enters the room and releases me, wrapping me in his arms. He is an indiscernible blur against the lighted hallway. How beautiful. The light in the hallway is a halo over his head. How beautiful. How gorgeous. His love... I can feel it pouring over me.

No.

Not God, after all.

I blink.

In real life he's an assassin of the H GROUP that kidnapped me. And he is here to torture and kill me. The ruler of my world, my GOD, or in other words, my murderer.

As it is above, so it is below.

I'm crying now.

How glad I am to become dirt and food for the President. So why can't I stop shaking? Why can't I stop the tears from falling? Why am crying so damned hard? "Please, have mercy." I find myself whimpering. "Mercy, please?"

"No. No mercy, dear."

God, I mean, the assassin, lifted me out of the chair and dragged me out of the room. He was as gentle as a lover and as beautiful as an angel and I was glad that this killer was the one to take me. It could've been anyone who dragged me to HELL but now I knew that God was dear and real and good because he let my killer be a beautiful beast of a man and not a monster as I had imagined he'd be.

"Please don't do this."

"I'm sorry dear, Andras requires your company."

"Your name, please?"

"Fifty-six."

"I see."

"And what is your name, dear," Assassin Fifty- Six asked me.

"Stella Johnson."

It was a contradiction. My life versus the will of THE COSMOS. THE COSMOS wanted me to die. THE COSMOS wanted me to disappear. THE COSMOS needed to sacrifice me because in the grand scheme of things, it doesn't matter if you were a bear or a cow or a young woman about to be murdered, when that little mark occurred in the universe that told HELL the deed was done and some future apocalypse would be prevented by my death, the point was that I had to die for things to continue going round, and I was a willing victim who wanted nothing to do with any of it.

Our fates are written out in such a way where life can improve and move forward and without my death, perhaps there would be no forward at all. Every little thing adds up to forever and perhaps my death would be the one to turn the world from death to life. Evil to good. Darkness to eternal light.

I am sacrificed, is what I'm trying to say.

Despite myself, I found myself kicking and screaming for help as he dragged me to the torture room and then left me there with my murderers. I watched him as he walked away, wondering why he hadn't chosen to save me instead.

I knew then what it was like to be a fallen angel. As we descended the stone staircase from the metal hallway, heavy fans whooshing above them, I fell from grace and saw the difference between HEAVEN and HELL, right and wrong, and the difference between life and death, that they were all equally valuable but not equal in terms of love.

Three is a big number in Christianity. The holy trinity. Three is divine.

There were three torturers on site in the room to hurt me.

They were called Seventeen, Andras leader of the H GROUP, And Aiden, Assassin number Two.

I was obviously in HELL.

They came to torture me.

It only took fifteen minutes to kill me.

I was dead and life continued forward. Life could go on as always now. The universe could turn and THE COSMOS could make way for newer and better things.

I'm dead now. THE COSMOS continues to turn. And if love were real, it would be the message I want to spread. That LOVE is GOOD.

That LOVE is RIGHT. That LOVE is RIGHTEOUS. AND that only through love can evil be cured.

Love and loss.

Why so eternal?

Why so sad?

In the end.

There's only bad.

But we can heal.

and we can grow.

And we can love.

Someday for sure.

So be it. End of that.

And the only thing I can do now is become the Earth and feed those in need with the fruit I bear.

* Stella Johnson, deceased.*

CHAPTER 2 prologue

"The way it was. The way it will always be.
The death of my sister.
Pure tragedy."

~Sarah Johnson

CHAPTER 2

I cried into my pillow. Sorrow is a tedious thing. It wears you out. I'm worn out from the death of my sister. I'm worn out.

I'm worried that I might be a bad person. For every instance that my sister was ever called a good person, I was only ever called a bad person. When I was little, my sister was the perfect one. The saintly one and for every saintly act of my sister is how evil I was. The one that got the perfect grades, and then went on to go to prom with the perfect boyfriend and get voted as homecoming queen. Then she graduated and got the perfect job as a lawyer. She was pretty much.... perfect.

I didn't like her at all despite the fact that she was my sister. I was very jealous of her. When she died. I cried with tears of both resentment of my situation and relief. Thank God, the bitch was dead. And then, how in the world could this happen to me? I was torn between grief and appreciation that there was such a thing as karma and that sometimes good things did come to those who wait.

I was now an only child. Just like I had always wanted to be.

The sorrow I felt from my sister's death was like a a drug so addictive it was self inflicted damage to my heart. How was I to know that I would be next. How was I to know that in my grievous longings for justice and forgiveness from the feelings in my heart, that I was the next one to be chosen to die.

There's nothing I hate more than thinking about the things I have no control over. I couldn't protect my sister and now she was dead and I wasn't sure if I cared or not. Maybe it was my fault. Maybe I was the one that killed her with my spite of her. Maybe it was me that had taken the knife and destroyed her with my jealousy of her. I could see myself making that mistake.

There was a knock on my bedroom door. I open it and a man dressed in a neat black suit is standing in my bedroom hallway. My eyes fall to the gun in his hand with the silencer over it.

I go instantly mad.

"Are you God?" I ask.

"No. I'm called Fifty-six. I'm an assassin."

"Why are you here?"

"I killed your sister. I'm here to kill you too."

He takes my hand.

"Where are we going?"

"We're just going to walk for awhile."

"I see."

We walk around the dark house, passing by my dead husband laying in a bloody heap over the couch, leaving through the front door and then through the front yard. "Can you comprehend," the assassin said, "that God is perfect."

"I know he is." I said.

"What would you do if you were him. What if perfect told you to murder human beings because they are inherently evil and need to die?"

"I would tell him that that was fine by me."

"Would you complain?"

"Well, you can't argue with perfect." I said.

"But don't you think perfect can be compromised in the name of mercy."

"Empathy." I mumble.

"Love."

"Cherishement." I continue.

"Then take it or leave it."

"I leave it. Kill me now and send me to Hell. I'm a bitch. Just kill me."

"Mercy is a sour medicine I think."

"Yes."

"Mercy is good and sometimes doing the right thing is evil. Does that make any sense to you. You're wrong to think perfect is more right than mercy."

"Will you have mercy on me?" I ask.

"In a way."

"What do you mean?"

"I'm going to kill you only," he said. "You can think of me as an angel. I've never tortured a soul before in my life. Only murdered them to free them of this suffered life."

I blinked. I'm still in my room and my killer stands in front of me. I realize that the whole thing had been a dream and that right before my death, my life had flashed before my eyes in a way I had never thought possible. I see the strange man in my house, with the gun in my bedroom hallway and I scream. I can only assume my husband is dead as well.

He quickly covers my mouth with his hand, presses the pistol to my chest and pulls the trigger.

The way it was. The way it will always be.

The death of my sister.

Pure tragedy.

How was I to know I'd be next?

I crumple to the ground and die. Blood rushing all around me.

The universe is pleased. And THE COSMOS continues turning, not the least bit mournful that I have died.

* Sarah Johnson, deceased. *

CHAPTER 3 prologue

"Can you imagine it?

A world free of time.

If such a world could exist.

I'd spend forever with you and it'd feel like a day."

~ Tara Jones

CHAPTER 3

I sit on my floor, shaking and screaming into the phone with the police. Both my daughters are dead now and I know why they have died. I had witnessed a murder days earlier and told the police about it. It was under investigation.

I feel regretful and sad about the murder I had witnessed and wish I hadn't been there that night after work to begin with.

I hang up the phone unable to concentrate on anything the woman is saying to me on the other line. I can hear my wife upstairs in her bedroom still sobbing over the deaths of our daughters. I fear for my wife's life and my own and our last and final daughter's life who is hanging on a thread as she is the last surviving daughter of our family.

There is a knock on my door. I open it and I am greeted by a man with a gun. I mistake him for God and ask him what he wants. "What can I help you with?"

"So sorry to interrupt you, good sir. I'm here to kill you."

"Shoot. I was just on the phone. Think you could come back another time. We're just about to sit down for dinner."

"I see. It's just that I'm very busy and I don't have a lot of time. I'd love it if you'd just allow me to kill you and your wife right now."

"Perfectly understandable, sir. Give me a second and I'll make arrangements for you. I'm never rude to a guest. Never rude at all. And I'd hate for you to feel unwelcome in our loving home. Welcome is what you are. You're welcome here."

"And I am duly grateful for your dear hospitality. Thank you, sir. Thank you very much."

I run upstairs, grab the wife and we both come down for cake and tea and cheerful conversation on the couch.

"The thing with religion," God, I mean, the assassin, says, "is that it implies a hierarchy is the answer which is in my humble opinion, depending on how you look at it, a concept that propels greed and selfishness, particularly when it comes to lives. It says that chain reactions are set off by the inherent belief that there is such a thing as a less valuable species."

"Like cows and deer and fruit, I think?" I ask.

"More like human beings."

"Maybe we are less valuable," I argue. "After all, we murder and worship suffering and there are children in Africa starving and no one does a damned thing about it but use it as a tool of comparison for why food isn't meant to be wasted. And for what? More money in your pocket. What do you do with that money anyway you saved from not wasting food? Go off and waste it on something else? What the hell does throwing food out have to do with a starving child?"

"Look, value is value and less is less, but I don't want to feel like less than a person. I want to think that somewhere out there, there's someone that cares. That if I get hurt, there's a God out there crying that I got hurt and and assuming he's not responsible for my death, mourns me." The assassin argues. He drinks from his tea cup. "I just want someone to care. I feel like the universe is cold and merciless and no one cares."

"Well, look at it from my perspective. Me and her, we're about to die, correct me if I'm wrong, aren't we?"

"True," the assassin said, "but I'm not quite sure what you're getting at."

"I'm saying, not all of us feel the way you do about equality, so what of that? Fuck, I like a little dying. I like a little hell once in awhile. I like getting hurt. But we have ridiculous babies like you complaining on my behalf. I don't want it and I don't need it."

"To each his own," the assassin or God, finally agrees simply, possibly hoping to calm me down, as I had been accidentally instigated with his words.

"A toast then," I agree finally. "To each his own." And I calm down. I do. For the wife's sake. For my sake. And for the assassin's sake as well.

We clank our cups together and smile as we toast. "To each his own."

"And may we have a Merry, Merry, Merry Christmas."

I blink.

I wake up from my spiritual dream.

The man is standing at the front door.

A gun is in his hand.

I try to shut the door again, but he pushes his way inside. My wife is coming down the stairs. "Don't come down here!" I yell. But my voice is cut off by bullets to my head. I fall over and die.

THE COSMOS, ever beautiful, ever present, and ever cold, it keeps on turning.

Bill Johnson, husband, deceased.

CHAPTER 4 prologue

"Night falls and you lay beside me.

If I could run away.

I'd do it now and spare the heartache."

~ Bee, Assassin Twenty -one.

CHAPTER 4

I come down the stairs, witnessing the death of my husband. The man turns his gun to me and I stare at him stunned.

He smiles at me and I'm seduced.

There are no other words. He's handsome and he kind of reminds me of an actor I used to have a crush on. "Hey there, stranger," I call out, eyes lighting up.

"Greetings, beautiful."

"Are you ready for our date?" I ask, smiling.

"Yes, I am."

"Well then, let's go," I'm dressed for the part, in a beautiful black gown with spaghetti straps. I hurry down the stairs feeling like a young woman again, and rushing to his side. I step over my dead husband and grab his hand. "Darling," I murmur. "A kiss."

"Always," the assassin replies.

"So," I exclaim, super excited for the date, "Assassin Number Fifty-six, what was it like killing two of my daughters and my husband?"

"Like chocolate covered strawberry, just a little sinful, but not too much."

"Amazing," I whisper. "Simply amazing. You're so exotic Assassin Number Fifty -Six. You're like a flower, a desert flower with no one around to appreciate you."

"I've been called many things before, doll, but never a flower. You flatter me with your sweet words."

We leave the house and go to his car. We drive to the movie theater and buy two movie tickets, before sitting down with a giant tub of popcorn and two sodas. We are watching <u>The Ten Commandments.</u>

"Thou shall not kill," I murmur to him. "Like, whatever, right?"

"Did I imply at some point at all during this date that I ever thought GOOD was relevant, real, or worth anything at all other than nothing? I don't think I did."

"If you think about it, killing is the upgrade from torture. Would you ever torture someone?"

"No, I've never tortured anyone before in my life. I don't want to and I don't feel like I have to. I just kill you. It's what I do. I kill you to ease the pain. I save you in a way."

"Why is everyone so scared of dying?"

"I don't know. Maybe because it's never implied whether it's HEAVEN or HELL that waits for you on the other side."

"Torture. It's torture I'm scared of. It shouldn't exist. Torture is a notorious thing. My daughter. They say she was tortured for a long time before she was murdered."

"I'm so sorry about your daughters."

"And my husband," I laugh. "Don't forget him. I really liked him. I liked him a lot. I'm kinda sad because I don't know if I'll ever see him again. Do believe in heaven? Because I don't really think heaven is real or expect anything to come from dying. I just kinda thought I might like to live the rest of my life out with him only."

"Don't be scared, dear. Being scared is the ruiner of humanity. It doesn't suit your beautiful face."

"Fear is the ultimate killer."

"Second only to sadness. Are you sad dear?"

"A little," I admit sheepishly.

"Well, don't be. I'm going to kill you gently. A privilege that isn't implied to humanity. You could've been raped or tortured or suffered, but I'm going to kill you only. Consider it a compliment."

"I do."

"Do you have dreams. I can grant them before you go."

"Yes, I have dreams."

"What are they?"

"To be a famous star."

"I can give you that."

"Thank you."

"Are you ready to go then?"

"Yes," I say, beaming. The movie has ended and we now are in the movie or are filming the movie or something like that. We're standing in the movie screen, speaking gently, the picture black and white. "I'm ready to die now, Assassin Number Fifty-six."

"Ready to film?" The director, called Andras asks.

"I'm ready everyone. I'm fucking ready. Get ready for me world. I'm going to be a star."

I blink. The assassin is aiming the gun at me. My dead husband glares at me from the living room floor. There's blood. Too much of it. I blink again. No, it's still there. Not a dream this time. Not a dream.

I turn around to run up the stairs again. I feel the bullet hit the back of my head and one into my arm and one into my back. I fall over and die.

And as for my stardom, I did become a star, I was on the front of every paper. My death along with my husband and my daughters were known as the Johnson murders. And I was famous and I was glad.

As for THE COSMOS, I don't think it even notices, because it just kept on turning.

Amanda Johnson Wife, deceased.

CHAPTER 5 prologue

"Michael, I would've liked to have known you better.
I wish we could've known each other for a little longer."

~ Tara Jones

CHAPTER 5

The assassin stood in front of her. She was Tara Johnson, twenty -
three and she was the third and youngest of the daughters. She was also
the last one of the immediate family to be killed by the murderers of the
H GROUP and shot down by Assassin number fifty-six. The cosmos
turned and turned and turned and it was her turn to die.

She stared at her assassin, and he stared back at her.

"Please, don't kill me," I beg.

He hesitated before replying. "Die now, dear. It's less scary that way."

"Please," she uttered. I began to cry. "I beg of you kind sir to spare my
life. I know you would never hurt me."

CHEMICALS.

"Your sisters and father and mother are dead. What is there to live
for? What good does it do to be the only surviving member of the family."

RUNNING ON PURE CHEMICAL.

HUMAN.

ROBOT.

THE HUMAN MACHINE.

WHY DO I FEAR DEATH.

BECAUSE I AM CHEMICALLY INCLINED TO DO SO.

I want love.

I want sad.

I want happy and good and right.

But most of all, I want it to be real.

I don't really, normally, do this, but I AM HUMAN. HUMANS
are petty, evil, and chemically driven creatures and that's all I claim to be.
A chemically driven creature. I don't think love is real. Perhaps it is right

and good and moral and just, but is love real? I doubt it very much. I don't believe in love. I don't believe in hate. I am no different from the murderer that stood in front of me. I am neither a saint as my oldest sister was, nor a devil of hate as my second sister was. I am more of a believer in all that is mechanical and hard and human.

We are nothing but robots.

My love for my family and my sadness over losing them is chemical only. It isn't real.

I never cried at my parent's funeral and sister's funeral. I think it's because I knew my sadness over the death of my family wasn't real. Yes, it hurt. Yes, I was chemically inclined to feel sad. But what was sad. Is that what I wanted? A simulation of sadness and guilt and a plea for mercy that did not exist in this world as of yet?

I want to truly mourn. I want to truly cry.

And most of all. I want to truly love.

"Isn't there anything at all I can say, to convince you to walk away?" I plead.

He frowns. "You're heart is pure, girl. Your mind is cluttered with fear. You're not thinking straight. But then again, neither am I." He fires the gun but not at me.

FEAR AND SAD.

LOVE AND LOSS.

TO REGRET BECAUSE OF CHEMICALS THAT FEEL GOOD OR BAD.

FEELS GOOD.

FEELS BAD.

I'm sorry but I don't want to be a machine anymore.

I'm a woman...

Not a robot...

He fires off to the side and wastes every bullet in his gun. When it is empty and there are no bullets in the barrel, he says. "So what? I could just reload. Right?"

"You could."

CHEMICAL INCLINATIONS DECLINING.

DECLINING...

"But I don't think I will. I think I'll leave it be as it is. I feel sorry for you, girl. You look like your sisters. If not more beautiful. I don't know what this feeling is but it is similar to regret," he said.

DECLINING...

"It hurts and I don't want to feel it anymore. You come from a lovely family and I'm sorry for what I've done. I don't want to kill you. Perhaps if I had met you first, I wouldn't have killed your family. I regret now. I do." he continued.

DECLINING...

He says, "I'm sorry for what I did. I'm sorry I hurt you. You've suffered enough. I don't want to hurt you anymore. And as for why that is, I don't really know. I don't really know why I feel so badly right now."

The cosmos stopped turning.

It belly-flopped. It strained. It lowered it's gun and sighed. It turned to look at her and it said... "Okay Tara. Okay. I'll let you live."

He lowered his gun and sighed. "Okay. I'll spare you. I'll do it not for you or for me or the feeling of regret in my heart. But in the name of love and loss and what your family meant to me, each one of them, a message from the heavens to set me free, and in the name of life itself in general, I have no intention of killing you." He turned around and left her home.

Tara felt stunned. Her knees were shaking. Against her will, she crumpled to the floor. There were tears in her eyes still and she began wiping at them frantically. It wasn't long before she was sobbing. She had been so scared. So scared. But he had spared her. For some reason, the universe had decided to let her live.

Love and loss.

Good and evil.

Right and wrong.

Why do we do the things we do?

Maybe we do come from a perverse society of greed and selfish and evil and meanness.

But why are you here?

Why am I Crying.

My heart foretells of future pains.

which you must understand.

after this moment.

We'll never be the same.

Forgive me for my impertinence.

Forgive me for all that I do and say.

I love you for sparing my life.

Please feel the same.

What does it mean to owe your life to a stranger.

Let's just say, the following feelings In my heart now portray a portrait of what I feel. And what I feel, is OBSESSION.

OBSESSION with life.

OBSESSION with death.

OBSESSSION with love and loss and hope and fate and destiny and anything that could imply that I was a fool for thinking it, but if it were even possible, I was now obsessed with this killer. And should I ever see him again, I should like to think that we could die in each others arms after a knife fight, a fight to the death after making love.

So is that love?

A mutual agreement to ask and recieve.

An awakening perhaps.

Is it gratefulness? That he spared my life?

Is it gratitude and affinity and even a mild confusion that he would spare me and not the rest of the world. Am I his only survivor.

Mechanically speaking, and robotically, as we are but human machines that try to carry the burden of appreciation of finer things and greediness I find myself thinking this now, I DO NOT WANT TO HARM YOU. EVER.

And it's not the gratefulness.

I can tell, somehow.

It's not the mild compliment that my family died and not me. A thought that if there were a God, would surely send me straight to Hell.

If love were real, which like I said, I don't believe in. My heart gliched for just a second, and felt it for my assassin who in his own mind, for whatever strange reason, decided not to kill me. And I think, I like him now. I like him.

The chemical pain over my family's death is sad and hurts. But it isn't real. This love. This sparse, glimpse of futuristic, anti-robotic feelings are a portrayal of real life emotion. I am no longer a robot. I am no longer human. I am an angel and I have felt love for the first time ever. Pure love. I feel love for the assassin that tried to kill me and chose not to. I feel love.

I am triggered. I am turned off as a robot and turned on as an angel. I no longer am chemical. I no longer am robot. I no longer am hard and metallic and destined to be alone.

I FEEL LOVE.

IT IS REAL.

And I realize, this trigger caused by my assassin could be the feeling I wanted ever since the death of my family. So I could tell my parents and my sisters how sad I am, that they are gone and I may never see them again.

Tears stream down my face.

True tears.

They are not fake.

They are not robot.

They are not chemically driven.

They are, in essence, in the very epitome of the word, real tears of love and sadness.

"OH GOD!"

Forgive me family.

For you are dead.

And here I am,

The one who should've died in your stead.

Forgive me family

I could not see.

I was a blind woman walking,

toward apathy.

Now I feel love.

And now I feel regret.

I no longer wonder.

What's real and what's not.

Love could be real.

And could be dear.

And forgive me for thinking.

I was more important than you were.

Essentially, what I developed was a guilty conscience and a soul that could potentially harbor love for another.

I am no longer a robot.
I am no longer a human being.
I am an angel.
And I am alive.
Alive.

* Tara Johnson, alive *

CHAPTER 6 prologue

"If I could love
and love is dear and beautiful to me,
I like to think I would've loved you the most."

~ Michael. Assassin Fifty-Six.

CHAPTER 6

I felt a wash of empathy rush through me. I had spared a life for the first time. I felt happy that I had been able to make someone else happy. It wasn't something I normally did and it left a strange inner fulfillment in my heart.

"Fifty-Six."

I jumped, turning around. "What's up?"

Bee, a fellow assassin approached me. She was pretty, with dark hair and pale skin, but she was little too short and thin for his tastes and he never desired her in the way that the other assassins seemed to want her. Besides, she seemed to be sleeping with Andras, the boss of the H Group Assassins, anyway. They walked together along the metal corridors, their footsteps echoing on iron floors. Bee handed him a photo of an elderly politician.

"Andras wants him dead by tonight."

"Gotcha." Fifty six, or Michael as he liked to be called when he was younger, said, and his eyes fell on blood crusted underneath Bee's nails and staining the front of her shirt.

"Oh this?" she asked, noticing his gaze. "I had a busy night?"

"Did you?"

"I even had to reload my gun."

"How unusual for you."

"Unusual indeed."

The lights went out.

His eyes wandered in the darkness, adjusting slowly to the narrow passage. "What's going on?"

"I have no idea."

Frowning, Michael made his way down the familiar hallway, his hand following the wall. The lights snapped suddenly back on again and the hall was illuminated once more.

Aiden, aka, Assassin Two, Wolf, aka, assassin number Ninety-eight, Heat, aka, Assassin number Seventeen, and George, aka, Assassin number Thirteen came rushing past him, cocking sniper rifles as they raced by.

A tiny figure in white emerged at the end of the hallway, covered in blood, as was his preference. It was Andras. The boss of H Group, Andras, was tall and skinny with a long face. Both his nose and chin were pointy, with thin lips that were always dry. He licked them constantly and they usually bled where they cracked.

"Fifty- six," he growled. "What are you doing just standing around?"

"The lights went out," I replied.

"I noticed. A criminal has escaped. He cut the lights and left through the north elevator. I want you to kill him Fifty-Six." He looked at Bee. "And what are you doing here?"

"I was just giving him his next assignment."

"That's your job now"

"But I just got back from the last one," Bee complained.

"I said now."

Letting out a growl, she spun around, walking loudly in the opposite direction. "This is fucking ridiculous," she screamed.

Andras turned his attention back to Michael. "Fifty-six," he said, handing him a folder. "Kill this man before tomorrow. If you don't, I'm sending Bee to kill you."

More of the same. Another day, another threat.

Letting out a sigh, Michael took the folder. "Thank you."

"No, thank you," Andras smiled. "You know...... you're my favorite assassin Fifty-Six. I love you more than any of the others, even more than Bee. I've loved you since the day you came here. You're like a son to me. You're my dearest one. My dearest. I promise you that. I couldn't love anyone more than you."

"Thanks Andras."

"You're welcome, Fifty six."

I leave the facility through the hallway and take an elevator shaped like a tree trunk to the upper floor. I leave the artificial tree elevator and find myself in the middle of dense woods in the middle of nowhere.

Location.

A secret.

I climb into the driver's seat of the waiting beside the tree and parked on the dirt road. The driver takes us off the dirt road and onto a paved highway. I hand the folder to my driver and we head to the target's location.

When we get there, a tall mansion with a large front yard, I get out of the car, and am fired at by a barrage of bullets. It turns out my assignment is actually here to kill me and not the other way around. Ducking, I fire my gun at him and kill him carefully. Then I climb back into the car and head home.

Andras had always made Michael feel uneasy. There was never a second he could go without feeling like he was being watched. Andras was obsessive. The boss found things he liked and he liked those things until they were nothing but blood and skin that hung from drying racks. Being loved by Andras was no compliment, no given honor. It was a terrible thing for Andras to like you. Simply awful.

I go home to my room. I sit on my flat grey mattress. I shared the bunk with Seven, who slept below me while he slept on top. He wanted to be alone to think. An open box of bullets lay beside him, metal shells spilling out onto the material. His empty gun sat in his lap, his hand brushing over it thoughtfully. He felt confused, and he felt alone.

The room stretched out about four-hundred feet in length and about half the size in width. Both men and women alike shared the space, with simple bunk beds that stood cramped beside one another in single file lines. The living quarters was located a floor directly above the cells where the prisoners were kept. Sometimes they could even hear their screams through the thick floor.

He climbed down when he saw Andras enter the silent room.

"Why aren't you dead?"

"You hired someone to kill me?"

"And why'd you skip Tara Jones?"

I raise an eyebrow. I hadn't expected them to notice so quickly.

"Ran out of bullets," I offered lamely.

"Right," Andras replied sarcastically. "I bet. Well, she's cute."

"That she is."

"Tall, blond. Big green eyes. Great look to her."

"Yes, she's very pretty." I'm growing frightened. What was Andras getting at?

"I'm saying I'm sending Seven to kill Tara and then we're going to kill you. Consider you two dead by sundown." He left the room and Michael realized he was no longer welcome at the H GROUP.

CHAPTER 7 prologue

"There's a world out there.
I want to explore the whole thing.
And become its king."

$\sim$ Andras Leader of H Group.

CHAPTER 7

Tara was curled on the couch. She was having nightmares. She dreamt she was tied to a chair. That the ropes that bound her were sharp and cut her like knives. They tore her to shreds. I feel scared as the assassin approaches me in the dream and kisses me over the lips. "I'm sorry I scared you." He hugs me and I let him.

Assassin Fifty-Six.

Longing.

Love and loss.

Would you believe it? I somehow long for you. To see you again.

I blink.

No, not real. Just a dream. It's night out, when I wake up.

I think of you and realize I am seeking out the source of my new angelic heart. I want you near me. The one that triggered me to evolve. I want to see you again.

I fall alseep again and dream of an army of robots walking in line with each other. They are human machines and they represent the end of the universe. I find myself with a machine gun, shooting them all down and killing them off one by one. I am traumatized. They form a circle around me and surround me and tear me apart.

A mirror appears and I stare at my reflection.

So it was.

And so it would seem.

With this love.

This heavy weight of love and angelic format.

Came the subtle consequence of hate.

Was this something my murderer had felt before? Could he comprehend these things? That love is a coin and in order to love, one must understand that it is a package that comes with hatred included in it. I did not know this on my journey to becoming an angelic being. And now that I am angel. I am drowning in feelings. In feelings of love, hate, regret, happy, sad, everything at all, and anything at all.

Assassin Fifty-Six. I hate you for taking my family.

But I love you too.

For your mercy.

For your kindness.

I awaken from the dream once more and find GOD IS SEATED ON MY COUCH.

I blink. No not God. It is the assassin. I am not dreaming. He is real, and as I had wished, he has manifested himself on my couch in real life. Not a dream this time. He is real.

I shriek.

He points a gun at me.

"Bang," he says. "Just kidding." He lowers the gun. "How are you doing?"

"I'm fine," I replied, stunned by his presence. "What are you doing here?"

"Just checking up on you."

"How'd you get inside?"

"You left your door unlocked."

"I see," I reply. I stare at him. He's tall and handsome with dark hair and grey eyes. Very pretty. She imagined he was pretty good looking when he smiled. He points the gun at me again and I frown. "Why are you really here?" I ask him.

"To talk to you, I suppose."

"About what?"

"Seven is coming. He is going to kill you tonight. I could either save you and we could run away right now, or we could commit a double suicide together. I could shoot you and then I could shoot myself. It would be beautiful. We could die in each other's arms. You can be with your family again."

Love and loss

Loss and love.

The way things are.

The way they'll be.

Don't forget me. Even when I'm gone.

I closed my eyes and when nothing happened, I opened them again.

"I just... I don't know what to do. I should kill you here and now but I just don't want to. What would you do if you were in my situation. If you were supposed to kill someone but you just didn't feel like it," he asked.

"I've never been in such a situation." I reply. "I'm afraid I can't relate."

"Here." He hands me his gun. "Kill me," he asks. His voice is almost begging. "Kill me and get me out of this. Then kill yourself."

I take the gun and press it to his temple. My hand shakes. "I can't do it either." I reply finally. "I'm sorry."

"Do it."

"I can't. Sorry." I lower the gun and hand it back to him.

He sighs. "Then we have a situation. We both don't want to kill each other. But both of us, we should be dead. Why is that? What are we going to do about it?"

"I don't know."

It's not that I don't want to die. I do. I'd like to die and be with my family again. But this is not necessarily the way I wanted to go. I want to learn more. On my angelic journey. I want to learn all there is to know about the world and I cannot do so without staying alive a little longer.

Fear is no longer an issue. I do not fear. I am not scared. Scared is for the human machine. I am beyond that now. I am truly fearless. And so, it is not fear that drives me to think these things, but pure and utter love and existentialism that makes me want to be happy and try to live and try to learn more and more and more. I want to keep evolving and growing and learning and Fifty-six, I think I'd like to get to know him a little better. If that were possible.

"Luckily I had a plan B, as I said. Don't say I never gave you anything." He hands her an envelope. "It's ten thousand dollars. Take it and go to Germany. They'll never find you there. I hope you feel better Ms. Tara. And I'm sorry I scared you so badly."

"Th.. .thank you."

"And you might as well take this gun too. Never know. You might need it."

"Thanks."

"I gotta go. But it was nice seeing you again. Even if it was just for a second. They'll find out I didn't kill you and they'll be coming for me later. I can't stay. I have to make a run for it too if you know what I mean."

"Who are these people? Who's 'They'"

"They're hitmen for hire. They're called the H group. Your father witnessed an assassination attempt and your family was killed for it. That's why we came after you too. To clean up."

"I see. And your name?"

"Michael. Just Michael. But they call me assassin Fifty-Six. So I'll be seeing you around," he smiled, "If you catch my drift. Bye Tara."

"Bye."

He leaves. I stare at the door even after he is gone. I take the gun and shoot my television. Bang. Just joking. What a jerk. I note the shattered screen and tuck the gun under my pillow before going back to sleep.

OBSESSION.

That's what this was. An obsession with a man I barely knew. And if love was real and I was in fact feeling something like love, how in the world was I supposed to act around this man that I sort of liked. I wish I had told him not to go.

I wish I had told him to stay the night. But I hadn't. I just, didn't have the nerve or the guts or something. I don't know. I think I messed up. I may never see him again. I stare at my broken television. Kinda like my tv now. Beyond repair. Never to see one another again.

If that's what love felt like. Maybe I didn't want it.

CHAPTER 8 prologue

"I don't normally do nice things.

When I do.

I feel like throwing up.

Saving Tara was like saving a mother.

I wish I had done it sooner

and resent the years wasted in regret and neglect instead."

~ Michael Assassin Fifty-Six.

CHAPTER 8

I awake the next morning.

Tara grabs her gun and purse and smart phone and orders tickets online for a one way ticket to Germany.

I pack my bags and fill up my car. Then get in and drive away.

Away I drive. Far away where no one will be able to find me. I feel crazy and scared and sad all at the same time. I feel alone.

Love and loss.

The way it is. If I could choose one person in the world right now to be with, it would be Michael. I can't lie. I am infatuated with the man.

I would even go so far as to say I have fallen in love with his concept.

What was love to me now?

Did you have to know each other for an eternity to fall in love or could you see each other for just a second and know right away that someone was right for you.

It had only been a day but I already longed to see the assassin again. I wondered where he had gone to and if he was okay.

What was love?

Did she really want to know?

Why did she feel this way and what could she do to ease the pain?

I'm thinking that maybe I detach myself from reality too often. What's reality mean to me? It's a cold truth that I don't want to approach. If so, approach with caution. That's what they say. Approach with caution.

The assassin.

Guns.

My broken TV.

My shattered reality.

I hope things get better.

Or at least if they don't, I hope they don't get any worse.

I drive for a very long time towards the airport. I stop at a gas station for gas and something to drink. I step out of my car and am shocked by a whizzing of a bullet past my head.

I turn around and see a car pulling up to me, windshield down, gun pointed out the open window.

I let out a small shriek and duck. Another bullet whizzes past me. I dodge behind my car and hide behind it. My right windshield shatters. I climb into my car carefully and grab for the gun underneath my car seat. I stay crouched low. Several more bullets shatter the windows of my car. My heart tightens in my chest. I see a man coming toward my car, gun raised. I cock the gun in my hands, keeping it low and hidden beneath the steering wheel.

The man comes closer and I stare at him. When he is only a few feet away, gun raised towards me, I pull out my own gun and unload ever bullet in the damned thing into him.

I'm scared.

I'm in disbelief.

I felt disturbed as the dead man crumpled to the ground.

Murder.

Blood.

My angelic heart has chosen to kill to survive on this journey of life.

I'm a murderer.

I have taken a life for the first time and I feel so bad I can't take it.

Without thinking, I turn my car on, and speed off. Fuck this. Fuck this city. I feel annoyed. My detachment is growing and I'm afraid I'm developing a mental disorder.

I head to the airport barely recognizing where I am. I head into the building and wait patiently for the plane to board. As I'm waiting, I think about things like ice cream and soda and how thirsty I am and how soda and ice cream make ice cream floats and those are actually pretty delicious on a summer's day.

I want to drown.

I'm in sorrow.

I have to leave.

I don't know where I'm going or why I'm going anymore. I feel confused and distanced from myself, as if I'm watching myself from far away. In this scenario, a me stands by the vending machines and another me stares out the window. I continue to sit.

The me at the vending machine turns to look at the one at the window and she walks towards the other. She starts a conversation with her, and then, like Spy vs Spy, they begin arguing and fighting. They pull out guns, have a standoff, and shoot.

I continue to sit.

I don't know how to explain that I don't like the sight of blood. I don't like blood or guts or anything that involves hurting someone else. I feel tragic. I know now that there is definitely something strange going on in the universe. I don't know what they mean by signs that the universe is about to begin or end but I think that the universe has turned on me. In sparing my life, I believe I have become something of a main character and am now co-dependent on violence to soothe the feeling of obligation and new found feelings of hate.

So, basically, who won the standoff isn't important but I believe it was the one at the window as she was quicker with her gun and when she won, she sat down beside me and told me not to worry because guns are the answer and if anyone tried to kill me I could always just shoot them again seeing as that had worked in the past, even if just the once.

Guns.

I needed new bullets.

More guns.

More bullets.

I feel convinced now that life is valuable and meaningful and not just a concentrated load of bullology. I'm suffered for sure but not unhopeful. I feel like life could be a good thing. That it is beautiful and rare and not meant to be taken unseriously. I feel convinced that the circle of life is broken now for my sake and I am flattered and confused. In what way am I worthy of such glory? In the rarity of life, I say, there are only a few things I ever loved in my life and one of them was a man that betrayed me for another woman, and in fact, I do feel hope and I do feel like I could be worth it. I feel like I'm worth this love and forgiveness that God has bestowed upon me. And I'm grateful.

I am spared.

And I am grateful.

But love.

How is one to live without love? I can't explain it. The hopeless and inappropriate romantic that I am and now that I have evolved and in my detached world where I sit and think and wonder what the point of life is, and thinking that even if I knew I wouldn't know what to do with it, I think that I would like to get to know someone a little better.

Love and loss.

To be helplessly alone.

I long for love, God.

If a journey is what I must go on, need I really be alone throughout the whole thing. I accept your spiritual journey and my new life as the main character of the story. But please, don't let me walk alone. I need someone to come with me. I'm not ready yet to be alone.

Someone to share my suffering with. Someone to share my joys with. If I could find love, I think I would be very happy indeed.

I'm lonely.

But I don't want to admit it.

I'm longing for things I don't have and am the center of a story I don't understand. But to have someone to hold at night would mean more to me than anything else in the universe.

I conversate with the me sitting beside me, the surviving me. "Do you think we'll find love in Germany."

"I'm sure we will," she agrees and hugs me.

"And if we don't?" I ask

"We'll just have to see then, dear." she says.

The plane is boarding.

I stand up and the two other me's disappear from sight.

I blink.

Back to reality.

I board the plane and head to Germany.

Assassin number One-hundred. Deceased.

CHAPTER 9 prologue

"Hold me, kiss me, don't let me go.
Once, I had a dream
and in it, I was a normal man."

Michael, Assassin fifty-six

CHAPTER 9

It is with great difficulty in my heart that I follow Tara Jones to Germany. I'm fascinated by her. By her grace. By her beauty. By her smile. I want to know more about her. But I'm a monster. I cannot hold a woman without being afraid she might wilt and die in my arms. I'm a murderer. I cannot love a woman without fear that she may disappear forever.

He had been seconds away from saving her from assassin One -Hundred, which was the name of the assassin who had attacked her at the gas station, before she had shot him dead herself, so Michael had stayed hidden in the parking lot of the station.

I'm torn between two worlds in my head. The first world is racing with thoughts of love and anger. And the second world acknowledges that once upon a time, I was once an evil person that had to kill to survive.

Love and loss.

Loss and love.

I wonder what love is. Is it a fascination with a woman you barely know? Is it to be obsessed. I find myself in such a situation. I'm obsessed. I'm thrilled by the thought of her. I touch her yellow hair in my head and think to myself that there is such a thing as perfect. Tara was perfect. She was everything I ever admired in a woman. She was elegant and sweet and I loved the thought of her.

Love at first sight is a complicated system of ignorances. I argue with myself that if I barely know her, then who am I to take claim to the word love. I find myself arguing back that love is intricate and complicated itself in its own right and that it's perfectly normal to be attracted to a woman for no reason at all but to believe you're in love.

What is love?

Is it the longing for a mother that died when I was young. Is it the will to succeed as father did if he did so much exist as more than just a figment of my imagination in my head. Is it to love a woman at first sight because I did in fact choose to spare her life.

Tara. Her life was my life. I had spared her. And now she was a beautiful butterfly that belonged to me. I drop to my knees and pray for forgiveness for all the bad things I had ever thought in my life. I love her but I don't know her. I need her but she's not here.

I digress.

Tara boards the plane. I board the same plane several minutes later. My seat is in the back and hers is towards the front. I watch her from behind as she brushes a strand of hair behind her ear. She doesn't know I'm on the same plane as her but I seem to know everything about her.

I think of Tara's family. Of Stella Johnson, of Sarah Johnson, of her father and mother who I murdered on command.

I never used to think about things like that.

It had been a simple life. To be told to kill and then to do so without a second's thought or hesitation or guilt.

What was guilt? To be told that you had done something wrong and to know it was wrong and to feel it was wrong and not okay and not good and not right. I feel sad thinking I had lived a long guiltless life when I had been made to only do things that should've lead to guilt.

I feel unnerved thinking that I had spent my whole life as a worthless creation that killed to be fine. By which I mean, what was the worst that could've happened by disobeying my orders? Sure, they would've come for me and murdered me too. But was that really such a terrible thing? To die a noble man that refused to take a life. In another world, in a parallel existence, someone who refused to kill, I think I would've liked to be that man.

I stare at Tara the entire plane trip. I am fascinated by her hair and neck and everything belonging to her. Her shoulders. Her back. Her shape and form. She was so beautiful and I wanted to be closer to her. I'm almost positive she will notice me staring but she doesn't and so I continue to stare, falling deeper and deeper into infatuative love with her.

I think of Stella Johnson again. She had been beautiful as well. Couldn't save her. She had been kind. But when it comes down to it, I couldn't even save one kind girl. This time would be different. This time, with Tara, I planned to save a life.

CHAPTER 10 prologue

"Jon,
Your deep broken heart,
I'll mend it with the blood of my victims."

> Bee, assassin number twenty -one

CHAPTER 10

Bee entered the German airport from the plane. I pulled out a tiny gun from my shoe and aimed it at Tara. Michael's hand twitched. He turned to look at me and our eyes met. Bee turned the gun to Michael and was surprised to see he had a gun of his own in his own hand.

He shot at Bee first, striking Bee in both shoulders and in the right arm.

I tried to lift the gun to kill Tara but realized my shooting arm was paralyzed. Shit.

I ran off. A car was waiting for me outside the building. I climbed in and we drove away.

Assassin Seventeen is waiting for me in the drivers seat, with Assassin One riding shotgun and me in the back seat. I begin to cry. I failed my job and now they were going to be angry with me. I felt embarrased and I was afraid to say otherwise.

"Are they dead?" they ask me.

I nod quickly. "Dead, dead, dead." I joke, frightened by my own voice as I lied to them.

"Good."

"Why are you crying?" Assassin One asked.

"My arm. He hurt my arm and I can't move it."

"We'll get you fixed up."

"Thank you."

We drove for several hours before reaching a private airport. We board a private jet, and fly back to the States.

CHAPTER 11 prologue

"By the infinite grace of God,
I am spared.
Please don't leave me."

~Tara Jones.

CHAPTER 11

I am traumatized by the sight of Fifty-six toting a gun and shooting at another woman with a gun. I have no idea what's going on. Michael runs up to me, grabbing my hand and pulling me forward. We race together out of the building and to a taxi.

He speaks German eloquently and tells the driver to take them to a hotel.

When he is done speaking, he tells Tara that he is glad she is okay and cups his hands around her face.

"Who was that girl with the gun?" I ask

"Bee. She's assassin Twenty-one. She's extremely dangerous. You must be careful. They followed us here somehow. I don't know how they knew we were here."

"I'm scared."

"Don't be scared. I'm here now. I'll protect you."

We pull up at the hotel building and we pay for two rooms. We go our separate ways and I think about Michael in a nice way. I go to a vending machine and buy some chips and something to drink and munch on it in the hotel hallway.

I feel fascinated by Michael. He is probably in his room now and I am thinking of only him. I think about how he had protected me and I am glad that he was there. I frown, drinking from the can of soda I had purchased and heading back to my own room. Who knew I'd run into him again. Hopefully they'd be seeing each other even more.

I go into the room and toss the garbage into the trash can.

Then I sit on the bed and turn on the TV. Everything is in German so I don't understand what they are saying but I watch mindlessly for a couple of hours before there is a knock on my door. When I open the door, Michael is standing in the hallway.

"Hi," I say.

"Hi," he says. "Can I come in?"

"Sure." We walk into the room and I sit on the bed and he sits in a chair by the window. "How are you doing?" I ask.

"I'm fine. I'm just thinking."

"What are you thinking about?" I ask.

"I'm thinking about us and what we can do to protect ourselves. They knew we were here so I don't know what to do to get them off our trail."

"We could move to England?"

"True. I'll save that as an option. For now, let's just hang tight and see if they come back."

"Michael?"

"What is it?"

"Why are you here?"

"I dunno." He sighs. "I guess I was just worried about you."

"Worried about me?"

"Yeah."

I smiled at him. "Thank you. I really appreciate that."

We sit in silence for a moment and I lay down in the bed, feeling tired. I cover my face with my arms and begin to cry.

"What's wrong?" Michael asks me.

"I'm sorry," I say, "I'm starting to feel sorry for myself."

"Don't feel sorry. I'll protect you. I promise. I won't let anyone hurt you."

"Why are you doing this?"

He hesitated. "I don't know. To be honest. I guess I just... like you. You're my friend. I like you very much."

"You're my friend too Michael. I'm glad we met."

I try to stop crying but I can't. I'm crying harder. Not because I'm sad or scared but because I'm very happy. I wonder how much longer the happiness will last. There's such a thing as hope. And for me, at this time, with the way it was and the way it could be, I hoped this moment would last forever. I wanted to tell Michael that everything was going to be okay for him too, because in a way I wanted to be able to protect him as well.

There were no words of my current sadness. They could die right now, today or tomorrow, and may never see each other again. In my mind, I saw a clock ticking away the last seconds of our life. How long would this feeling last? How much longer before she never saw Michael again? How long before their luck ran out? She didn't know. But for right now. Let the day pass in the company of this stranger. She welcomed the time passing by.

Several hours passed and it felt like seconds. Michael stayed with her in the room and they chatted nonchalantly. It was wonderful. The feeling of his energy. It felt absolutely wonderful. Can you imagine it? A world free of time. If such a world could exist. I'd spend forever with you and it'd feel like a day.

I enjoyed his company. Later that night we went out for dinner and it felt like we were on a date. He took my hand as we went out to the restaurant. We walked to the restaurant across the street from the hotel and were seated at a small booth table by the window. He ordered two pastas and wine and water for us, speaking German to the waiter.

"I like being here with you," I admitted.

"Thank you. I'm enjoying myself." He smiled and I wondered what I could do to only see him smile.

He takes my hand and we stay like that for awhile. I wonder what it would take for a moment like this to last forever.

When we are done eating we head home and to our separate rooms. Seeing as I am a virgin, I do not invite him to my room for the night. I let him show me to my door though and I let him leave me alone with nothing but my thoughts.

CHAPTER 12 prologue

"I wanted him to know I loved him.
But to tell him
would be the death of me.
My heart,
It aches with uselessness.
For as it was before, and how it has always seemed,
there is nothing I can do."

~ Tara Jones

CHAPTER 12

"Michael..."

The voice was gentle. Michael looked around him carefully, wondering where it was coming from. He was in a dark woods. There was snow. The trees were nothing but tall shadows in the fading night He watched as the flakes fell softly around him, landing on his skin.

"Michael.."

He saw her then. She called to him. Her long dark hair went down to her waist. She reached out for him with slender arms, a smile forming on her delicate face. His mom. She was his mother.

"Michael."

A red line formed around the woman's thin neck, splitting the skin open. Droplets of red dribbled down her flesh.

He remembered.

The knife that slit his mother's throat.

The gunshot that pierced his father's body. He trembled, wanting the memory to disappear.

Blood poured from his mother's wound, soaking into her blouse and she fell forward, disappearing into the white snow.

A voice screamed out. "Save Michael. Someone save Michael." He could see her beautiful face, with dark hair and gray eyes and slender hands that grasped for him and clawed at their attackers. He saw himself as he was dragged away by men in black suits, guns raised. His father lay dead in the middle of the floor, his clothing soaked in the pool of blood around him. Michael's father.

Michael blinked.

The night faded away and soon both images were gone.

Michael. He liked it when Tara called him that. It was a warm feeling that brought back vague flashes of running around through a house bigger than he was. Very vague. It was so real that he couldn't help but believe deep down that he hadn't made it up. It was real. As real as the dark haired woman that cried out his name, and the man that lay in a pool of blood.

His second memory came flooding back to him.

Sitting on a bunk bed.

Assassin number Seven below.

He wasn't sure who he was or where he had come from. Blood streaked his face and his body was bruised. He felt sad. Lonely and sad. A rifle was grasped in his small hands.

He blinked again.

When he opened his eyes he was laying in a car. He looked through the glass, watching as a small girl with dark hair shot Tara with a gun. He tried to reach for her. There were no doors in the car. He couldn't get to her. He was sealed inside the car.

He pressed his hands to the glass, yelling as he slammed his fists against the window.

Tara fell to the ground, her head turning to him.

"Please help me," she said. Michael could hear her voice ringing clearly in his ears. "Don't leave me. Save me. Please."

It wasn't the first time someone had asked that.

The woman that called herself Stella Johnson, one of Tara's sisters. She had been a saint. Couldn't save her then. Couldn't save Tara now. It haunted him. The fear of failing to protect Tara Jones was traumatizing him.

Fear.

It destroyed him.

Stella Johnson and the Johnson family. He wanted to forget about them.

Stella had been so pretty. She had been older than him by about ten years, possibly thirty one or thirty-two. He remembered she had clawed at the door of her prison when they first caught her, screaming for help that fell on deaf ears.

He had watched her silently through the dark window of her cell, unbeknownst to her. He remembered that moment the most. She was an angel. And he had acknowledged her pain, acknowledged her beauty, and acknowledged her tears. Nothing more. Then he had gone in to get her. Had taken her to the torture room to be killed by Andras.

The morning after, he had found her in pieces on the floor.

Her decapitated head lay with wide eyes staring at him from the floor. An arm lay across the table. A leg had found its way into the hall. Michael had looked down at the torn chunks of flesh, feeling strange and detached from the world. Save her. Why hadn't he? Only kill.

To kill.

To only kill.

He had killed so many people.

Killed so many people that hadn't deserved to die.

Why?

Why had he killed them all?

Because Andras had told him to.

He had killed so many, many people.

It wasn't his responsibility. Why ask him? What could he do?

He couldn't do anything.

Not even save Tara.

He beat on the windows of the car still, trapped inside the metal cage. Tara lay on the ground, looking up at him from the snow. Blood gushed from her wounds and she grew as white as the winter snow as the blood began to puddle around her body. "Please save me," she spoke, her voice weak. "Save me. Please save me," she spoke.. "Save me. Please help me. Don't just stand there. Do something. Help me."

He wanted to. He really did. He wanted to help her. He wanted to save her.

"Please help me, Michael. Please. Please save me. Please."

Michael was a little boy again. He trembled with the gun in his hand, looking behind him. Seven approached him. Seven was a year younger, with dark hair also and wide brown eyes. They had been friends since they had met a couple years earlier.

He turned around, his eyes watching the dark tunnels wearily. Another test. He hated them. They were frightening and he always ended up getting hurt in the end. A sharp pain hit him in the arm and he glanced down at the bloody lump forming on his skin. The bullets they shot at the boys with were made of rubber only.

Michael looked around carefully catching sight of the trainer as he ducked behind the corner of the wall. He aimed, staying low and pulling into the shadows. Their trainer turned his head around the corner and Michael fired, hitting the man between the eyes with a rubber bullet. The man groaned falling back, his hand to his forehead.

Seven ran up to the fallen trainer, firing him with his own round of rubber bullets.

A red light flashed and a buzzer sounded.

"Mission successful. Round Two." A mechanical recording sounded from a speaker.

The tunnels were dark and wet, with slime that dripped from old cement. Michael and Seven stood beside one another as two men came running out, replacing their fake guns with real handguns. The sound of gears and creaking sounded as a long line of wire was pulled forward in front of them, from the furthest part of each end of the tunnel, from right to left.

At a terrifying fast speed, dead, mutilated corpses hanging from wires were rushed in a line before them, their gaping mouths and bulging eyes gazing back at them. The wire was threaded through their arms and shoulders, poking out of the skin through the wrists.

They lifted their guns for the target practice, aiming at the moving bright red stars painted across the dead victim's forehead and chest. They fired mechanically, blowing off rotted limbs and exploding jaws from leering faces. The smell of decay was strong in the air. They reloaded at the same time, firing again and again. The star on one of the bodies exploded, sending chunks of the man's head in all directions. They fired more, hitting two more stars painted over the corpse's faces.

A red light above them flashed again, the buzzer sounding.

The machine blared through the speakers. "Thirty-five percent accuracy. Mission failed. Round Two. Repeat Mission."

Sighing, Michael reloaded his gun, watching as more and more bodies flew by in front of him. He watched them as they blurred before his eyes, loud groans sounding from the cranking machine that pulled them past the two boys.

He watched as the dead faces before him glared back at him, as their hanging mouths twisted into sadistic, wide smiles and began laughing loudly at him. They laughed at him maniacally, the corpses with bulging eyes that never blinked. Their eyes followed his every move, watching everything he did, every mistake he made.

The blur of laughing corpses grew darker before him. A blur of dead bodies too fast to see.

Love and loss

Love and loss

The loss of his parents.

The loss of his freedom.

And much later to come, the loss of Seven.

It was all too much to bear.

Michael felt dizzy and fell back. They laughed louder at him. They called him names. A stupid, scared little boy they called him. "Michael," they screamed. "Scared little Michael!" They laughed still, until their voices were high and shrill and pierced his ears. "Scared little Michael," they screamed. "Scared little Michael. Just a scared little boy in the dark. That's all he is." They laughed.

Scared.

Sadistic smiles in the darkness.

The corpses laughed at him.

It drove little Michael crazy

That's all he was. A scared little boy.

That's all he was.

A killer, called Fifty- Six.

He blacked out on the cold, damp ground.

They told me to kill the dog and I refused.

They are mad at me.

I don't want to kill and I don't want to justify my suffering.

Andras grabbed me by the arm, ripping me upward and pulling me into the air. Michael wouldn't kill and it had gotten him in trouble more than once before.

They threw him in a small room and locked the door, imprisoning him. I closed my eyes, wondering what it would feel like to just die right now.

I thought about the universe and my place in it and what it meant to be that kid. The one chosen to have a terrible life and not know what happiness felt like.

When the stars aligned and the moon had shined its light, saying someone had to be sacrificed for the world to keep turning, the planets had painted a portrait of Michael and God had chosen him to suffer.

Chosen to suffer?

Was that all he was?

Someone sacrificed so that someone else could live?

Did that really make him happy?

He didn't know anymore.

Somewhere in the world, in the turning comsos, there was a "if this, then this" clause. It said that love could value another human's life over another, a victimizer's hierarchy that had always sickened Michael. Why kill so others could live? Why die so another could be born? Why the hell was there such a thing as a more precious person?

If his death spared others could he find joy or sorrow from such a fact?

Why in the world would he want to suffer for a fucking woman or man he had never met before. If that was love, I didn't want it. Perhaps, if I had known Tara back then, I would've understood what it meant to be a good person and sacrifice yourself to save others without questioning the existentialism behind the whole thing.

I was locked up for about a week.

When they pulled me out I was weak, dry mouthed, and half- delirious. I was given a small meal and water and my broken arm was wrapped.

I felt sick and feverish all day long and I thought about God and the COSMOS and why I had to be the one that had to get locked up for a week and what I had done wrong in past lives to lead me to such a life.

God is real?

Is God real?

God, if youre real.

then why do we suffer so much?

Why are we always in pain?

I want to live on a star.

A star so high and placed afar.

and if i dream

I dream of life

a life without pain

no suffering no gripes.

I feel the world is nothing but evil
And if the H Group were God.
Did that make Andras the Devil.
If you can control.
The way things are.
and nothing is broken.
Just shattered and scarred.
Then maybe we have.
No choice in it all.
I hope that this time.
We happen to fall.
Deeper and deeper
into our pain.
and thoughout it all
it all stays the same.
and nothing can change.
and I'm sorry i told you.
that I would be good.
because they threatened to kill me
if I did what I should.
and I long for my mother
who no longer exists.
and pray for a father
that I can't remember well enough to miss.
God are you real.
and if so, why so sad?
Did you intend to hurt us.
Or save us instead.
Why are we here and who are we really.
because without love.
we lose credibility.

The next day, Andras pulled Michael aside taking him to a bright hallway that the children rarely saw. It was completely unlike the tunnels. Dry, with neon bright white lights above them, giving it a strong glow. Michael had to shield his eyes, stumbling through the blinding glare. From below, he could hear cries and screams coming from beneath the floor.

Pounding sounds.

He furrowed his brows in confusion.

"The prisoners are kept in the floor below us," Andras explained. "It's where much of the business is conducted."

Not sure what to say, Michael just nodded, keeping his shielded gaze to the floor.

They walked for a ways before Andras took him to a small lit room. Michael found the light from the glass lamps only slightly more agreeable. It shined as a golden glow that lit up the warm and comfortable looking living area.

He felt awed by the place. A table sat in the middle. It was fancy looking, with candles glowing, casting its rays on the white cloth that lay across the tabletop. The floor was soft against his bare feet. Soft and fluffy. The walls were colored in pleasant browns and with lovely pictures that hung from them. He cocked a head to the side, flooded with flashbacks, of living in a house, of having a house and a soft floor and warm lights and lamps and feeling safe.

Andras led him to the table, taking a seat on one of the tall chairs. He looked at him coldly. "You can sit," Andras spoke.

Michael hopped up on the chair opposite the man, looking around him. He didn't know what the boss wanted with him. From their last encounter, he didn't expect much. Maybe the man was going to kill him because Michael refused to kill the dog. Was that what it was?

A woman appeared, holding two large plates in her hands. She set them down, one in front of the boss and one in front of him. Michael looked down at his own plate in surprise, finding large slices of speckled meat and brightly colored vegetables. It smelled amazing and looked delicious.

He looked up at Andras who was already cutting into his own food, juice pouring from the grilled chicken as he sliced through it.

Andras looked up at him, the fork to his mouth. He chewed. "You can eat too." He said.

I nodded slowly. Taking my own fork and clumsily poking at my own plate.

Andras continued speaking, eating as he spoke. "I wanted to tell you how sorry I am for leaving you in jail for so long. I don't want you to think badly of me."

Michael didn't reply. He didn't know how to reply.

"My father did the same to me when I was your age. He stole me from my mother. As if getting her pregnant in the first place wasn't evil enough, he canceled out any love and good that could've come from the arrangement.

Then he killed her. And he took me down here." Andras stopped, swallowing a bite of food. "But he made me who I am today. Fifty-six, one day you'll understand. When you're grown up, you'll see that I only do the things I do out of pure love for my family here. I have to be strict. If I wasn't, nothing would get done. It's not easy being leader. I'm sure you can understand that. It's a hard job, and if it weren't for my father's brutality I wouldn't be able to do that job as well as I do. For that, I thank my father, and I know you think I should hate him, as most people do, but I don't. I respect him only. As respect is the answer."

Andras lifted a cloth to his face, dabbing at the corners of his mouth. "Fifty-six, why do you fight us? Why do you still refuse to kill?"

Michael stopped eating, dropping the fork to the table and looking away. He should've known this was going to happen. Andras was going to punish him for not killing the dog.

"I asked you a question."

"I just don't want to," Michael said finally. "I don't feel like it."

"You don't feel like it?"

Michael shook his head. "Yeah, I guess."

"Killing is human nature. I know you may not know this but above ground they kill people all the time. They have wars. They steal. They murder. They do these things for no reason at all, sometimes. What makes you think you're any different? It's the human condition to kill. When you grow up, you'll come to understand that."

"But it feels wrong."

"It's not wrong to kill, Michael. Even as you speak, you're eating something that got killed. A chicken died so you could live. There's no such thing as right and wrong. They're just concepts. They're made up. They aren't real. They're just there to confuse you. Good and bad don't exist. There's just the here and the now, and what you choose to do with that time is completely up to you."

A world that chose me to die instead.

A world that sacrificed me the chicken so someone like Andras could have something to eat.

Was that love.

If that was love, then maybe love was evil and hatred had been the answer after all.

Michael sat quietly, touching his wrapped arm lightly with his fingers. "Is that how it is?"

"That's exactly how it is. That's exactly the way the world is, Fifty Six. And don't let anyone tell you anything different."

He stood up. "Let me show you something Fifty-six."

He led Fifty -six out of the room, locking the door behind him. Then they made their way down the corridor and to a staircase. They went to the level below, suddenly surrounded by the sounds of screams and haunting energies.

They entered a room, where a mangled corpse lay in the middle of the room on the floor. Fifty- six gasped when he realized the man was still alive.

"The human condition," Andras spoke again. "Is to kill." He took a knife and handed it to Fifty-six. "Now kill him Fifty-six."

Michael hesitated, not sure what to do.

The human condition?

A cosmos that wanted him to suffer.

And the following justification for such.

Was this my fault. If I did what Andras wanted, did that make me evil?

Was there a God who'd be angry by these things?

I wasn't sure.

I wasn't sure about anything anymore.

"Kill him." Andras urged. "What are you waiting for? Do it."

I refuse to move.

"I said kill him." Andras began yelling. He stomped a foot on the ground. "Kill him kill him kill him right now. Kill him or I'll kill you."

I was shaking. I didn't know what to do. I wasn't moving. I stayed frozen in place.

He felt a hard shove of the gun against his scalp. It stung. The metal stung the skin on the back of his head. Fifty-six finally spoke. "To end his suffering, I'll do it. You can get me to kill someone but I'll never help you hurt him. Is that a deal?"

"Deal. Now kill him or so help me I will pull this trigger and end your suffering instead."

It was then that I realized that sometimes it was like that too. That when you killed someone, it could be the most loving, most generous thing you can ever do for a person.

Was that really true then?

Or did this justify Michael's own suffering even more.

The second I took that knife, did I just justify every bad thing that ever happened to me before?

He closed his eyes slamming the knife down hard into the miserable man's chest, blood spurting out all across his face. He pulled the knife out and stabbed again, tears flooding his vision as he did so.

Stab.

Stab.

Again and again he stabbed the man until there was no life left in the man and there was nothing left of his suffering.

He stabbed him and stabbed him and stabbed him.

Past the point of death, I stabbed and stabbed and stabbed him until there was nothing but blood and death and a guilty conscious left behind.

So basically the dream is over now and I am left with my memories only.

I feel sad. In case you're curious about what happened that night I dropped by Tara's apartment, this is what happened immediately beforehand.

Seven stood waiting for him outside of H Group headquarters. He was obviously there to kill Michael. And Michael felt betrayed. He supposed somewhere in his heart, he had really thought that Andras would forgive him. However, despite the false promises of love and forgiveness, Andras had sent an assassin, not just any assassin, but his best friend Seven to off him for failing his mission to kill Tara Jones.

No forgiveness.

No coming back to H GROUP.

Just sadness, betrayal, and heartache.

Michael watched him, his own gun raised in front of him. They faced one another in a standoff, neither moving nor breaking their stare.

"Andras sent you?" Michael asked even though it was obvious. The rage was impossible to suppress.

"You know I don't have any choice, Fifty-six," Seven said, sounding angry and frustrated. "You never should've failed. You should've just killed the stupid bitch."

"Fuck you, Seven."

They fired, moving quickly in opposite directions. There was no turning back. It could never be the same again. He wasn't welcome there anymore. The H Group was his enemy, along with everyone in it. Michael dodged behind a bush and Seven did the same at the opposite end of the lawn. They were all enemies now. He didn't have any choice but to fight them.

Michael made a dash forward toward Seven, narrowly missing a shot to the throat, and fired at Seven once more. Seven jumped back, falling when the bullet entered his leg and he fell to the ground. Michael regained his balance and they were aiming at each other again. Michael aimed downward and Seven's gun raised from his place on the floor.

Seven hesitated, as if regretting their battle, and Michael fired mercilessly. The bullet entered Seven's chest. Narrowing his eyes, Michael fired again and again until the sound of empty clicking sounded only. The devastated body lay in a heap on the floor, blood pouring out from the open wounds. Michael watched him for a moment, watching as the life poured from his companion's body.

It was over.

Seven was dead.

It hadn't been on purpose. It was wasn't his fault.

He cried. Seven was dead.

It hadn't been on purpose that he killed Seven,

but the betrayal had been too great.

It hadn't been on purupose that he had killed his dear friend.

So that was that. I turned my head left and right, finding myself sitting in the dark room of my hotel room.

He stumbled to his feet, moving to a lamp and switching on the light. It was already late. The room was empty and silent.

He wiped at his face, feeling uncomfortable as he did so.

Not his fault, he thought.

It wasn't his fault that he killed Seven. The betrayal had been so great, that he hadn't any choice but to finish him off. He put his hands over his face and began to cry.

Assassin number Seven, deceased.

CHAPTER 13 prologue

"Love and loss
and no real difference.
It's people like you
that make life worth nothing to me."

     ~Jon Assassin number Forty-five.

CHAPTER 13

Tara awoke to the sound of knocking on her hotel door. She opened the door and stared at Michael who stood in the hallway.

I feel sad, thinking that he himself looked sadder than usual today and I wondered why. I wanted to tell him that everything would be okay but I didn't know what to say so I stayed quiet.

We went inside and sat on my bed.

He still looked depressed so I asked him what was wrong.

"Nothing," he replied. "Bad dreams, maybe."

"What kind of dreams?"

"Dreams about my past."

I nod, not sure what to say and finish eating. "I'm sorry to hear that...."

Bad dreams.

Love and loss.

I ask, "May I ask, what kind of dreams you have about your past?"

"When I was little, I was kidnapped."

"What happened?"

"I was raised as a killer. That's why I was an assassin."

"That's terrible."

"Yeah. I ran away because I couldn't take it anymore."

"I see."

Bad dreams

and love and loss.

And no real difference anymore.

Was that the point of life?

To be disturbed and sad forever?

To wonder about things like God and the Devil and wonder if they were real and haunting us even as we spoke.

"It made me think about things like religion and existentialism," he continued. "And why we're here and how I came to be in the predicament I was in. To kill or be killed. It was all I lived for for so long. And if there is a God. Is it possible I justified my miserable existence as a victim every time I picked up that gun? Do you believe in God and Devil? And if so, are they right or wrong? Be they kind or cruel? What the hell is going on here?"

"I do believe in God and I do believe he is kind Michael. I was raised a Christian girl."

"Do you think that they divine our fate?"

"I have no idea."

"Maybe we're just puppets."

"Like human machines?"

"Yes. Maybe we don't deserve to exist. Maybe someday, God will be so disappointed in us that he will just put us right back and never let us come back to life again."

"Put us back?"

"To heaven or to hell," he said. "To be with him or not. He will put us back to death and we'll never see the light of day again."

I feel bad.

And sad.

Forever and ever.

I love you

but you don't know me.

I love you

but you don't see me.

I need you.

but you don't need me.

I want there to be a God.

So that you can be happy.

and safe and know that all is not for nothing.

It is divine and real and propels toward a better future, not no future at all.

I dream of a better world. Of a world free of violence and cruelty. Of a world that knew that Michael was a good man and, in fact, not a terrible person regardless of his deadly past. I feel bad for him.

I feel bad.

I think that if I could choose between God and Devil as being kind or cruel, i would choose kind, because that is my hope for the world, is that kindness is real and the answer and all there is and the only way we can possibly be happy someday is to believe in him and GOOD truly. Let him be kind in your heart and you will live forever. Think he is cruel and he IS cruel. Think God is kind, and he is kind. This was real to me. The belief that belief rules over our judgement. The theory that in the name love and loss, there could be a world of no loss and only love and only if, we knew God did these things for us and not against us.

"I want to think God is a good thing." I say finally. "Do not fear God, Michael. For I swear, that God is good and would never hurt you. I think your fear that God is trying to suffer you or justify your suffering is unfounded and not real. You are a wonderful man and I don't believe that you were born in this world just to suffer. I feel like happiness is possible for a reason. So that we can seek it out and try to be happy forever someday. I hope you can understand.

Michael. I love you.

I want you to be fine.

I need you to be fine.

Michael is so real and so right and so my life and I am no longer obsessed with him and his concept but am truly in love with him now. My little crush had turned into a giant force of nature and it was propelling me towards some greater accomplishment in evolution. This love is real Michael. Feel me. Feel my heart. And know I love you. Understand that this love so real that it is more real than you and me put together. I LOVE YOU MICHAEL.

I love you so much...

This was real.

This was what love felt like.

My love had grown and grown and grown until it was as tall as a tower and as beautiful as a flower. My love. My life. I feel like my heart is encased in a deep sorrow. How sorrowful to love you so much and not know if you loved me back.

Was there a God?

and if so,

What in the world could come of doing such things to this man? I think we thought too long and too hard about it. But in the end. Just know this, the things that do come of this, may they bring us toward a better future where nothing bad ever happens. That's called faith. "Michael," I say. "You must have faith. If God is real then God is good and your faith in him is all you need. Just feel his love Michael. Feel his love and feel my love for you. There's nothing wrong with love Michael. Let it pour over you. The things that hurt you can hurt you no more. We've run away. Now let's learn to be happy and I will try to be happy too."

"I see," he says.

"I'm sorry I spoke so much."

"No, really, it's okay," he replied.

"I just," I continue, "want to know more about you. I want to know everything about you."

I wasn't sure what I was saying.

But what I was trying to say, was that I felt better knowing that he was able to share his life story with me.

When he was around I didn't feel lonely anymore.

There was no more conversation between us.

He excused himself and left the room without another word.

Some time went by with me alone.

I decided then to sneak away for some time to myself and a place to think. Deciding on the beach, I grabbed my purse and a big hotel towel to take with me.

I boarded a taxi and it took me to the beach which was more empty than normal despite the time of year being a heated summer.

I laid a beach towel out and laid over it. I drifted to sleep.

When I was asleep, I dreamt about my family and their death. I dreamt that I was there with them during their murders, watching as a black figure shot them dead. I dreamt in terms of vivid sadness and despair and felt so sad that almost awoke from the agonizing pain in my heart from loving them so much and losing them so badly.

I dreamt that music was playing as I stood like a statue over a stone cement block, posing as if like the Virgin Mary, and I was praying and crying and hoping that God would come down and save us all.

I dreamt that Michael was staring straight into my eyes as a violin strummed gently in the air. His eyes, so deep and pretty, gazing deep into my own. I didn't know what to do so I blink and he's gone.

I open my eyes and wake up, finding it is later in the evening. The violin is still playing even though I am awake and I realize that the music had been real and that a young man was standing there playing music on his instrument only a few feet away from me. I turn to look at the man. There is no one else on the beach, just me and the strange man in question.

He is blond and tall and has blue eyes and looks young for his age which I can only assume is somewhere in his early twenties but maybe not.

I smile at him and he smiles back at me, continuing to play on his violin. I feel enchanted and borderline frightened by the music. It is so hauntingly beautiful that it makes me feel uneasy and happy all at once.

The man stops playing and I clap my hands loudly. "Beautiful, beautiful," I say. "Wonderful," I say in German.

"Thank you."

"Oh, you speak English," I ask.

"Yes, I do."

"And your name, Sir?"

"Why, I'm called Jon."

"Jon lovely name."

"Thank you. I'm actually better known as JOn forty five. Assassin number forty--five that is."

"Excuse me?"

"You heard me. I'm assassin number Forty-five, and I'm here to kidnap you, Miss Tara Johnson."

I try to run away.

"You can run away if you like," he said, still smiling. "As a matter of fact, you can do whatever you like, but it won't do you much good."

I keep running. The sand catches in my toes and slows me down but I keep going.

"Won't do you any good," he yells again. "Because it's too bad, I didn't come alone."

Two more men appeared from behind trees and began chasing after me. They caught up to me, grabbed me and dragged me to their car. They drugged me and I was made unconscious.

When I awoke again, I was in an apartment and surrounded by blood.

Jon forty-five stared down at me, kneeling forward. "Oh, you're awake," he smiled. "That's good."

I was tied up and not sure what was going on. There were two other men, the ones that had brought me there, they were on the couch and two headless corpses on either side of them. Jon stood up and went to the kitchen. He returned with a bowl of food. And began eating it hungrily, sitting down on the carpet beside me. "People." he replied. "In case you were wondering." He smiled again.

I felt sick, almost understanding what he meant by that.

I realized the two men on the couch were eating from plates too and drinking from beer cans.

"What we're eating that is," the man on the left continued, "is people." He lifted a can and shook it. "This is their blood."

The man on the right gestured beside him to the corpse sitting next to him. "His blood to be exact."

I felt more sick but tried to hide it.

Maybe they were joking?

"I was hoping you'd wake up soon. Are you hungry too? There's plenty of stew left over for you to have some."

"Last meal," The man on the left laughed out loud

"Why didn't you just kill me?" I ask.

"Waiting for Michael." Jon replied. "You're bait. Let me tell you something Miss Tara, because this is how I feel. Love and loss and no real difference. It's people like you, that make life worth nothing to me. And that's the way it is."

I begin to cry. Why was I crying? Perhaps I was just sad that I may never see Michael again. I never should've left him. I never should've gone out alone.

Michael decided to go looking for Tara after she disappeared from the hotel. He caught sight of her entering a taxi. I called the same taxi and asked where the girl had gone to and he answered the public beach. I asked for him to take me there too.

When I got to the beach, I watched as Tara was dragged into a car. Jon Forty-five was on the beach and two men were shoving Tara into the vehicle.

It was quite suddenly that I felt a kick to the back of my head. Stumbling forward, Michael swung around quickly to face his attacker. His hand went to the handgun at his side. Bee was staring straight at him.

"Bee," I hissed. "What are you doing here?"

"You know why I'm here Fifty-six." Her clothing was all black, her long hair pinned up to the back of her head, as it often was when she went off on assignment. Her gun was poised before her, aimed steadily at my forehead. "It doesn't have to be like this. We can talk things over. You can still come back Fifty-six."

"Andras wouldn't let that happen. He'd make sure I was dead first."

"I can talk to him," she insisted. "We can talk to him. It doesn't make sense for us to fight like this."

It didn't happen often but it did occur every so often where one of the H Group would fail a mission or try to run away. Obviously there was no room for second chances. Their mutilated corpse would be hung in the dining room hall, arms outstretched as they dangled from metal walls, a giant iron spike impaling them through the center of their chest. They served as examples to the rest of them. "What makes you think I'd believe you."

"I wouldn't lie to you."

"Then what makes you think I'd ever do something like that?"

Bee narrowed her eyes at him angrily, her lips curling into a scowl. "Don't say I didn't try, Michael."

She fired her gun at him. The bullet barely let out a whisper through the silencer as it passed through it.

Anticipating the shot, Michael dodged it a split second sooner, sending a gun shot in her direction. As expected, it threw her off, and she lost her balance as she tried to avoid it. He ducked along the side of a car, until he was in front of the car from which she was standing.

He could see her through the passenger window, straight through to the other side, and to her crouching form outside the driver's side door. He pressed the tip of his gun through the window firing a bullet through both panes of glass, from passenger to driver and watched as it entered her shoulder.

He heard her shriek and glanced through the splintered glass trying to spot her. She was out of sight. When he looked again, she was standing on the roof of the car, a tall figure glaring down menacing at him and leaping forward. Her foot made contact with his head and he went teetering backward as a second kick sent the gun flying from his hand. Before he could recover, she kicked him hard in the chest, sending him sprawling on his back.

Jumping down from the car, she slammed her foot down roughly on his stomach pinning him to the ground. She lifted the gun with her left arm now, her right one a bleeding mess hanging at her side. "Nice try," she muttered. She aimed the gun at his face.

He swiveled his right leg quickly to her ankle, tripping and knocking her to the dirt. Pulling himself up, he tried to get a hold of the gun in her hand and was stopped with an elbow to his nose. Bee slammed the side of her hand down hard on the back of his neck, knocking him forward. He pulled his head back up instantly, knocking her forcefully in the chin with the top of his skull.

His hands wrapped around the gun in her hand and tore it away from her, pulling it up and firing at her. She ducked racing away and heading into a forest of trees that lined the outskirts of the sandy beach.

He grabbed his original gun from the ground, now holding a gun in each hand. He raced after her into the trees.

When he reached the woods, he found Bee had completely disappeared from sight. It started to rain, and he watched as droplets of water rolled off the bare branches and landed on his skin.

He glanced around himself carefully, both guns raised in the air. To his surprise, Bee came speeding down from a tree top, landing with a crash in front of him and jamming a knife into the center of his abdomen.

When Michael did show up, which he did, he came pounding in through the door, gun firing.

His torso was wrapped and there was red on the front of his shirt.

The two men on the couch turned to look at him in surprise, before pulling out their own guns and shooting back at him and he dodged, ducking into the kitchen.

"Shit," one man mumbled, and the two men stood up.

Jon continued eating not looking up from his meal.

The sound of guns firing.

The sound of bullets and the smell of gun powder.

The two men went down silently and Michael emerged, from the kitchen with blood pouring from his left shoulder.

I wondered what Jon Forty-five had planned.

Love and loss.

And no real difference anymore.

The human meal the men had shared.

I wondered why I had gone to the beach and what I could've done to prevent the bad things in my life.

It's people like you Jon, assassin number Forty-five, that make life worth nothing to me. You jerk.

Jon twitches, as if he can hear my thoughts.

I watched as he throws his bowl of stew at Michael, steaming hot food, splashing over Michael's face and eyes and the bowl smashing into his nose and breaking it immediately. Michael dropped his guard for a moment to wipe at his face. Blood smeared across his cheek from his broken nose.

Jon rushed forward, punching Michael in the gut and Michael fell forward. Jon lifted his knee and kicked him in the face as Michael fell forward and Michael flew backwards, crumpling to the ground. Jon Forty-five, pulled a gun from his belt and put it to Michael's head, to my horror, and I thought for sure that Michael was done for.

But Michael threw his head forward, and headbutted Jon in the face. Jon teetered back, the gun flying from his hand.

Michael went to shoot him and pulled the trigger, the sound of an empty barrel sounding. He was out of bullets.

They raced for Jon's fallen gun and Michael got to it first, shooting at Jon, who dodged him and ran out of the room, disappearing immediately from sight.

Michael untied Tara and helped her to her feet. "Are you okay?"

"I think so."

"You came for me," I breathed, still in disbelief over what I had seen.

"You thought I wouldn't?"

"But why?"

Michael shrugged. "It's like I said before. You're my friend. I would do that for you."

We head out of the apartment through the broken open door and Michael practically carries me to a taxi waiting for us. "What happened to your stomach?" I ask.

"Stabbed. Bee, Assassin Twenty-one got me. She almost killed me."

"Are you okay?"

"Yes I'm fine. I'm worried about you? Are you okay?"

"Yes," I lie, not wanting to talk about it anymore.

"Okay then," he replied helping her into the car.

We drive home to the hotel room. He follows me into my room and I go to bed, falling asleep on the bed. He stays with me, falling asleep on the chair beneath my window.

CHAPTER 14 prologue

"You're in my heart,
you're in my mind,
if you were gone,
I think I'd die."

~Michael assassin fifty six.

CHAPTER 14

In the morning, we dress his wounds and I'm relieved to see they aren't as deep as I had thought.

I ache thinking I had almost lost him. Time was painful. It could go on forever or for one more second and either way I'd never know when would be the last time I'd see him again. I want to tell him that I appreciate him, that I cherish him and most of all that I love him but time is short or long or backwards or forwards and I have no idea if we're even going to live through this or not. I may never see him again someday. How was I to know what tomorrow would bring?

We could die at any second and I'd never even see it coming, just a quick bullet to the head that would lead to eternal darkness. I don't know. Maybe I'm just a pessimistic person by nature.

I love you, Michael, but I can't tell you, Michael.

Love and loss.

Loss and love.

There was something about him that made me want to cry.

I long for you but I never tell you.

In the end, it was people like him, that made life worth living.

So fuck Jon Forty -five and his cannibal assassin friends.

Fuck Andras and his big gang of assassin bullies.

Fuck the world for never knowing the difference between good and evil and right and wrong.

Fuck me for loving someone that probably thought of me more as a friend.

I love you Michael. Please don't leave me.

He lays in my bed recovering from the injury. I don't want to bother him so I sit in his seat in front of the window and watch him as he sleeps.

I glance through a magazine that is in German and I still haven't learned a lot of the language so I mostly stare at the pictures and ads for perfume.

The pictures blur before me. I see Michael get up from bed, well again. He wraps his strong arms around me and begins to kiss me. I feel enamored and hungry for him. I kiss him back.

Love and loss.

And the way it feels when you're around. I love you Michael. I want you near me always.

He pulls my clothes off and we have sex.

His bare skin against mine is the most sensual experience of my life.

You're in my mind. In my head. In my heart. In my dreams. I can't forget you.

Maybe you're perfect.

I can't forget about you or get away from the thought of you.

White suits...

Soaked in blood...

I wanted him to know how I felt.

But love is a silent killer.

And I didn't want to cry anymore than I already had.

I drink in your scent and and bite your ear and kiss your neck.

You're everything to me.

My world.

My life.

My existence.

I'm not sad when you're here. Despite it all. Despite the fears and paranoias in my heart, as long as you're here, everything feels like it'll be okay again.

I awake from the dream and blink.

Michael is still laying in bed and there was no kissing and no sex and nothing I could really brag about later to anyone at all. Just an emptiness in my chest. I guess the whole thing has just been a delusion of my own. I sigh, and stare back at the magazine, thinking I had fallen asleep by accident and fantasized too hard about my favorite person.

I stare at him a little longer, feeling almost guilty for my sexual fantasy about him and get up, leaving the room and shutting the door behind me.

CHAPTER 15 prologue

Here I am.

Voodoo girl.

I don't know why I love you.

I just do.

And I hope that doesn't inconvenience you.

in the way it has inconvenienced me.

~ Tara Jones.

CHAPTER 15

I'm worn out and fatigued and tired.

I don't want to be here but I am. I'm drowning in my solitude. I head to Michael's room and grab him some clothing and bring it back to him.

I go back into the room and set the clothing on top of the dresser in front of the mirror that is above it.

I'm tired of running and tired of fighting. I want to give up but I can't seem to have the guts for it. For Michael's sake, who I love now and who has been so very careful with my life, I feel like I have to survive even thought I no longer want to, so I have rejected the knife to slit my wrists, and thrown out the pills to overdose on.

I think of all the times I ever had regretted or not appreciated life but to be alive was a beautuful and apparently very fleeting second of our existence. I don't want to lose it but I don't want to try anymore. I'm tired Michael. I'm thinking about giving up. I just want to throw it all away and perhaps spare you the heartache of finding my life more valuable than your own.

I go for a walk.

A long one.

In an attempt to commit suicide perhaps by being out in the open.

Should I live or should I die?

I don't know which is more right anymore.

I want to give up, but I don't want to disappoint Michael.

I think of you

of throwing out my life.

and even if I try

I leave it in fates hands.

and am drunk off of you

and think that maybe I'll give life a chance.

So long as nothing bad happens in the meantime.

What I'm trying to say is,

fate can decide for me.

Once again, I leave my life up to destiny.

and hand my will over to God.

When no one comes for me and I am annoyed.

I walk around, going to the store to pick up something to drink and some microwaveable dinners. I bring it home.

I go out again and go to a casino to gamble for a few hours.

When I am done, I head home again.

Nothing interesting had happened. No bullets whizzing past my head. No one had attempted to kill me in days now and I'm beginning to feel neglected. I give up on my assisted suicide and go back home again to Michael who is still sleeping.

I go against everything inside me telling me this would be embarrassing to do and I crawl into bed beside him and go to sleep too.

My attempt at assisted suicide lasted for three days. Yes, I was kidnapped again on the fifth day and yes, I did feel a little disappointed with the world and God and Goddess for putting me in a situation where I was to want one thing and have happen another. My dream of being kidnapped with my consent was something too expensive to afford and I could not have it.

So, as for my suicide, or at least, my try to kill myself, I walked in and out of the rooms as Michael slept. I ran out of the motel room, ranting and screaming and even took a taxi to the beach as I had the other day to hopefully repeat the incident. But this time I wanted to die. And that was probably why nothing happened. So I gave up and went home and for three days straight, leaving and going, leaving and going, and hoping something interesting would happen that never did.

On the fourth day, Michael is well and up again and we are headed out for dinner. I call it a date. He calls it something else, probably, but I'm sure he would've been annoyed if he knew I was considering it a chance to get to know him better so I didn't say anything. I didn't make a big deal out of the beautiful dress I bought at the thrift store to wear for dinner or make a big shabang out of my perfectly in place makeup and carefully groomed hair. I didn' t say anything special to hint that I loved him and the quality time I was spending with him.

We leave and go out to dinner and sit down to eat and I am ecstatic the entire time. We order cheeseburgers and fries and ketchup and I order wine and he orders water. I clear my throat.

"How do you feel?" I ask him.

He smiles. "So much better thank you."

"How are you feeling?" he asks me himself. "You had quite a scare the other day. I was worried about you. I was worried it made you sick. You barely slept and you're restless. How are you feeling today?"

"I feel great," I replied quickly, smiling. I knew it was a stretch of the truth but I didn't want to tell him I was still scared of death and of God and Heaven and Hell and of the end of the world and of killer bees and of clowns and such and decided to tell him something else. I said, "There's something about tonight that I just love."

"What's that?"

"Well, being with you for one," I say. "And for two, it's a beautiful starry night and the moon is out and I just love it that you're here with me tonight."

"Thank you," He replies. "You're a good friend. I love being here with you too."

"Do you think the world is GOOD place, Michael?"

"Well, it definitely has its ups and downs."

I say, "Well, I ask because I think the world is a GOOD place, Michael. A very GOOD place. I think God is right when he says that we are all dear to him, and that GOOD is the answer. I think GOOD is precious and right and good and wonderful. What do you think?"

"I think good is a good thing too."

"Do you think we'll be happy someday?"

"We're happy right now," he replied.

"No, I mean happy. You're such a GOOD man, Michael and I want you to know I really appreciate you. I'm so grateful for everything. For you. For God's forgiveness. For your protection of my life. I value the world now. I value the small things. I value love and life and the way things are and I feel like it could get better and better forever."

"Thank you," he smiles. "For telling me that. It means a lot to me."

"What about you? Are you happy? Happy to be alive?"

"Tara, if it weren't for you, I don't think I would be alive at all right now. I'd have done myself in a long time ago. Your friendship has meant the world to me. I'm so grateful for you."

I smile. "Thank you Michael. I know I haven't done much yet. I know I haven't really given you much back in return or done anything to make you truly happy but I will someday. I promise. I'll give back to you. In the way you always gave so much for me."

"Don't worry about it," he says, drinking from his water. "You're wonderful. You don't owe me a thing. Just promise you'll never change."

The food comes and we eat in silence.

When we are done, we leave and we lay down in the parking lot and gaze at the stars, pointing out the constellations and making the world a softer place to live in. He wraps his arms around me in a tight hug as we lay there and asks me. "Why so philosophical tonight?"

"It's just thinking about things like death and what it means to be alive and what it means to survive such strange ordeals," I say. "I finally feel safe. I think it's over. I don't think anyone will ever hurt us again. And I'm grateful for that. I'm so glad it's finally done with. I feel safe with you, Michael. Even safer than before the H Group began stalking me."

"I'm glad you feel that way."

"Do you think love is real? Or just our imagination?"

"Real. It's definitely real."

I blurt out finally, "Because I think I love you. I love you very much."

"Thank you, Tara," he replies, pulling off of me. "I love you too but only as a friend. I'm afraid I can't be with anyone right now. I'm not the type."

I nod, beginning to cry. "I understand. I hope you're not angry. You're not angry are you? Now that you know I love you?"

"No, I'm not mad at you. And love is real Tara. Just keep holding out. Hold out for someone and you'll find the right man for you. Someone brave and strong that can take care of you forever. I'm not that man. I'm afraid I'm not the one for you."

I cry harder. "It just hurts so much. It's not easy to give up but I'll do it for you. I'll give up on you if you really want me to."

"Please do, Tara. I'm no man. I'm a monster. And I don't think I'm the one that can make you happy. Through it all, I'm nothing but a murderer. A stupid assassin NUMBERED Fifty -six."

"Can't you just be Michael for me?"

"I can't. I'm Fifty-six and I'm not a strong man. Just a man. and I can't protect you, just delay the inevitable. We all die eventually, Tara. It's just a matter of time. And I can't be that handsome knight that saves you every time you bruise your knee. Forgive me. I have to go."

He gets up and leaves.

I try to follow him but I lose sight of him as he is faster than me and I cry into my hands when he is gone from sight. I walk the twenty minutes back to my hotel room, head inside, and then lay in bed and go to sleep. I feel embarrassed and saddened by his rejection of me. And I realize, this may be it, the day I never see him again.

CHAPTER 16 prologue

"I feel like the days go by,
and I get old.
and pretty soon they're all dead.
All dead.
Except for me.
And I find myself being the last one of my generation left."

~ Aiden Assassin number 2.

CHAPTER 16

I stand in front of the vending machine of the hotel. I haven't seen Michael all day, and it is now the day after since our failed date. I buy a snack of chips and pretzels and pop a few into my mouth and chew.

Here I am.

Voodoo girl.

I don't know why I love you.

I just do.

And I hope that doesn't inconvenience you.

in the way it has inconvenienced me.

I lose you and remember the point of life.

I've lost you and only one thing matters now.

The world has ended for me and all I have left now...

Is food.

I hear a noise and look up. An older man, one in his late fifties comes toward me and smiles. "Hi there," he says.

"Hi."

"How are you doing young lady?"

"I'm doing well, thank you. What can I help you with?"

"I was just wondering what you were doing out so late at night. It's not safe."

"Oh, good point. Thank you."

"Are you a religious woman?"

"A little? Why do you ask?"

"How do feel about fate?"

"Why, I think fate is a bad thing."

"Why's that?"

"I want to think I have more control over my life than that?" she replied.

"But you believe in God?"

"Yes. Are you a reverend?"

"Maybe in another world I would've been. Not so lucky this time. Maybe next life around I'll get it."

"What do you do?"

"Drink," he joked. "I drink and drink and drink. That's all I do."

"That's funny," I laugh.

"I have a story to tell you."

"Go ahead," I reply.

"Once upon a time, there lived a stupid little boy. He claimed to be good and moral and know all there was to know."

"So what happened to him?"

"Well, one day his girlfriend comes and sobbing tells him that her mother is dead and a man named Jack is her murderer. The stupid little boy gets upset and promises to fix it for her. He runs off, murders the murderer and tells his girlfriend that the deed is done and he has saved her life by avenging her mother's death. The girl sobs even harder than the first time she spoke to him and tells him he's a terrible thing and that he should never take a life for anyone's sake no matter what."

"What's the catch?"

"Well, she tells her boyfriend, the murderer of her mother was actually her father and that now she has lost both her mother and her father in this lifetime."

"I see. That's terrible." I replied.

"The point of the story Miss, is that no suffering is the answer. You can't just go around getting revenge. Love is the answer and that person he killed coulda been anyone's mother or father or son or cousin or best friend. We're all connected, you know. In a web of relationships. We can't just go around killing people."

"That's a very good point." I reply.

"Next story. Once upon a time, there was an angel that fell in love with a human. He wanted the human to become an angel too. He begged God to change her from a human being into an angel, and God told him he would have to bring him the heart of his true love in order to transform the angel into a human. The angel went to his human love and began to raise the dagger that would end her life. Then he felt a change of heart and changed his mind. He decided to let the girl live and never hurt her no matter what. He went back to God and told God that he couldn't do it. He couldn't bring his love's heart to God because she would cry and her loved ones would mourn her death. God smiled and told him that he had passed the test and that he could instead turn the angel into a human so that he could descend to earth and be with the girl of his dreams. Beautiful right?"

"Very noble. Your stories are full of nobility."

Last story then.

Once upon a time, a man believed that there was gold at the end of the rainbow. He walked forever and never found it. Which led him to write a book about never doing things by assumption but only by proof of existence. It's one way of saying no suffering is the answer. Kindness has never failed a man, but cruelty is proven to lead to more cruelty. There's no gold at the end of the rainbow, dear and if you look for it, you're not only a fool, but could be saying you condone suffering which, of course, I don't.

"Of course."

"I'm a pacifist at heart. I long for peace. I long for love to be the answer and things to get better in terms of forever."

I ask, "Do you think it'll get better someday?"

"Yes. For sure. It'll get better. It'll get much better someday. You do believe in heaven, don't you?"

"I do."

"Well, that's a good thing, Miss. I feel like the days go by, and I get old. And pretty soon they're all dead. All dead. Except for me. And I find myself being the last one of my generation left."

I frown. "What do you mean?"

"I mean that I have to kidnap you, Miss. Please, forgive me."

I probably should've run away right then. I should've called Michael. I probably could've done a lot of things right at that moment. But instead, I stood frozen with fear as a group of men surrounded me and gagged and tied me and dragged me to a car. They drive me away to an H Group hideout, dragging me to an artificial tree with a camouflaged elevator in the trunk. I'm shaking. I'm crying. I'm scared but I don't fight them. And

I'm glad it's finally over. No more lucky breaks. No more cat lives. I'm going to die, and I'm fucking glad.

I'm dragged down a ragged metal corridor and I feel frightened by the sight of blood streaking the walls and metal floor.

They tie me up to a chair and lock me up in a dark room.

I'm here now.

In God's loving arms, I tell him I'm sorry for all the things I did wrong.

Then I wake up.

And I remember where I am.

I'm tied to a chair, kidnapped, beaten and scared. I don't know who they are or what they want from me. All I know is that I am going to die.

Love and loss

Love and loss.

Love and loss.

To live and let live. To die and let die.

I think that in retrospect, I would've liked to belong to something before I` went. I would've liked to know I had saved a life or left behind some great momentum that taught us that love is real and good and right. But I didn't get a chance to do any of those things. Instead, I was a lonely girl, who lived a long lonely life and hadn't had anything at all to do with anything at all. Nothing of importance anyway. Nothing that could make a difference.

My body is bruised and broken and tied to a chair. The room I'm locked in is dark and silent. The bottoms of my shoes stick to the grimed red floor.

I feel sorry for all the not nice things I had ever thought in my life and regretful for any feelings I may have hurt.

I try to move but can't. My wrists are bound behind me and hold me fast.

A scream echoes from the hallway and through the closed door to my room, and I feel frightened again. I'm ridiculous. I know that now. A ridiculous soul to think that in the scheme of things, I mattered more than a microscopic organism in space.

When they killed me, I knew I'd become dirt and dirt becomes trees which bear fruit and feed deer and expecting mothers and people like the president so at least I could leave something behind when i was gone other than nothing. A wasteful life would become a wholesome death of me giving back for once instead of just taking.

Who am I?

I'm no one.

That was what I learned.

I learned that I'm no one and they are everyone.

Who is they?

Everyone other than me. Not so much on an individual level but as a whole.

I reek of fear and chilled skin and yet a quiet resolution has fallen upon me and I am prepared to die.

I sit and realize I am essentially reliving the nightmare of my sister Stella Johnson. It's as if I have reincarnated as her. I cry, thinking that she had been here too and that she had been as afraid as I was right now.

I feel angry. As if I had been ripped off in life. Who was I? And why was I here? Why did God save me just to kill me later? Why would he do such a thing? What the hell was going on here?

In terms of transcendence, if I would've known this were going to happen, I would've asked Michael to just kill me right there and then weeks ago when he had invaded into my apartment. I couldn't believe it. This was the worst of all kinds of luck.

Michael.

I wondered if I would ever see him again.

My life was over. But at least I could die without regret. Because Michael knew how I felt. And that's all that mattered to me.

There are two things that mean the most to me in terms of love and respect for each other. It's heaven and hell and to be in between that makes all the difference in the world. I think there's such a thing as loving someone too much and being forced to be together or apart, thus the Heaven and Hell, and I don't want to be in any of those situations at all.

I feel like with Tara, I'm either forced to be with her or without her. I love her but I don't want to. I need her but it hurts to be in love. When I awoke and found out she had been kidnapped, I was devastated. I knew it was my fault. I had rejected her and now she was gone. I immediately regretted my decision to tell her I did not care for her.

But at the same time, I'm remorseful.

Love.

Who was I to love?

Love and loss

And the sympathetic overwhelmingly simple math that goes into a relationship.

Who was I to care enough to be that guy that settled down and married the woman he cared about more than anyone else in the world?

It's not you Tara, I wanted to say.

I'm the one that's not ready. I'm the fool that doesn't know what to do.

I'm the one that can't hope to love without fearing he'll crush the girl and kill her with his neglect and paranoias. I'm a monster, Tara. And I can't guarantee I can make you happy in the way a normal man could.

I thought all these things as I raced to a payphone and called Andras' cell phone.

"Hello," a male voice answered.

"Where's Bee?" I asked.

"Killed herself. Dead now. Shame. We really liked her. And Jon Forty-five too. They went down together they did."

"Then it wasn't her or Jon that did it. Then who's this?"

"Seventeen."

"Fine. Where's Tara."

"Good question. I was just about to get a hold of you. We took her back to German HQ. We're going to kill her if you're not here by the end of the night."

"What's the catch?"
"Your life for hers."

"Kill me instead of her?"

"False," Seventeen said. "We'll let her go if you stay here and become the boss's heir to the H Group. He wants you to take his place when he dies. If you die. It's up to me. Which means you're my enemy Fifty-six. I wanted to be heir, but it's your show so take it or leave it but don't make a big deal out of it. I might get jealous, you know."

I sigh. "Can I at least think about it?"

"Yes. Think all you want. You've still got eight hours until sundown. Good luck getting here in time. If you don't, good for me. If you do, good for her and you. Either I win or you two win. It all depends on if you get here in time. And even now it's wasting."

"Fine. I'll think about it."

"Tik tok, tik tok, Fifty-six. Time's a wastin'. Hope you can think real fast cause there's not a lot of time left."

I hang up and head to the hotel. I get dressed in a neat black suit with tie and jacket and brush my hair and wash my face and hands. Then I sit down on my bed and think. I think of Tara and how much she had meant to me. I want to save her. I really do. But could I really sacrifice my life and go back to being an assassin for them? I had hated that life so much. How could I just give up my freedom for a woman I barely knew?

Sighing, I cover my face with my hands.

I'm so stupid. I'm a stupid man with a stupid life and a stupid way about himself. I saved her and now it was up to me to make sure she stayed saved no matter what. How could I do that to her? How could I spare her just to let her live a few days longer. It was my responsibility to help her. It was my responsibility to make sure she was okay.

When I was little, the skeleton figures had laughed at me. Had called me a scared little boy. Afraid to kill. Afraid to become what he hated the most. A justified prisoner of suffering. Someone who deserved the harsh life he had lived. I regret. I do. And I hate that I do those things.

When I got older, I killed my friend Seven to be with Tara. I ran away from the H group and did everything I could to stay gone. What was freedom if Tara wasn't okay? Not much. And I think that my love for her, my love for her that had manifested itself as admiration and friendship could've possibly grown to be more if we had gotten to know one another a little better. I feel like I could've really gotten attached to a gal like that. I could've really gotten close to her. Felt her heart by mine. Felt her love in my chest.

Love.

What was love?

And who was I, a monster, to think love was right for him?

One woman.

Love and loss.

When I couldn't even protect one woman, one sweet, beautiful woman from danger. I think of Stella Johnson and how her fair hair reminded me of Tara's very much so. I think of how kind Stella Johnson had been and how sad I had been to lead her and her family to her death without saving her. Save her.

Why hadn't I?

It had been possible, hadn't it?

To save her?

Why didn't I ever think of these things sooner.

Why didn't I ever come to these conclusions before these things happened instead of afterwards.

I blink.

Tara or Stella or the Johnson family or Seven or my parents or whoever it was I had lost in my life. Why did I let those things happen?

This time.

This time...

Could things be different?

To be without the loss of love.

Could that person be me?

Tara. I do. I love you. I love you very much and I don't want to lose you again. I don't want to lose you in the way I have lost so many others in my past. Please. Forgive me. Even if it means never seeing you again, I do have to save you. I will save you. I will save you.

I WILL SAVE YOU.

I

W

i

l

l

S
a
v
e

Y
o
u

My life.
My love.
Hold me,
Kiss me,
don't let me go.
Once I had a dream
and in it, I was a normal man.
It's dreams like this,
that make me cry the most.
Because marrying you is closer to being a dream,
than being my reality.
I've never known love.
Now that you're gone.
I never will.
Please forgive me.
For making you fall in love.
With someone
so heartless.
who couldn't even tell you he loved you too.

Bee Assassin number 21 and Jon assassin number forty -five. Deceased.

CHAPTER 17 prologue

I loved you so much
it broke my heart.
I'm sorry it ended.
With us never seeing each other again.

~Tara Jones

CHAPTER 17

I am drugged. In my unconscious state, I dream of my family and of red-eyed cats clawing at my door. They tell me. "Wake up, Cinderella. The ball. The ball. You must get ready for the ball."

When I awaken, the cats are gone and a man in white stares at me. He taps me on the forehead before acknowledging I'm awake now and nods at me. "I'm Andras," he says.

"Andras." I repeat groggily, still dazed from the drugs they had given me.

"That's right."

The one that Tara had heard so much about from Michael. He had finally manifested himself phsycially in real life for me.

"Love. Do you believe in it?" He asks, pouring a glass of wine from a canter.

I look down and realize I am tied to a chair. The room is distorted and messy, with slashed photos of a woman hanging from the walls, and a dead, stuffed woman seated at the table across from me. I started to scream but I stop as he pours the wine into my mouth and pulls my head back forcing it down my throat.

"Never waste wine. Especially, expensive wine," he murmured, making sure I had drunk it all. "It'll leave you cursed." When he is done, he sits down beside me in the third chair and gulps down wine from his own glass. "Red wine, white wine, pick your poison."

"Where's Michael?" I ask.

"Probably on his way."

My eyes widen. "What do you mean?"

"He likes you. I think. He would do that. Come back for you. He's the type that would come back for a woman he likes and then sacrifice himself in order to spare her life. I'm sparing you, you know. I have no doubt in my mind. No doubt at all that he'll show up. His life for yours. That's all I wanted. Would you accept that? Would you ever let a man do that for you? 'Cause if you would, maybe you don't deserve him."

"I doubt he'll come," I mutter more to myself than to him. "And I would never accept such a sacrifice. How dare you even imply I would ever do such a thing."

"Do you believe love is real, Miss Tara."

"Stop asking me that."

"I just want to know. Because love is real and dear to me, Tara. I would do anything in the name of love." He points at the dead woman in the chair across from them. "That's Bee. I loved her once. I loved her too much and never told her how I felt. I guess you could say it was somewhat unrequited. Now that's love. To long for someone forever and never have them love you back in return. That's true love. Do you think Michael loved you?"

"No. And I'm over it. I'm over it. I'm over it. Just kill me now and get this over with. I'm sick of being your puppet. I won't let Michael sacrifice himself for me."

"Well, he does love you. Because I know him better than he even knows himself. He loves you and he doesn't want to admit it because it hurts to be a man. A normal man. That's all we dream of. Of being normal. But we can't have it. It's far away. Like the sky itself. Too high to reach. The goal of being normal and kind and good and righteous." He sighs shaking his head. "It's beyond me. Beyond him. Beyond both of us really. That's why I need him. He's so much like me. He'll make a good heir to the H Group. A very good heir."

"You want him to rejoin you," I ask in disgust.

"Yes. Indeed. And you can just go on home once he gets here and never think of us again. You are, as I call it, spared, Miss Tara. A spared woman from a very dangerous league of demons. You're lucky."

"You call this lucky," I spit out, struggling in my seat.

"Well, all social commentary aside, I'm afraid I have to get some business done. I'll return later when Michael is here. You'll wait for us won't you."

I felt tears flooding my vision. It was the first time in my life I didn't want to see Michael again. The first time in my life, I didn't want Michael to come.

I've always been known as a killer. As an assassin, Assassin number fifty-six to be exact. I don't do love. Love is for the young and happy. I am neither a young man nor a happy man. Love. Not for me. But I do believe in soulmates. I think Tara was my soulmate. I enjoyed her company and missed her when she wasn't around.

I don't know what that's called.

Maybe I'm being immature.

I long to set things right. To change the past or the future or the present or some part of my life that could make the world pure and nice again where Tara and I could run off and get married and be together forever. But that's not always the option we're given in life. The option to be happy. I'm sorrowful. I'm sorry God, but I don't like this world. I don't like it and I don't want to live here any longer.

When I get to Tara, she is tied up in Andras' room at the dining room table and she is obviously delirious from being drugged.

"Michael," she cries when I show up. "Why did you have to come? You fucking idiot. Why did you have to show up? Just go home. Just leave me here. Please. Just leave me here."

"Tara," I mumble, heading towards her.

Andras is on his bed, reading from a book. "Oh good, you're here," he states, pulling himself up, and taking off a pair of reading glasses. "Took you long enough. Another second had gone by, I'd have killed her myself. The bitch wouldn't stop complaining."

I go to Tara, ignoring Andras and begin to untie her.

"Please Michael. Don't be here. Go home. I don't want you to save me. I just want to die."

"Shhhh, you'll be okay," he says, helping her up from the chair. "We're going to send you back home to the States. Everything's going to be just fine. And I'll stay here with Andras. It'll be fine. Everything's going to be okay."

"I love you, Michael."

"I love you too, Tara."

"How sweet," Andras says. He gets up and comes toward them. He pushes a button under the table, and a monitor turns on. "Send for Seventeen to come bring Tara home."

"Coming," replies.

"I hope you two realize the situation you've just survived from," Andras continues, circling the two, Tara in Michael's arms. "Fifty six, or Tara's Michael as she likes to call you, you two are what I call the luckiest people in the universe. Good luck to you Tara in all you do. You can go home now. Fifty-six. You stay here with me. A deals a deal after all. And never forget Tara as you grow old and wither away and die from old age, that you let him do this for you. Never forget that you sacrificed the one you loved just to live another few decades or so. You would do that. Never forget. You would, is the point."

"Don't listen to him Michael. It doesn't matter what he says. I don't want you to do this, Michael," Tara cried. "I want you to run away."

"I have to, love. Please, don't be angry. I can't stand to see you get hurt. I love you. Never forget that. I do. I love you. And I'm sorry for ever making you think otherwise. I have to save you."

"No, stop," Tara said, tears falling from her face as she dropped her face down over Michael's shoulder. "Stop Michael. Don't do this."

Seventeen comes in with a gang of men and they drag Tara away, who cries and screams the entire time.

"Goodbye Tara." I mutter.

There is a TV monitor of the hallways of H GROUP HQ. They watch surveilence video of Tara being dragged through the hallways and out of the underground lair.

"Funny, huh."

"Yeah, real funny."

"I know, Fifty-six. It's men like us, that don't appreciate the woman. We covet her. We long for her. We want her. It's men like us, that don't realize what we have, until she's gone."

Fifty-six touches the screen of the surveillance and kisses the image of Tara, nodding slowly in agreement.

"Until she's gone," Fifty-six repeats gently.

THE END OF BOOK 1.

BOOK 2

A Killer's Instinct:
Bee and Jon Forty-five's story

CHAPTER 1 prologue

"Hands entwined.

I hold him in my arms.

So lucky.

I smile. Yes I'm smiling.

Dear Jon, thank you for making me so happy.

I kiss him deeply.

Jon.

I love you.

I love you so much."

~ Bee, Assassin Twenty -One.

CHAPTER 1

I wake up from my dreams and I'm in Andras's bed. I sigh loudly, feeling like a bitch as I climb out of bed and put my clothing back on. God, did I hate Andras. More than that. I loathed him.

I go to the kitchen and make myself some eggs and toast. I juggle three eggs for the fun of it before frying them in oil, salt, and butter. I sit at the dining room table and start eating. Andras looks at me and I strain a fake smile. "Mornin' Darlin'. How's life?"

"Just dandy, whore."

I roll my eyes and continue eating.

"Looks like you didn't make me anything to eat."

"I'm not a maid."

"No, but you're a whore for sure. A dirty whore."

I want to kill him. "Shut up." I mutter. I drink some orange juice and then I get up. I jump onto the bed, landing on my knees. "So, what's the mission today, Pops."

"Oh, go to Seventeen and get the package. And leave me be. I'm tired."

"Whatever."

I walk out of the room pulling my shoes on and yawning loudly. I pass by Jon Forty-five and we stare at each other for a long time before passing by each other completely.

Jon.

My love.

My idol.

The only one I truly cared about in this God forsaken place was him. We had slept together only once before and it had meant the world to me. We never spoke again. But it was a silent relationship we shared. It was a silent understanding that made me feel both happy and sad in my heart when I thought about him.

Jon, your deep broken heart. I'll mend it with the blood of my victims. I promise.

I go to seventeen and fetch my target's name and address.

The driver sends me there and I shoot him dead.

I stand before the dead body and kick it hard. Stupid person. Why did this always happen? Why did you have to die? You know, you don't have to just do whatever I want. I sigh, turning around and then out of nowhere, get punched in the face by a bodyguard.

Shoot.

He knocks the gun from my hand and punches me again, this time in the stomach. I grab my stomach and fall back. Before he can punch me again, I kick him hard in the groin. As he fell forward, I retrieve my gun and shoot him dead in the head.

My nose is bleeding and I'm worried it's broken.

I wipe at my sore nose and spit out a mouthful of blood. Asshole. What a jerk. He hurt me. I leave and head back to the car.

"You okay?" The driver asked.

"Not really. I'm kinda in a bad mood."

"Why's that?"

"I dunno. Just thinking."

"About what?"

"None of your business," I joke, pushing him lightly as I climb into the car and ride shotgun. We collect the money from our client that hired us for the kill and drive back home.

When I get there, the driver, Assassin number Seventeen drops me off and drives off to pick up another assassin from another mission. Jon is standing guard outside by the elevator. He smiles at me. I carry a briefcase full of money in my arms. We enter the elevator and head down to the underground station. My nose is still bleeding. I clear my throat and say hi to Jon.

"Hey." He smiles. He gently touches my face. "Why the blood?"

"Body guard," I smile, feeling flattered by the attention. "He hit me."

"What a shame. Doing that to such a pretty girl. Such a shame."

I blush and cough into my hand, feeling shy and nervous all of a sudden. "Thank you."

He no longer speaks and we go our separate ways once we are out of the elevator.

I drop the money into a drop box, and close it, then I turn around, watching Jon Forty-Five as he walked away from sight.

CHAPTER 2 prologue

My life
If I could give it to you
The sacrifice would be the
closest thing I've ever felt
to joy, my entire life.

Bee

CHAPTER 2

I cross the street to the gas station. It's about 2:45 in the afternoon. I run into Jon Forty-Five as he is purchasing a coffee and a donut. I smile at him, blushing shyly, and he smiles back. I like him but I'm afraid to tell him how I feel. What we had was a friendship that was beautiful in its own right and I didn't want to ruin it.

I pick up a box of cookies and a soda and buy it, passing Jon by as he heads out of the gas station's foodmart. I pay for the food and head out. Jon is parked right outside the foodmart entrance, waiting for me.

"Hey there, stranger," he says.

"Hey," I smile.

Jon leans forward and opens the passenger side door. "Want a ride?"

"Sure." I climb in, flattered by the gesture. I shut the door. "Where are you going? Are you on a mission?"

"Yep. Wanna help?"

"Okay."

He starts to drive and we head off, turning north onto the freeway. I roll down my window and enjoy the sensation of wind through my hair. Love. What did it mean to be in love? Was I in love with Jon? If so, was it possible he could ever love me back?

I push the thought from my mind, feeling self conscious about it. I glance over at Jon and watch him as he slides on a pair of sunglasses.

"So how's life with Andras," Jon asks.

"More of the same," I laugh. "It's all fun and games until someone gets hurt, right?"

"Right."

"So what about you? A lady in your life?"

"Yes."

"I see." I feel annoyed but I try to hide it. "What's her name?"

"Jennifer."

"Jennifer?"

"Assassin number 55."

"I see," I say again. My annoyance is growing. My heart aches but I don't tell him. I'm starting to wish I had never asked. "So what sect is Assassin Fifty-Five from."

"Sect BB. They're stationed in France."

"Is she French?"

"Qui. She is."

"I bet she's beautiful." I sigh nonchalantly, picking at my nail.

"What makes you say that?"

"Just seems like what you'd go for. Someone really, really beautiful." I smile, pushing away jealousy and guilt from jealousy and pretending to not care.

"Thank you," he replied to my awkward comment.

We arrived at the mansion of Walter Figgs. Quietly, we head inside and find Walter seated on his couch. He yells out at us as we pull out guns and begin firing into his body. When he is dead, we tuck the guns back into our coats.

"I have an idea," Jon says, the mission completed. "Wanna be a little mischievous?"

"Okay."

He takes my hand and we begin to explore the giant mansion of the now dead target. "I'm going to show you something I've never showed any woman before." He continues. We find the kitchen and he begins to boil a pot of spaghetti.

I don't notice anything unusual until he excuses himself. He leaves and comes back dragging in the dead man.

My eyes widen. "What are you doing?"

"We're going to eat him."

I gasp, my hand flying to my mouth? "Jon, you're joking."

"No. I'm dead serious. This is something of a hobby of mine. I eat the bodies of my victims. I try to ease their ascension to heaven by eating their corpses. It's a kind of kindness. I wanted to bring you to my world and show you what I do. Is that all right? Now that you know this, is that okay with you?"

I don't know what to say to him. I feel shocked but I don't want to disappoint him. Love... What was love? To what extent would she be willing to push herself in the name of love?

Was this love?

Is this what love looked like?

I nod blankly. I had no idea. I had no idea he was like this.

I watch as he turns the arms of the man into meatballs for the pasta and cooks it. He explores the cupboards and finds spices to add to the meat.

I feel like I'm driving in a car.

I'm driving fast.

So fast that the lanes blur.

My desire for Jon is so great and big and giant that I can't take it.

I want him so bad. He's everything I ever wanted and all I ever needed. I love him.

We're racing.

My car versus Jon's.

We drag race down the street, fighting to be faster than the other.

I can't take it. I can't take it. I can't win.

His car pulls ahead of me and he wins the race.

I'm scared and I don't know what to do.

I'm not thinking I was ever the most moral woman in the universe. I was kidnapped when I was about four or five, like everyone else in H Group. I killed to keep from being killed. And that pretty much summed up my life. If ever I had parents, I don't remember them. If ever I had been happy I don't recall what that felt like. I don't know.

I'm sorry. I don't want to be too moral. I don't want to be that bitch that thinks she has a right to judge someone when she herself is a murderer.

I find myself sitting at the dining room table.

Jon serves me a plate of pasta and human meat sauce.

In my mind I'm standing on a street. Jon is driving towards me. I stand frozen in fear and my eyes widen as his headlights head straight toward me. I don't flinch. I don't run. I don't try to shield my body. I stand there and let the car run straight into me, shattering my body.

I close my eyes.

My life

If I could give it to you

The sacrifice would be the
closest thing I've ever felt
to joy, my entire life.

I open them again.

Smiling, I take a bite of the meat, without a second of hesitation.
Without throwing up. Without judgmentalness. Without crying. Just
love. Just pure and utter love. Love and admiration for Jon.

"Mmm," I say. "It's actually pretty good."

His eyes light up and he smiles back. "Oh, wonderful. I'm glad you
like it." He fixes himself a plate and we eat in silence for a few minutes.

My desire for Jon.

My love for Jon.

My inner longing for Jon.

God, can you blame me?

I just want to be happy.

I just want to feel what joy would feel like. And joy came to me
dressed up as a cannibal. Lol. Figures, huh. Such is life. My life anyway.
But who am I to complain? I think I can honestly say, this is the closest
thing I've ever felt to happiness. Being with Jon, is my only salvation. My
only solace. I love him.

Love
My life
If I could give it to you
The sacrifice would be the
closest thing I've ever felt
to joy, my entire life.

I think again.

We finish eating in silence and I don't feel the least bit like vomiting
it back up again. As a matter of fact, I feel full and happy and excited to
be with him.

He comes closer to me and kisses me. I kiss him back. It's lovely. I'm
happy. I really am.

Hands entwined.

I hold him in my arms.

So lucky.

I smile. Yes I'm smiling.

Dear Jon, thank you for making me so happy.

I kiss him deeply.

Jon.

I love you.

I love you so much.

The kissing becomes more desperate and he begins to pull my clothing off. We have sex and I am filled with every sensation known to man. It's amazing. To be a wash of emotion and feeling.

Guilt.

Love

Joy.

Sadness.

Acceptance.

Sex.

Gladness.

They wash over me and I feel ecstatic. There's nothing in this world I would trade this moment for. He kisses me and I kiss him back. The only sensation that is missing is hate. And trust me, hate has always been a theme in my life. Hatred for my past. Hatred for killing. Hatred for Andras. Hatred for my victims. Hatred.

Hate.

Hate.

Hate.

Everything but hate.

Jon was fixing me. He was fixing me.

I want him to know that if I could pick one person to be with forever, I would pick him. I love him so much I can't take it. Jon, please, love me too?

God.

There's such a thing as regret.

I do.

I regret.

I only ever have.

Please don't hate me for this one moment of joy.

CHAPTER 3 prologue

Jon,

I just wanted to be happy.

Maybe that really was too much to ask for.

                                 Bee assassin number twenty one.

CHAPTER 3

The next day was business as usual. Jon didn't say anything about our day together. As a matter of fact, he didn't even speak to me at all and barely acknowledged me as he walked by.

I turned around as he passed me, wondering if I should go talk to him or not. I wanted to be with him, and our one night of ecstasy had left me wanting more.

I decided to go up to him so I did, and Jon smiled at me. "Hey there, Bee."

"Hi."

"Did you sleep well?"

I nod. "What about you?"

"Not so bad."

Andras appears in the distance and Bee stepped back, suddenly feeling frightened. If Andras found out she had slept with someone else, would he kill her?

She gave Andras an awkward wave. "Andras, how are you?"

Andras frowned. "What's with the chit chat. Why aren't you two working?"

"Sorry," Bee replied quickly. "I'm actually on my way to pick up my next assignment."

"Oh." He paused. "Good. Hurry up, then."

He stepped away and Bee waved goodbye to Jon.

"Can you pick up my assignment too while you're there?" Jon asked.

"Sure, I'll talk to you later," she mouthed before hurrying off.

I go to seventeen to pick up Jon's next assignment and my own.

When I get it, I am surprised to see it is Fifty-six, a former ally is Jon's next target and Tara Jones is my own. Andras hadn't said anything

114

but apparently he had figured out that she hadn't successfully killed them and had forgiven her?

"Seventeen, "I begin blankly. "You're joking. Not Fifty -six." Shoot. They weren't even mad at me.

"I'm afraid so. He's gone rogue. We have to off him. Since someone apparently failed to do it herself."

I switch the assignments, thinking Jon would be better off taking care of Tara Jones than Fifty-six. Maybe I was conceited. But I felt like I was a better assassin than Jon and was afraid he'd get hurt if he went after Fifty-six himself, as she had only weeks earlier. "Here's your assignment," Bee sang, handing him the folder. "Tara Jones. Easy enough. Hope you don't have to waste too much time with this one. A waste of time, she is. A waste of time."

"Which one is yours?"

"Fifty-six."

"Why do you get to kill Fifty-six? That was always my dream to do."

"Don't you want to kill Tara?"

"You know how I feel about Fifty six."

"You don't like him?" I asked.

"No, I loathe him." Jon Forty-five replied sharply.

"Sorry I brought it up."

"It's okay," he said. He smiles then, unexpectedly. "Don't worry about it. Actually, I wanted to ask you something. Would you like to come with me today on assignment. I have two, the first ones I'm headed to now and Tara Jones, I'll do tomorrow. Would you like to come with me today?"

"I'd love to," I replied immediately. "I'd love to come with you."

"All right then. You just made my day. Let's go." he continues.

We head out and our driver is Aiden, assassin Two. He drives us out to Jon's assignment and we head into the house, Kidnapping a wealthy woman named Melissa and killing her security guards on sight. We then proceed to turn the guards into stew and eat them, as is the favorite hobby of Jon's, and then we drag the woman Jessica into the car's trunk and lock it.

"What took so long," Aiden complains.

"Sorry for the wait," Jon smiles. We climb back into the back seat of the car and Jon instantly leans over and kisses me.

"No hanky panky either," Aiden complains.

"Cock blocker."

Aiden rolls his eyes and drives us to the next targets location. It is for a wealthy man named Jefferey and we drag him out of his home, kicking and screaming and throw him into the trunk as well.

The two are shipped back to HQ, stripped of their clothing, and locked up in a cell together to be held hostage for ransom.

Jon takes me back to his dorm room and we have sex on his bottom bunk. It is the most wonderful experience of my life. If I could've made that moment last forever, I would've.

But time is no friend of mine. The worst days last too long and the good days, are far too short.

I think that if I could've, I would've cried then and there
but out of petty pride
and fear of embarrassment,
My eyes stayed dry and my pride intact.

CHAPTER 4 prologue

You're like leather,
Soft and sweet,
and most of all,
Dead to me.

                    ~Andras, leader of the H Group.

CHAPTER 4

The next morning, before her assignment to kill Fifty -six, Jon Forty -five asked me gently, "Would you like to be my girlfriend?"

I was ecstatic. We lay in bed, the covers over our naked bodies and I replied. "Yes, I'd love to," with something of a stammer in my voice. I was happy for once. Too happy. Jon was returning my affections and it felt lovely.

He kissed me and I closed my eyes, thinking that if this were a dream, I never wanted to wake up.

Long stares.

Hands entwined.

Give me your heart.

and I'll give you mine.

I let him kiss me and I am glad

If it weren't for you Jon,

I'd have gone mad in this place a long time ago.

You make me normal.

You make me well.

You make happy.

While I'm in hell.

I kiss his hands, his fingers, his arms. He's too much for me. He's too much. I'm glad for him. And hope he will be able to find happiness too, in a place like this.

She stops him and pulls away. "I better go to my next mission," She begins. "I'll have to fly all the way to Germany to kill Fifty-six. Do you think I'll succeed? Fifty-six is one of the best. Do you think I'll live or die?"

"You'll win for sure," he replied quickly.

Despite Jon's jealousy for Fifty-six, probably because he had been Andras's favorite and had been next in line as leader of the H GROUP, followed by Seventeen, she had no real grudge against Fifty-six. But her loyalty to Jon was too strong. She didn't want Jon to get hurt. Therefore, she decided, she would kill Fifty-six for him, and keep him out of danger. It wasn't easy fighting another assassin and she couldn't bear the thought of losing Jon in the way they had lost Seven.

I drop out of bed and begin to pull my clothing back on. "And you'll win no matter what," I smile. "I promise. I have some work to do for Andras. I'll see you around, Jon" When she is dressed, she hurried out of the dorm room and made her way to a private jet that Andras would let her fly during missions. She brought with her a knife and a gun and tied her dark hair back to keep it out of her face.

She flew the jet to Germany, which took several hours to do. Then she landed on German H GROUP HQ landing space deep in the woods and got out of her jet. When she was done, she took an H GROUP car to find Fifty-six. The tracer that was embedded in every assassin's body, some with or without their knowledge, told her that he was at the beach only 30 miles from German HQ. She was one of the few with the privilege of knowing about the tracer at all. I drove there without hesitation, my adrenaline rushing through my veins as I prepared myself for the upcoming battle with my ex-friend Michael, assassin number Fifty-six.

CHAPTER 5 prologue

Love can be fickle.

Love can be blind.

The most happiness I ever felt.

Was when Bee said she was mine.

~Jon assassin number Forty-five.

CHAPTER 5

I waited for Michael at the beach, spotting him appearing as Jon forty -five finished kidnapping Fifty-six's little girlfriend Tara. Good. They hadn't noticed Michael just yet. I raced after Michael before he could confront them and keep them from driving away.

I kick him hard in the back of the head, knocking him forward and off balance. He teeters back and then rebalances himself on his feet and I am aiming my gun at him. Bee," he hissed. "What are you doing here?"

"You know why I'm here Fifty-six. It doesn't have to be like this. We can talk things over. You can still come back Michael."

"Andras wouldn't let that happen. He'd make sure I was dead first."

"I can talk to him," She insisted. "We can talk to him. It doesn't make sense for us to fight like this."

"What makes you think I'd believe you."

"I wouldn't lie to you."

"Then what makes you think I'd ever do something like that?"

Bee narrowed her eyes at him angrily, her lips curling into a scowl. "Don't say I didn't try, Michael."

I fire my gun at him and he dodges it quickly. We fight like that for quite some time before I finally succeed in stabbing him in the abdomen.

Let's just say this, I get cocky.

I feel like every time I ever thought I won in life is when I find out there's more to it than meets the eye. This was one of those times. I stood there, instantly reloading my gun and when I looked up, Fifty-six had already removed the knife from his abdomen and was stabbing me in the throat with it.

I gaped at him in horror, fell backwards onto the floor and felt the blood rush from my face. I felt weak and sick. The blood poured from my throat and I ripped the knife out, pressing two hands against the wound. Shit. What was I thinking. I was going to die. I was going to die and never see Jon again.

I felt tears in my eyes.

Jon

I just wanted to be happy.

Maybe that really was too much to ask for.

CHAPTER 6 prologue

I don't like to think about God.

About the after life or the cosmos.

After everything I've ever done wrong in my life,

I think God might be really angry at me right now.

And Jon, even in hell,

I promise to love you

~ Bee assassin number Twenty-one

CHAPTER 6

I woke up in a hotel room. Jon was sitting beside me in bed.

"Are you okay?" he asked me gently.

I wasn't sure how many days had passed since my injury but it was still hard to speak. I mouthed "Yes," and he smiled at me. My hand goes to my injured neck which is now tightly wrapped in bandages.

"You were out for two weeks." He said. "I watched over you. Here you should try eating something. I brought you some soup. There's no people in it this time. I promise. It's vegetable stew. I thought you might like it."

I mouth, "Thank you," and allow him to spoon feed me the stew. It tastes delicious and I am starving and thirsty all at the same time. He brings me a glass of chocolate milk and I down it in one gulp.

"Does that feel better?" he asks.

"Yes," I reply, my voice barely a whisper.

"I wasn't able to kill Fifty-six for you," Jon continued, looking distressed. "As a matter of fact, it looks like you were unable to kill fifty -six as well. I called HQ and Andras had only one thing to say to me."

"What was that?"

"He said that we're no longer welcome there."

"Really?" I ask, in surprise. I remember my two failed attempts to assassinate Michael and Tara and realize what I had done. I had been forgiven the first time when they had figured out I had failed. Now they were no longer willing to forigive us for our incompetence.

"Is this a joke?"

"No. No joke. I removed the tracers from our bodies and threw them into the ocean. They probably won't be able to find us."

I think with great surprise that maybe he wants to run away together and I ask him, "Do you think we could be like Michael and Tara?"

"What do you mean?"

"Do you think we could run away together like they did? We could do that you know? Be on the run forever. We don't have to die just because they want us to."

"No, I'm afraid I have no intentions of running away."

I frown, disappointed by the reply. "Why not?"

"The last thing I want to do is run away from The H GROUP and never be acknowledged by Andras. I need him to notice me. I need him to make me the heir to the H GROUP."

I feel tears in my eyes as he speaks. "What are you saying?" I ask.

"I'm going to go back to the H Group and assassinate Andras. He will make me heir or he will die and I will make myself heir. I must be leader, Bee. I must. There are men that would follow me, men that would serve me and they will help me make this dream of mine come true."

"But it's a death trap there," I say, tears in my eyes. "What if you die, Jon? What if you die?"

"Not only am I not going to die," Jon replied, "But I'll make you my princess, Bee. There's a whole world out there and I want to own it. I want to be it's ruler. I hated it. Every second that man ever touched you. I'm going to kill him and rule instead."

It was then that I realized it.

Then that I saw clearly.

Jon wasn't the type of man to have eyes for love.

He was the type of man to have eyes for hate.

He was the obsessive type. I think I knew that about him before but it became ever so clear now. He was the type of man to hate someone so much that he was blind to the love that was right in front of his eyes.

I suppose, I really thought he'd run away with me.

I really thought that was what he was getting at.

But no, no matter how much I saw Jon, all Jon could see was Andras and the H GROUP and power and a desire to be heir. I could cry all I wanted but Jon wasn't able to hear me. He was too power hungry and obsessed with the details of his takeover to understand me. I felt alone. I realized that throughout my whole life and forever afterwards, I have only ever been, alone.

My heart.

My mind.

It aches for you.
Open your eyes Jon.
And see me.
Truly see me.
Here as I am.
I don't like to think about God.
About the after life or the cosmos.
After everything I've ever done wrong in my life,
I think God might be really angry at me right now.
And Jon, even in hell,
I promise to love you.
Even in hell,
I promise to never give up on you.
I love you.
Forever.
So, why are you doing this to me?

CHAPTER 7 prologue

Karma is real.

Love is real.

Hate is real.

Never assume.

That's all I have to say about that.

~ Andras, leader of H Group.

CHAPTER 7

My mind is shaped in blacks and reds. I can only see the darkness and it stares right back at me.

Bee is my light. My energy. My strength.

But I'm a creature that feeds off the darkness, and light is not my thing, energy is overrated, and strength is just a figment of our imaginations.

I don't really need Bee, despite the fact that she clearly needs me. And even if I could feel love, which I don't, I can't help but think she could do better.

My obsession with becoming Heir to H GROUP is deep. It hurts it's so deep. I'm OBSESSED. And by OBSESSED, I mean that I cannot not think or breathe without fearing it will ruin my chances at becoming king.

I love Bee in the way I love puppies. They're cute and fun to play with but not something I would sacrifice my future career for. I know. I'm a terrible person. But what do you expect from a man as sick and deranged as myself.

I never claimed to be nice, or normal, or relevant to society. I never claimed to be good or righteous under the eyes of God. But I do think that I might be Evil. And Bee is borderline Good. I think that in a different world, she would've been a good hearted Christian girl and I would've been something of a Satan worshipper. I can't have that. I can't have a precious dear such as Bee suffering for my sake.

So, I will make her a princess. Make her queen. Worship her even. But love. No I'll never love her. Just long for her forever, distanced from her by the leagues of darkness in my mind and heart.

I could desire Bee all I wanted.

I could long for her and want for her and wish I was with her in the way a man is normally with a woman, but that wouldn't change the fact that I was evil.

So in reality. Who was I?

Just a sad person, unable to feel love, but truly, truly, truly wishing he could.

I left Bee in bed that morning, hoping she would get better and not die. She was still precious enough to me that I feared she might get hurt. I loaded two guns, tucked them into my jacket and made my way to the airport to fly to American HQ. I take a cab the rest of the way there and walk to the artificial tree elevator hidden in the middle of the woods.

Love can be fickle.

Love can be blind.

The most happiness I ever felt.

Was when Bee said she was mine.

I'm wrong to think things are finite.

I'm wrong to think there's such a thing as implied.

And as it has always been

and how it will always be,

I hold you hostage.

Just to feel you close to me.

The elevator goes down to the first level and stops, the doors sliding open.

I exit the elevator, raising a gun in each hand.

And proceed to shoot everyone there.

CHAPTER 8 prologue

You are my world.

You are my life.

You are my husband.

And I'm your wife.

I love you Jon.

Why did you have to betray me?

~ Bee. Assassin number Twenty-one.

CHAPTER 8

As I approach Andras's room. I am overwhelmed by the number of men attacking me. I punch one man in the face, twisting his head backwards instantly and grabbing the gun from his hand, using his corpse as a shield from then on and shooting in front of me.

An assassin goes down. Then another, then another.

Here I was, about to do the best thing I had ever done before in my life.

And the only witnesses were the dead.

I fire at another assassin, knocking him back. The corpse I hold in front of me as a shield is riddled in bullets.

I break into Andras' room, dodging whizzing bullets. Andras is laying in bed. The man jolts up, a gun in his hand and he fires at me repeatedly.

The bullets graze my shoulder and I wince, hesitating from my firing and my gun lowering unsteadily. Andras jumps out of bed, races out of the room through a secret door in the back of the room that few knew about and disappeared out the back.

I tried to follow him.

I did.

But someone shoots at me from behind and I feel stunned by the sensation of the bullet entering my back. I turn and shoot at the assassin who has fired at me, killing him instantly with a bullet to the head. The bullet seems to have missed my spine and is deeply embedded into my right side.

I fire a few more bullets with dead accuracy, killing off three other assassins and begin to feel tired. A new bullet enters my leg and my arm and I am feeling drained. I'm worried I can't go on.

Bee.

I wanted to make you my queen
and rule the world with you.
Now.
I may never be able to.

I am about to give up when a glint of silver catches the light. I see Bee, running toward me, blade in hand, and she dodges from one man to the next, slitting their throats. She grabs my arm, and I follow her quickly out of the underground lair.

When we reach the exit, we race to her car and speed away, headed immediately into the traffic for our getaway.

CHAPTER 9 prologue

The worst thing that ever happened to me,
was thinking perfect eternity could come in the form
of fourteen short days.
Goodbye Jon.

> ~ Bee, assassin number Twenty-one.

CHAPTER 9

Two more weeks have passed, and me and Jon have had a wonderful life together. Things have gotten better since I had saved his life that day. He is attentive and sweet, and this time it's me, feeding him vegetable soup and tending to his wounds.

I sit in a chair beside him and we watch TV together, in the hotel room.

I tell him, "We can run away together for sure now. Just like Tara and Fifty-six. It'll be so romantic. They'll never find us. We can move to Canada or Mexico or even Korea. They won't find us there. It'll be amazing."

"So you've been saying," Jon replies. "It's just that I want to be heir so badly." He sighs. "Can you comprehend that? I need it."

"You're obsessed with power, Jon. And you're obsessed with Andras. You have to let it go."

"I know. I know. But I can't seem to see you, Bee." He let out a breath of air. "I do want to see you, Bee. I want to see you and hold you and tell you everything will be okay. I want to say, yes, we'll run away together. But I can't bring myself to do it. Something's wrong with me. Why'd you have to fall in love with someone so evil?"

"You're not evil."

"Yes. I am. I'm evil. And yet you come home every day and tell me I'm not. Why is that? Why do you love me so much?"

"I don't know. I guess I just can't live without you."

He smiles. "You're sweet. A sweet girl. I'm sorry I'm like this."

"It's fine,

"Jon," I say. I think about life and God and Heaven and about all the things I had done wrong before. I think about every precious second I have spent with Jon and how much I love him and I realize that maybe things aren't as bad as they had seemed before. "Maybe... maybe we're forgiven Jon. I feel happy for once. I'm finally happy."

"Forgiven? By who?"

"By God. I feel like, I spent my whole life thinking he was mad at me. And now, maybe we're forgiven. Maybe he's finally forgiven me for the horrible life I've chosen to live."

"Sweet," Jon said again. "You're so sweet. Maybe someday we will run away together. Would that make you happy Bee?"

I smile, tears in my eyes. "Yes. Jon. That would make me very happy."

"Then we'll do it. Just like you said. Just like Michael and Tara. We could do what they did and run away and never die and never get caught. It's possible, right? We could run away together and be happy."

"Happy," I repeat.

The days pass,

and you're here with me.

Maybe, we're forgiven.

Maybe, we're finally forgiven.

I think of you and I'm glad.

When youre around.

I'm never sad.

You are my everything.

You are my dream.

Dearest Jon,

You mean everything to me.

"You're my favorite thing, Jon. My favorite."

He leans forward, and kisses me over the lips. "You're my favorite, too, Bee. Whatever that means."

We watch TV in silence then, holding hands.

Jon's spirit is ever present, ever close to me.

We are together and I am so happy.

So very, very, very happy.

Every so often,

I wonder,

what is sad?

I've been so happy for so long now,

I've forgotten what that word means.

But maybe,
as I am starting to realize.
The worst thing that ever happened to me,
was thinking perfect eternity could come in the form
of fourteen short days.
Goodbye Jon.
Becausae you can't trust a man like Jon.
You can't hope he'll stay forever.
And you can't dream he'll love you back.
Peace and tranquility.
Love and hate.
When youre around.
I've found my fate.
To be with you.
To be with me.
There's no such thing.
As being unhappy.
You are my world.
You are my life.
You are my husband.
And I'm your wife.
I love you Jon.
Why did you have to betray me?

CHAPTER 10 prologue

There's no such thing as justice,

When I'm with you.

our love is a crime.

I never should've told you we'd run away together, Bee.

~ Jon assassin number Forty-five.

CHAPTER 10

Betrayal.
To betray.
Love and loss.
Love and loss.
Love and loss.
To love and then to lose.
To lose in the name of love.
I stare at you, Bee, my dear.
And I know I have done something wrong.
Dearest Bee,
I am going to betray you.
There will be no running away.

No, trip to Korea or Paris or Tokyo or Carribean. There will be no marriage on the hilltops. No stories around the campfire of our daring escape. There will be no cottage with the picket fence and the pet dog running around the front yard.

I have to leave you, Bee.

I have to kill Andras and become heir. I'm sure you would understand, if you knew. Once I have killed Andras, me and my men will be able to take over as we had intended to begin with. I just need to kill Andras. My dream. My hope. My future. I see a world, and I see myself ruling over it.

I know you're angry.

Or at least, you would be if you knew.

I'm leaving you, Bee.

To do what I have to do.

There's no such thing as justice,

When I'm with you.

our love is a crime.

I never should've told you we'd run away together, Bee.

Because I had no intention

of ever fulfilling such a promise to you.

Didn't I say I was evil?

If you had believed me then,

this wouldn't have happened to you.

Bee lay in bed, sleeping in the hotel room. She doesn't suspect a thing. I am going to leave her, to disappear and never come home again. That is my plan. I am going back to HQ and I am going to kill Andras. With or without Bee's approval.

Betray.

Betrayal.

To betray the one you care the most about. Your favorite person.

I'm going to leave you, Bee. And who knows, maybe we'll never see each other again.

I kiss her over the lips as she sleeps and whisper I'm going out to get us something to eat. She nods quietly, then flutters back to sleep.

She trusts me.

Which is even worse than the betrayal on my part.

She trusts me too much.

If this were another man's story, she'd be dead by now with so much trust. She never should've thought I'd run away with her. She never should've thought I'd choose her over power. And most of all, she never should've believed me when I said I would never hurt her and love her forever.

Words are empty.

And love is blind.

And my heart is evil.

And so is my mind.

and with this in mind,

I leave Bee behind.

Leave behind her beautiful face wrapped in covers. And think that maybe she wasn't so beautiful now that she was being betrayed. I left, never planning to come back again.

Goodbye Bee,

May we never meet again,

in this life or the next.
Or if we do.
May you be a less trustful, naive girl,
and me,
a decent, kind, man that knows how to treat you.

CHAPTER 11 prologue

For sleeping with Bee and stealing her from me,
I'll drink your blood and eat you eyes.
Jon.
You fucking, hateful fiend.

~ Andras leader of H group.

CHAPTER 11

Andras hung up the phone. It was days before the kidnapping of Tara that had brought Fifty-six home to him

I wiped a handkerchief across my forehead and then tucked it back into my breast pocket. The night was dragging on longer than I had ever wanted it to.

I sat in an elaborately decorated master bedroom, seated in a cushioned seat before a wide desk located furthest from the door and against the opposite wall. The kitchen was to the right of me.

Andras had finished a conversation with Thirteen, hardly feeling better about the entire situation. He had much to do. Jobs to finish. Jon assassin Forty-five and Bee on the loose.

Bee.

He growled, slamming a fist down hard on the desk. He slammed it down again and again, watching as dark mahogony wood splintered and blood dripped from the torn skin on his hand.

He had never felt so angry.

For sleeping with Bee and stealing her from me,

I'll drink your blood and eat you eyes.

Jon.

You fucking, hateful fiend.

Maybe Thirteen was right. He was glad that Tara Jones would finally be out of the way for good. She was an escaped target, hardly worth his time and effort at all and yet, here she was still alive and thriving and in the way.

One less thing to worry about. It was about time.

Bee.

He knew and yet... to see it. To feel and know it was real, he had always known about their affair and yet somehow, the proof, it ripped at him.

Karma is real.

Love is real.

Hate is real.

Never assume.

That's all I have to say about that.

Never assume a man will never fight you back. Because that was exactly what I planned to do to Jon Forty-five, was fight back.

He felt his chest ripping at the sight of her that night, protecting Jon Forty-five like he was so precious to her. He couldn't stand it. He couldn't take it! It ripped!! It tore and killed him to see it.

Jon Forty-five would die. Not just die Andras would drink his blood and eat his eyes. He'd pay for the mockery he had made of the H Group that night.

He turned around in time to catch a kick to the face. He flew back, landing hard against the hardwood floor. Jon Forty-five stood over him, laughing like a madman as he lunged forward, grasping Andras by the hair and stuffing a gun against his skull. "Hi Andras. It's me."

He pressed his face to Andras' cheek, chuckling to himself.

"Let go of me, Jon," Andras said through gritted teeth.

"I'm not going to let you go, Andras," Jon shrieked, laughing louder. "I'm going to fucking kill you, you fucking maniac!"

The attack had taken him completely by surprise. It took Andras a moment to regain his composure to think clearly again. He let out a small breath. "We can talk about this, Jon," he said calmly. "Just put down the weapon. You don't want to do this."

"You're so presumptuous," Jon murmured. "You always think you know what's best. You always think you know what I want. But let me tell you something, Andras, you don't know. You don't know anything. And I think you think you do. Fifty-six isn't better than me, Andras. I should be your heir. I should be your son. I'm going to show you why."

Andras could hear the sound of breathing in his ear. Jon had always been a little off. He wasn't stable. Andras had to think quick. The boy was hesitating. He could feel it. He was afraid to pull the trigger. I decided to take advantage of that. "You're not well, Jon." I said gently. "I can help you. I'm sorry if I hurt you. You don't know how hard this had been on me letting you go." Jon paused. He was listening. Good.

Andras made a swift motion with his arm, knocking the gun from Jon's hand. He lunged, grasping the fallen gun from the floor and fired it several times at Jon.

He watched as the bullets entered the younger man through the center, knocking him back to the floor. "I'm going to enjoy this." Andras smiled, stepping forward and pulling a leg back, kicking the man hard in the side of the head. There was a cracking sound as Jon's face fell limp on the floor.

He tucked the gun into the loop on the inside of his coat. Bending down, he grasped both of Jon's ankles and started to drag him from the bedroom floor. If he left the boy there too much longer, the blood would start to stain the expensive rugs, something that was unacceptable. He felt the corners of his lips curling into a thin smile. He couldn't have asked for more.

Jon had come to him.

It was perfect.

He felt a vibration in his pocket as he dragged Jon Forty- Five into the hall. He paused, pulling out a small phone. "What?" he asked, feeling annoyed.

"It's bee. She's back." A voice said urgently. "She's killing everyone."

"Tell the men not to fight her. You can inform her that she can find both me and her boyfriend in the torture chambers." He licked his lips.

He'd drink Jon's blood and eat his eyes.

You're like leather, Jon,

Soft and sweet,

and most of all,

Dead to me.

His gaze fell to Jon's limp body. He couldn't have asked for more. "Tell her, we'll be waiting for her there." He dropped the phone to the floor, grasping Jon's ankles firmly once more and pulling his body across the ground.

A trail of red streaked the floor with every step they took, seeping from the jacket that hung from Jon's frame. The boy's blonde hair had turned pink as Andras pulled him along, and the man felt his anticipation growing by the minute.

"You're not well, boy" he said again, speaking quietly to the unconscious man. "I'm going to help you. You stole Bee from me. Swiped her away, just like that."

When the man didn't reply, Andras stopped angrily, kneeling down and slapping the boy's face again and again. "Wake up! You fucking shithead. Wake the fuck up!!!" Jon stirred, grunting as his eyes fluttered open, wide and blue from his dusty face. "I want you to be awake for the whole thing," Andras hissed. "Thief. You stole her from me. I'm going to make you hurt for it."

He grasped Jon's ankles again, pulling him through a doorway to a staircase. Jon let out moans as Andras dragged him down the stairs, his body and head thumping down each and every step as they went down. He moved his head back and forth, dizzy and disoriented as Andras pulled him up against the cold cement.

Andras strapped Jon's wrists and ankles tightly with leather straps, until the man hung in the standing position, his head hanging forward in a daze.

Andras made his way to the door, pulling the slab of iron shut. He locked it, glancing through the square bulletproof glass window near the top of the door. Bee. He contemplated whether she would be next or not. She'd be coming right to him, after all. It made him sick, knowing she'd come. She was going to come and try and stop him. Try and stop him from hurting Jon. His eyes felt damp at the thought. The cheating tramp. How could she?

He pulled away, shaking the thoughts of Bee and Jon from his head. He grasped his face, groaning and muttering to himself. Bee was a cheater. Bee was a cheater. Bee was a cheater.

Bee was a cheater.

He grasped the long knife, plunging it deep into Jon's chest and dragging it downward.

Bee cheated, Bee cheated, Bee cheated, Bee cheated.

Nothing could make it better.

Nothing would take it away.

Bee was a cheater.

He lifted the knife again, slicing the right side of Jon's face open, splitting skin and muscle apart and watched as blood squirted out from the pulsing flesh.

The whore.

The tramp.

She was disgusting.

Never again. Her long dark hair. Red lips. Her pale skin. Never again.

He hated her.

"Andras stop."

The scream pierced through the air, echoing throughout the small room. Andras turned around, trembling as he did, his eyes falling on Bee's blood splattered face through the glass. Just like he knew she would. So predictable. It was unbearably sickening.

He smiled at her, turning back to Jon and digging his fingers into the long gash slicing Jon into two and pulled them apart, exposing bone and organs, blood pouring from the open hole.

"Stop it!!" Bee screamed. She shrieked, pounding on the door loudly from the other side. "Don't do this, Andras! Please stop it."

"Whore," Andras murmured. He grasped at organs, ripping them from the red nest inside. They fell in soft plops onto the floor. Jon cried out in pain, his head rolling to the side.

"STOP!!!" Bee screamed it. She screamed it. She screamed it. The whore screamed it at the top of her lungs. Andras caught sight of the tears streaming down her face. She cried loudly, shaking the door handle and pounding and scratching at the window. "Stop Stop Stop Stop Stop Stop It STOP IT STOP IT STOP IT STOP IT STOP IT." She cried. "JON JON JON JON JON! STOP!! JON!!!" she cried. The whore cried. She cried until her face was swollen red, pounding her entire body against the door.

Andras dug his knife across Jon's arm.

No more Bee.

No more tears. The door shook. Screaming. The whore screamed and screamed and cried. The door shook and rattled. She'd never get in.

I dug out chunks of flesh from his arm, throwing out pieces as if they were trash on the floor.

"JON!!!" Bee cried. "JON!!!"

Andras refused to look at her. He couldn't look at her. He tore the knife this way and that. He dug into the man's eye, gouging out the tender soft flesh. He leaned forward, moving a tongue along the blood and liquid that dripped from the gaping hole. He'd drink his blood and eat Jon's eyes for touching Bee. He'd drink his blood. He heard a gunshot.

Andras stopped.

Bee was gone.

Andras moved to the door, the knife hanging from his hand at his side as he unlocked it and pulled it open. Bee lay on the hallway floor, a hole through her head, the gun she had shot herself with still clenched tightly in her hand.

She had killed herself.

He felt fresh tears in his eyes as he bent down over her. It wasn't long before he realized that he was sobbing and shaking uncontrollably. He lifted the knife in his hand, stabbing it hard into her still, dead body. He lifted it, bringing it down again and again. "I never would've hurt you," he whispered. "Why? Why did you do this to me? Why?" He cried, dropping the knife and lifting her in his arms. "Whore, you're a stupid whore." Her destroyed face hung lifelessly as he lifted her body.

For Jon.

He knew she would never die for Andras.

He cried burying his head in her chest.

Stupid whore.

Under different circumstances, he wanted to think she would've chosen him instead over Jon. He was probably just kidding himself to even think it. Stupid whore. If only she had never cheated. Wiping at his face, he pulled himself back to his feet after laying her down again.

He took the knife back into his hand and headed back to Jon

He stepped into the torture chamber, his eyes narrowed at the man that hung from the wall, his insides still pouring out of him. "Jon," he said, walking towards him. The room spun. "Bee killed herself." Jon lifted his head weakly, his good eye turning to look at Andras. Their gaze met. "She's dead because of you." Andras lifted the knife, slashing it quickly across Jon's neck and watched as blood poured from the wound.

Dead.

The things people did for love.

For love, they did the oddest things.

He wondered, if there was any way he could use that.

BOOK 2 END

BOOK 3

A killer's instinct: Andras Story

CHAPTER 1 prologue

"You're the worst one for thinking no one hurts like you.
We all hurt, Andras.
We all do."

~ Assassin number Thirteen's ghost

CHAPTER 1

A week had passed since Bee's death.

The wonderful paintings by famous artists were torn down from the walls. Andras had valued them more than anything during his lifetime. Rare works of art. They meant nothing to him now. They lay in shredded piles on the floor.

All business had been completed from his bedroom from then on. He hadn't left. A maid brought his meals for breakfast lunch and dinner. She was the only one he opened the door for. He hadn't changed from his robe and bed clothes for days. He worked through his phone on the desk, directing his hit men from the comfort of his own room. He imagined they had all heard about Bee already, and it made him feel vulnerable to think they knew he was grieving.

Bee.

He was distressed.

He couldn't think of anyone else.

He had always hated her for cheating. He had always held it against her. There was no way he could've known how devastated he'd be if she died. There was no way he could've known how awful the pent up rage he kept inside would be when it was let out. The years of hating Jon. The years of secretly wanting to destroy him for his crime of stealing her away.

Andras looked at the walls that surrounded him. The ruined paintings had been replaced with blown up portraits of Bee. He hadn't known how many pictures he had of her until he started to enlarge them and use them to decorate his walls. Her smiling face covered every inch of wallpaper. Her smiling face watched with dozens of pairs of eyes from every corner of his room. He sat on his bed, gazing at them with empty vacant stares, his mouth in a grim line.

Eventually, he stood from his bed, walking slowly to the portrait of her face. He lifted an arm, his hand outstretched in front of him. His sweet Bee. His fingers met the smooth surface of the photo and he leaned forward, lips pressing to the picture of hers. His sweetest. "Bee."

He turned around, facing the body seated behind him. "You're probably wondering what I'm doing, aren't you." He took a step back, regaining his composure and admiring the photograph with newly focused eyes. Her hair was down, long and flowing down her shoulders. "I think that's a good picture of you," he said. "That's all. You don't have to be jealous. I like you even better now than you were before."

His eyes fell on Bee's corpse dressed in a long scarlet gown and propped up in an expensive chair with a high back. Her flesh had started to decay, taking on a grayish-green color. The hole in her face where she had shot herself had begun to shrivel and shrink inward. She sat at a small table for two, across an empty seat. He stepped toward her, setting himself down in the empty chair. "We've gotten a lot done today," he commented.

His hand slid under the table, pressing a small yellow button. A woman in black clothing came rushing into the room, a large silver tray in her arms. She carefully and silently set a large plate in front of Bee as well as him. Then she poured two glasses of red wine for each of them. She hurried out just as quick, shutting the door behind her and locking the door as well. Andras smiled, lifting his glass with a nod. "A toast? You can if you'd like Bee. It's completely up to you. He continued to smile, sipping it slowly. "That's so like you."

It wasn't that he didn't know she was gone. The lie soothed him was all.

He hated Jon Forty-Five for taking her from him and he hated him for killing her. Unfortunately, the man was dead, and no matter how much Andras longed to rip him to pieces all over again, it was no longer possible. Jon Forty-Five's corpse was hung from the dining hall, his head removed and made into a centerpiece for the long dinner table in the middle of the room. It brought Andras little consolation. Nothing could alleviate the pain.

"You're the only one that understands," Andras said finally, lifting his fork and placing a chunk of rare steak to his mouth. He chewed thoughtfully and slowly. "The H Group will disappear without me," he said quietly. "It's just the way it is. My grandfather started this group. He knew it too. Just like my father knew. The unfortunate truth of the matter is that men aren't born killers. Despite my attempts to convince them otherwise, the truth always prevails, regardless of whether it's beneficial or not. They're born tools. The're born followers. They're natural instinct is to do whatever the hell I fucking tell them to."

It was something he had discovered throughout his lifetime. Men were nothing but useless followers, followers begging for guidance and answers. They weren't intelligent creatures inclined to war but pathetic insects working to please the queen ant. Throughout his leadership, he had tried to convince the men that human beings were nothing but creatures born to kill and destroyed. He had called it the human condition.

"They do as they are told," Andras said. "I tell them to kill, they kill. I think them to die, they die. If I tell them to do none of the above, then they sit and do nothing until they receive their next order. They're nothing without people like us, Bee."

He breathed heavily. "You're quiet today. I think it's because you don't like what I'm saying. You know I can't live forever. When I die, the H group will dissolve into nothing. They're worthless without a voice to tell them what to do. There's nothing I can do about that. I tried to make them leaders but they refused to hear me. They're animals incapable of learning.

He looked up at her, acknowledging the gray skin flaking at the edges of the torn wound and dried blood. Her once beautiful eyes were dry and lifeless. He stood walking to her and taking a napkin into his hand. Gently, he pressed it to her cheek, bending down and placing a small kiss against the oozing flesh. "Don't cry Bee. I have a plan. I want Fifty-six to take my place when I'm gone. He's the only one that can. I trust him."

Andras didn't have any children, nor would he ever. Fifty-six was the closest thing he had to a son. He was almost perfect. He was intelligent. He was strong. And he could be very cruel. But he had his weaknesses too. He was afraid to accept his own demons. He fought them. Just as he fought Andras. He was afraid to be himself. Something had held him back his entire life from going completely and utterly insane and uncovering his true potential. Fifty-six was the only one that could lead the H Group.

Andras knew people did strange things for love.

He had seen that for himself. Had watched it unfold before his very eyes only days before.

Even if Fifty-six wouldn't go willingly, he had a feeling he'd give in to persuasion instead. "I'll let them fall in love for now," he said to Bee, turning from her. When it was all over, Fifty-six would be successor and leader of the H Group. If things kept going the way they were, he'd have no choice. He knew the things people did for love. They were strange.

He walked slowly to one of the large portraits of Bee, his eyes fixed on the grinning face. He stopped in front of it, and ran his fingers lightly down the surface. If he imagined hard enough, he could think the printed hair were real and soft and in his hands. He ran a thumb through the image of dark strands. The illusion was almost perfect. "You sound uncertain," he said. "There's nothing to worry about. I'm certain it'll work out." He laughed. "An optimist? Now really, Bee. I'm hardly anything of the sort."

He turned around to look at her corpse. The room had become more real than the rest of the world. This bedroom was all there was now. It was a madhouse. It was a trap for the unwell mind. He doubted he'd ever escape it. He was happy in his blissful delusion. Was it so wrong to live a lie? Surrounded by the one he loved, he felt safe and truly alive. Loving her gave his life value. A value he had neither realized nor appreciated before. "You've barely touched your food," he said quietly. "Aren't you hungry?"

He smiled. "I think that way too. I felt that way since he was a little boy. He's kind of like a son. Fifty-six would've been our son if we had ever had children. That's the reason he has to take my place."

The phone rang and he turned to look at it, feeling odd about it. The sound was an unpleasant reminder of his work. He hated getting calls during dinner. Stepping toward the phone, he lifted it to his face. "What?"

The call was from one of his killers on a mission. "I need the target's current location," the man said.

Sighing, Andras reached into his pocket, pulling out his miniature computer. He clicked on several buttons before replying. "892 Fort Road. Anything else?"

"No."

Andras hung up. He decided it'd be a good idea to check up on Thirteen while he was on the phone. Dialing Thirteen's number he waited for an answer. Thirteen picked up almost immediately. "How are Tara and Fifty-six." Andras asked.

"They're good."

"Anything interesting happen?"

"Not really."

Nothing interesting. Andras tapped his desk with his free hand thoughtfully. "How does... How does Fifty-six treat Tara Jones?"

"Good... I guess. Why?"

"No reason. Just keep watching them. I need you to to watch them for me."

"Got it."

"Call me if anything comes up," Andras said. "I'll check up on you later tonight." He hung up the phone, his hand resting on the receiver for a moment.

He was certain his plan would work. He just needed to give it a little more time to guarantee his success. When the time was right, certainly he'd be able to sense it. He'd feel it in his blood. The time to strike would ring out to him, calling and begging for him to continue on and finish the deed. His ears perked up and he turned to Bee. "I'm glad you agree," he said smiling. He headed back to the table, taking a seat in his chair across from her. Lifting his glass in his hand, he replied cheerfully, "Bee, I think You're absolutely right about that."

CHAPTER 2 prologue

If you were a normal man.

I wouldn't love you as much.

Is that okay?

I hope you understand.

My love for you is real.

As real and as heavy as I can carry.

~ Snow white, the maid.

CHAPTER 2

It had started some eighty-nine years ago. The H Group had been formed by Andras' grandfather. When his grandfather was murdered, Andras' father had taken over, and when Andras' father had been murdered, Andras had taken over. It had been a cruel, though surprisingly simple cycle of life.

Unfortunately for himself, Andras had no children of his own, nor did he have any intention of creating any. He wasn't the fatherly type. It never worked out, even if he had tried. His hope had been that Fifty-six would be the one to take over when Andras passed away. He had been training the killer with the intention of making him capable for the job.

Andras chose his name because he felt like it suited him. In demonology, Andras was a great prince of Hell who's only purpose was to hunt and kill men, as well as bring havoc to the world. Like himself, the highly dangerous demon commanded legions of other demons in hell, and used men's own rage against them.

Andras' real name was Edward James. His mother had named him after her uncle. She had been a prostitute living in the ghettos of Los Angeles. When he was five, his real father, the current leader of H Group at the time, had come to take him back from the hooker he had impregnated years back. When Andras mother had fought him, his father had slaughtered her and taken him anyway.

But such was life.

Still, he had a feeling it was the reason he had never considered children himself.

Andras sat on the quilted mattress, wrapped in a burgundy colored silk robe that was worth around ten grand alone. He loved luxury and he had luxury. His sheets were made of silk and spun gold and his blankets were thick and rich and trimmed in gold thread.

His bedroom was nearly as big as the first floor of most people's houses, with plush carpet, and rare paintings stolen from museums lining the walls now shattered and laying on the floor and replaced with photos of Bee.

The world.

I want it.

I want the whole thing, to hold the entire thing in my arms and cradle it was if it were my own.

There's a world out there.

I want to explore the whole thing.

And become its king.

Dear God,

if you exist.

forgive me for my sins.

And let me rule your universe with an iron fist.

I sigh. I don't know what to do with myself. I sit on my bed and think about life and what it must look like from a distance.

He imagined, it must remind someone of a loony bin.

A king, I'll be.

A King.

I gaze at Bee's dead form laying beside him on the bed. Andras stands up and lifts the corpse of Bee in his arms, twirling her around the room, his eyes closed.

They were dancing.

Simply dancing.

His men were dancing with Tara and Fifty-six.

And he was dancing with Bee.

On their way now. On their way now. The classical music played loudly from the speakers. Violins strummed dramatically. Low base notes filled the air.

The air moved with sounds.

It moved in dark swirls.

It moved so thickly he could feel and see it in motion. The sound moved in the air in spiraling bouts of music.

He danced with Bee turning her body gently with the rhythm. Her head fell backwards unnaturally, from her neck as he carried her, tearing decayed skin and exposing bone. Andras stopped moving, holding her in front of him, just brittle bone and dried blood. She didn't bleed. She was nothing but pus and green and rot. Bee was dead.

Dead.

Bee.

She was dead.

Love and loss.

Loss and love.

She was dead and he was never going to see her again.

He let out a loud sob, crying loudly as he threw her down on the ground and walked away from her. Bee was dead. He knew Bee was dead. To constantly be reminded of it was a crime. He cried harder, stumbling to the wall beside him and tearing down a large glossy portrait. He broke the frame, shredding the picture of Bee in pieces.

He tore down another and sobbed to himself. The music continued loudly and dreadfully without end. She wasn't there. She wasn't there anymore. She wasn't coming back. Her soul had left. And as much as he had longed for her to stay, she had left him. She was gone.

The men were on their way but Bee was gone. He stayed there for a moment, breathing heavily. Time didn't heal. It made it worse. The agonizing reality of losing her became a heavier and heavier weight on his shoulders. It was a pain that never lessened. It only grew.

"I have to fix you" he said. He moved to the dining room table and pressed the small yellow button underneath it. The door to his room opened immediately and his maid came rushing in. She looked distressed, straightening her dark clothing awkwardly at the sudden call, "Yes, sir," She asked.

"My doll is broken," Andras breathed. "I need you to stitch her up again."

The woman looked frozen, as her gaze fell on the mutilated corpse. She looked like she may throw up, her hand flying to her mouth. "Stitch her, you say, sir?"

"Yes, my doll is broken." Andras said again, lowering his head. "I need you to fix her."

"Yes sir. Right away, sir." She made her way to the body and bending down, picked up Bee. She carried the corpse with her as she hurried out of the room.

Andras took a seat at the table, putting his head down in his folded arms. His Bee had become a ragdoll. To be stitched and sewn back together again. Her soul had departed. Just a doll. The music annoyed him now. He pressed the button once again, calling in the same maid.

The door flew open, and the maid came hurrying back in. "Yes, sir?"

"Turn the music off for me," he said, "It's annoying."

"Yes, sir." She hurried ahead of him to the sound system on the shelf flipping the switch off. The silence came immediately. It was soothing. He felt more relaxed.

"That's all," he said.

She nodded and hurried away, the door closing behind her. Andras remembered, her wealthy family had been slaughtered by the H Group years earlier when she had been fourteen. A child caught up in the politics of human greed. She had begged for her life, so frightened to die that she had agreed to serve him in return for her continued existence on Earth. If she could call this much of a life. To sacrifice her freedom just to live. He had thought she was strange then, and now that seven years had passed, he thought her even stranger than before. He called her Snow white for her fair skin but as for her real name, he had never learned it nor bothered to care that he hadn't.

That's when the whispers began.

They came to him when it was quiet.

He heard them as if they spoke to one another in constant distress.

Voices called to him.

They called to him, mocked him, pursued him relentlessly.

"Leave me alone," he murmured. The voices continued, overwhelming him completely. They whispered in one ear, then disappeared and whispered in the next.

When he lifted his head again, and looked up, a dark shadow stood on the table in front of him, staring at him with blank eyes. "Take me death," Andras whispered. "Take me if you must. But Bee. Did you have to take away my Bee too? Death you've come for me now. Please tell me it won't hurt."

I hear you death.

I let you hold me and as you do, my body falls apart.

There's not much I can say about wanting to live and fear of an afterlife or of nothing or of reincarnation or Hell or some other otherworldly absurdity that I can't even begin to imagine.

Please death, be kind to me.

I beg of you.

As I fall apart,

and my mind disperses into little pieces.

CHAPTER 3 prologue

I'm a fool of a man.
A fool.
For love, however sweet and kind is love.
Is how much I am capable of hate.

~ Andras

CHAPTER 3

It came to my attention weeks later that Thirteen had died from old age.

Andras felt sad, thinking that Thirteen had been something of a friend to him. He had lived longer than most of the other assassins, hitting an age of 62, and had died in the middle of dinner, his head falling forward into his plate of meat.

He had been a good assassin, and it had been a sad shame to lose him. Just as it had been a sad shame to lose Seven and so many others as of late. Pretty soon, there would be no one left but him and he'd have to start the whole thing all over again. Perhaps.

I don't normally talk to ghosts, Andras thought, but when Thirteen's ghost came to haunt him, he replied very loudly, "It's a shame indeed. A giant shame that you've come back for me too?"

"Not just yet," Thirteen's ghost replied. "Not just yet. You still have unfinished business Andras. You must get Fifty-six to come back."

"I know that. I know that."

"Do you believe in the afterlife?" Thirteen's ghost asked him.

"A bunch of rubbish," I replied. "But knowing my luck. There's hell only and that's all."

"So it would seem. You're the worst one for thinking no one hurts like you. We all hurt, Andras. We all do." said Thirteen's ghost.

Andras turned to Bee, stepping behind her and resting his hands on her bony shoulders. Her flesh was rotted and ivy-colored and her skin had shriveled until it resembled a dried apple. He had her dressed in a long turquoise gown that morning. She looked stunning.

He paused. "Do you think?" He pulled his hands from her body, clasping them behind his back and turning away from her. His eyes fell on a particularly lovely portrait of her sitting on his bed and smiling at him. "I think that when the time is right it cries out for acknowledgement. Do you believe in signs Bee?" He smiled. "Of course you don't. But in this business, you do begin to believe in that sort of thing. Signs to guide you when all else seems lost. I think Thirteen's passing is a sign. The universe is watching us, and if you listen hard enough, you can hear its voice."

He let out a loud, long groan. Putting a hand to his head, he pulled out a handful of hair. He looked down at the ragged strands in his hands, watching as they blurred in and out of focus against his pale skin.

"The universe talks to me, Bee. I hear it. It drives me mad but I hear it calling to me. It tells me the most amazing and terrible things. I long for its secrets yet it rips at my soul in return. You must hear it too. I can't be alone in this." He sighed crouching on the ground and resting his head on the floor. "It's quiet in here. How can I help but hear things. When there's nothing but silence, how can I help but find what's beyond the silence? Do you think I've gone crazy, Bee?"

"No, I suppose you're right. The sign was Thirteens death. His death announces the arrival of the new beginning. He was the offering. The sacrifice. His death will give birth to Fifty-six's new life as leader of the H Group." Andras turned his face until it was pressed to the rug. He dug his fingers into the material, breathing heavily. "Do you hear it, Bee? The universe is telling me I'm right. The universe knows it. It calls to me. It wants me to know that all is not for nothing. Losing you wasn't for nothing. My loss was our gain. My life is over. Fifty-six will take my place. The end is near. The new start is here. Listen to it Bee. It calls to us both."

A knock sounded on the door and Andras jumped, letting out an inhuman cry. He stopped himself, listening to the familiar voice of his maid from the other side. Closing his eyes, he rolled his head until he had made a full circle around his neck. He cracked his jaw, tilting his head awkwardly as he pulled himself to his feet. He made his way to the door, his hands falling on the cool surface of the wood. "Not now" he said finally, "I'll eat later."

"Yes, sir."

He heard the voice from the other side of the door. He slid down down it to the floor, listening as the set of quiet foot steps made their way down the hall and disappeared. He still hadn't left the room since Bee had died.

He was spiraling.

He feared his mind had decayed away along with Bee's sweet flesh. "If I think I might be crazy, does that make me crazy, Bee?" he asked quietly. "The voices are real. If I told anyone they'd think I was imagining things but I'm not. They're real. They talk to me now. There are so many of them. Once I knew they were there, there was nothing I could do to stop them. They thrive on my awareness of them."

He lifted his head, turning to look at her. Bee's mouth now hung open from her shriveled face, wide and gaping. The hole in her cheek had pulled itself open until he could clearly see through to the other side. "I'm losing my mind. The light is playing tricks on me. I see things that aren't there now, bee. The nights foretell of my demise. I can hear them whispering. They know I'm going to die. I don't have much longer to find an heir."

"I see his bony finger beckoning to me." Andras laid himself on his back his arms spread out on either side of him. "He wants me to follow but I dare not think it. I'm frightened to go. Death is here. His voice pierces my skull with empty rushing of wind through matter. Don't let him take me, Bee. I'm not finished with my work yet. I'm not ready for him."

He closed his eyes. "Death eternal, sees me now." He breathed. The words left his lips in a slow and quiet song. "See me, Death. Take me, Death. Watch me, Death. I hear your voice. Let the darkness come for me as night falls."

"Bee," he said. "Thirteen's death was a sign. The time is here. I'll tell the men to capture Fifty-six and Tara Jones. They'll be back in the country by tomorrow morning. "And Thirteen, I hope you'll forgive me, but I have no intention of forgiving you for dying before me. I hate it. To think that your death must indeed be a sign of change. To do something I hadn't thought of before and make things right again."

"Take it as you will, "Andras, the ghost replied. "Just know this. If you ever shall fall, the H GROUP will disintegrate with you. I can't guarantee you will succeed."

"My death is soon. I know this."

"Then hurry and make your preparations for a heir. It won't be long before it'll be too late to make one. You have very little time left."

The nights foretold of Andras' demise. It wouldn't be long before he was swept away with the darkening sky, never to see the world as it was again. A life of murder and exotic pleasures, to Hell it would send him, where all the bloody amusements he had bestowed on others would be bequeathed upon his ravaged soul. He wondered, such a life, had he wasted himself with it.

CHAPTER 4 prologue

Bee was my everything.

My only.

I never should've put her in that situation.

A situation that could hurt her.

~ Andras

CHAPTER 4

My maid is starting to act strangely towards me. I don't know why I noticed but I did. She is staring at me more often and I'm beginning to wonder if she has gone as insane as I have.

I ask her if she has gone mad and she replies no, before chuckling to herself and blushing softly. "It's just, such a nice day today, isn't it? I went out for groceries and you wouldn't believe how warm and bright the sun is out."

"I'll tell you when I start to care," I mutter, spoon-feeding my dear Bee. It dribbles down the dead doll's face and I sigh. "Napkin."

The maid rushes to my side and drops a napkin into my hands. Her fingertips linger over mine for just a short second before she pulls back. For the first time, I notice how fair her skin is and how drab her short auburn hair is, pulled back into a bun. I notice the freckles on her cheeks and the raise of her brows as she speaks.

Nice.

That's what she was called. Very nice.

And I hated that about her.

I hated nice women who were kind to everyone other than themselves.

I wipe at Bee's mouth and sighed. "You can go now."

"Thank you, Sir."

I think of my maid. She is bright and smart and nice. Nice. Nice. Nice. Why? In a place like this? In a world like this? Did we need someone so goddamned nice?

I sit down beside Bee and ask her if she is jealous of the maid. "Are you jealous, darling? Because if you were, if I ever find out you are jealous I will do whatever it takes to set things right again between us. I adore you.

I love you. I need you and you alone. Please don't be angry. My wandering eyes only have sight for you. You are everything to me. The sky. The ground. Heaven. Hell. The world itself. You are my air."

Bee is silent. and I laugh to myself. "Very funny," I murmur. "Very, very funny."

A woman like Snow White, their fairy tales never ended well. They lived short tragic lives, longing for a happiness that never can fall onto their laps for free. They dream of princes that ride on white horses and carry them away to make them some kind of princess.

Ha.

Well, good luck Snow White. Because in real life, it's the evil queen that wins, not the humble servant girl.

I sigh.

Good luck Snow white.

Good luck.

I fear of cold winters.

And hear your voice sing.

As if the outside is not freezing enough as it is already.

I would long for you.

Really and truly I would.

But evil beckons me.

And summer does not exist in my heart.

I am not a warm man.

I am barely a man at all.

Please forgive me dear.

All I can do is wish you luck.

And know that in life,

it's girls like you.

That don't succeed.

Gobbled up,

by humanity's greed.

I'm a fool of a man.

A fool.

For love, however sweet and kind is love.

Is how much I am capable of hate.

So good luck in life Snow white.
And may your failure to find joy hurt
as little as possible.
For when the evil queen comes to slay you.
May your death be gentle.

CHAPTER 5 prologue

"The irony of it all,
is that for as long as I've known you.
You've never acknowledged me
as more than just a figment of your imagination.
I'm real, Andras.
And my love for you is eternal."

CHAPTER 5

Andras sat in his room, Bee sitting beside him and speaking to his own shadow, who he had named Fourteen.

He explained to Fourteen, "For love. The things a person will do. Isn't that right, Bee? Don't mind her." He said to Fourteen. "She's been quiet ever since her lover died and I think she may be jealous of the maid. Bee was my everything. My only. I never should've put her in that situation. A situation that could hurt her. Where she would have to hurt herself to protect her heart. So now, as I was saying, why wouldn't I use love to catch a couple of crooks."

His shadow replied quite fervently. "But to use love as a bait is a sin. God will be angry. Surely you know this Andras."

"Here and now my friend. I'm not worried about tomorrow. It's the here and the now that I care about."

"And the here and now is worried about you, you fiend."

"A fiend, he says," I laugh. "Well now, Haven't we gotten conceited. You are the fiend. Mr Fourteen. And I beg for you to please hold back on the harsh language."

My maid enters the room and sighs, the conversation between myself, Bee, and Fourteen interrupted. "Good evening, Mr Andras," she smiles. "You look very engrossed in what you're doing. May I ask what you're so excited about?"

"Nothing that concerns you, wench."

"Forgive me for speaking out of turn," she replies quickly. She sets out two plates of food. One for Bee and one for myself. "Love is beautiful, isn't it," She sighed, nonchalantly.

"As beautiful as a unicorn. By which, I mean, it doesn't exist."

"Not true at all, Andras," She pushed, as if trying to further the conversation. "Not only do I believe love exists, I have hope for the future to one day find it myself."

"My condolences to the victim. May he rest in peace in his Hell."

"Your sense of humor is improving," Snow white points out. "How clever." She mumbles to herself. "Very clever. You'd be funnier if you smiled when you said it instead of frowning though."

"Don't patronize me, you bitch."

"Another joke?"

"Hardly."

"Well, I hope you enjoy dinner. What would you like for dessert?"

"A beautiful whore would be nice."

"Would you like me to order you a strip tease?"

"No, I'm not in the mood. That was a joke. I guess," I smile at her somewhat sincerely. "You're too nice, you know that. You could get away with that in heaven but not in hell dear. Which is where we live. Pure hell. And I'm sorry for the attitude. It's just that you're to damned nice and it's starting to piss me off. Respectfully, that is ma'am. And I'm sorry but I really can't talk right now. Not that you're not interesting to talk to. But you're a bit of everything I hate and love in life, a saint that can't stop jabbering about how saintly she is. So why don't you go fly back to your cloud and leave me be, angel. You're too much for an evil man such as myself. And as a matter of fact, maybe you should quit."

"I'd never leave you," Snow white insisted. "Please don't ask me to leave."

"Then accept the consequences," I mutter. I reply louder afterwards. "You're something of an idiot to me. You know that, don't you?"

"It's just, you're all I have in this world, Andras."

"I know that. It's stuff like that. Stuff like that, that makes me so mad at you. You should be angry at me. The audacity. To make myself all you have in life. How could I do such a thing. How could I betray you in that way. I've hurt you, angel. Not helped you. I am not your savior. I am your destroyer. Why can't you see that? Why can't you just be a little bit more angry about it."

"But I love you, Andras."

"I'm sure you do, in the way that cows love grass, but that doesn't mean we have to go about in this way forever. Take this warning once more. Leave, dear. Leave me be and go find yourself a life in the outside world. It would do you some good to have some freedom. You could find your prince. You could get married. You could be happy. This is your chance to run away from the H GROUP. This is your chance to be free."

"No. I won't go." She smirked. "I'm sorry. I like it just fine here. As a matter of fact. I'm never leaving and you can't force me. But I'll go for tonight. And I'll be back tomorrow with breakfast and lunch and dinner as usual. So goodnight, Andras. And forgive me for my impertinence."

I sigh.

The idiot.

She leaves and I leave my mind.

"How unfortunate for Snow White," I say to my shadow Fourteen. "How unfortunate, that the princess doesn't even know a good thing when she hears it."

The shadow replies. "You're cruel. You're a cruel person to let her keep thinking that this is all there is."

"I offered her freedom and she defied me."

"That's because she can't even comprehend what freedom is. She was practically born in this dreaded place."

"Are you threatening me?"

"No, but I'm warning you. It's girls like that, Andras. Girls like that, that can change a man," Fourteen continued. "She could make you NICE. You could be NICE too because of a girl like that. You don't want that. You'll have to fight her."

"I know what you're thinking. Fight off her love and then I will be able to continue on with my miserable existence as an evil person for all eternity. Sounds delightful."

"Then fight her. Fight off her advances. Fight off her NICE words. Fight off NICE. You don't want to be NICE by accident. NICE will destroy you. NICE will kill you. NICE will make you feel bad for the things you've done in your life, and all the people you've hurt before. NICE is your enemy, Andras. Never forget that."

"And that, I never will."

CHAPTER 6 prologue

All I ever wanted was to be a strong man that knew what
he wanted and got it.

The time goes by,

and now I fear I've wasted my life.

Is this what regret feels like?

Andras leader of H Group.

CHAPTER 6

Some days later, and it was during a time of great despair over the conversation I had had with Fourteen, when I noticed this, but my maid was watching me once more. She stared me straight in the eye. Then she kneeled down and hugged me and told me everything would be okay, and not to worry about Bee because she was in heaven and happy now. It was the first time I ever heard her in a way that did not annoy me quite as much as she usually did and it was then that I felt compelled to kiss her to erase my sorrow, and to forget about the world and Fifty-six and Bee and everyting that had ever made me feel bad in my life.

All I ever wanted was to be a strong man that knew what he wanted and got it.

The time goes by,

and now I fear I've wasted my life.

Is this what regret feels like?

Because if so,

then maybe guilt is real and I was a fool for not knowing I felt it too.

I watched us kiss, as if from a distance. And then, I was relieved when it was over. I felt better for once and I told her that she had a sort of calming effect on me for once instead of the normal opposite effect of her pissing me off until I can't take it anymore. I know Fourteen told me to fight off Snow white's love, but I'm something of a sensation seeker and I don't do well with rejecting what feels right, right this second. So I accepted her love for just that one day regardless of my regret immediately later.

The calming effect, was one that Bee had never had on me. Bee. All I could remember was feeling angry and frustrated every time she was around. And wondering if she would come back or not or run away with Jon or whatever she was trying to do at the time. And I hated Bee for that.

Bee was a tremendously beautiful woman. I could never forget her and I don't want to. She was so supremely strong and confident and everything I had ever admired in a person. And Snow white was something like a mother to me. She was sweet and kind and soft and gentle and everything I hated in life. That's why I let her kiss me. That's why I chose to mix pain with pleasure.

She kissed me again and I wanted more. Believe it or not. I wanted more.

The wolf in me desired Snow white, probably to eat her which is more my kind of thing. But bare scarce humanity still remaining in my soul said, "run Snow white. Run. You don't want me to devour you whole. I'm nothing but a wolf and you are prey. It was naive of you to think I would never hurt you. I'm not for you snow white. I'm really not."

When she was done, she kissed me on the forehead and I told her once more, "You should really think about quitting."

"I'd never leave you Andras. You need me. I love you. You need me and I need you."

"Leave or regret not leaving," I say again, pushing her against the wall. I kiss her neck. "Leave or regret not leaving. I promise you. You'll wish you had left if you don't."

"No. I won't." She lets me kiss her. "I'll never leave. I love you forever."

My time goes the slowest.

I'm ruined by Bee.

I'm ruined.

I sigh and push the woman off of me. I send Snow white out of the room. When she is gone, I drop down to my desk, putting my hand to my forehead. I'm tired. Disturbed and tired. I hadn't expected that and I wondered what it meant to hate and love someone so much you didn't know what to do about it. That was how I felt about Snow white. Like I loved and hated her the most.

Ruined.

Love and loss.

The difference between right and wrong and the fine line he had failed to find years ago.

I write myself a note on my desk that maybe it was okay to forgive Bee for leaving me, and went on to bed and go to sleep.

Love and loss.

Loss and love.

And the fine line between what's love and what is hate.

I feel my death coming towards me.

You know it when you're about to die. You know it when death is just so close it's nipping at your ear and licking the tip of your nose. I'm saddened to realize that death is so close to me.

Bee. Please, don't be angry. I know now that your jealousy was relatively justified. You're jealous of Snow White. Then be the wicked witch and kill her for me. Kill the maid for me and save me from this ache in my dead heart.

I'm fighting two worlds.

A world of happy.

A world of sad.

I feel so scared.

It drives me mad.

Which road do I take?

Which line do I cross?

I feel you in my heart.

And we're never apart.

I know you're disappointed, right?

With so many options to choose from,

you really thought I'd pick happy?

CHAPTER 7 prologue

Hell is something you fear for a reason.
What is Hell?
For me, it was the day I realized
my NICE maid was in love with me.

'Andras Leader of H Group

CHAPTER 7

The next morning my maid comes in and tells me that she loves me again and that she always had.

"If you were a normal man, I wouldn't love you as much. Is that okay? I hope you understand. My love for you is real. As real and as heavy as I can carry." Snow white spoke gently to me. "Could you ever find it in your heart, to love me too? The irony of it all, is that for as long as I've known you, you've never acknowledged me as more than just a figment of your imagination. I'm real, Andras. And my love for you is eternal."

I am shocked to say the least. I'm starting to think this love thing wasn't a joke on her part. I'm starting to think she wants to fuck me or something. Or get married. Who knew what the hell the woman was ranting on and on about.

And by the way, just to warn you ahead of time. I did choose evil, not good. In this role playing game of life, I chose sad.

Hell is a frightening concept.

I don't want to think about it.

Considering the fact that I'm probably not too far from taking a permanent residence there when I die.

And all I can say is this,

Hell is something you fear for a reason.

What is Hell?

For me, it was the day I realized

my NICE maid was in love with me.

The idiot.

Love.

Hate.

Forever and always. I pick Hate.

You were stupid to think I'd choose otherwise.

And now the girl thinks she's in love with me.

The fool.

What in the world did this poor girl know about love?

And in what right mind had she the right to claim she loved me.

"You think you know love?" I asked, my voice almost raising into a state of semi-hysteria. "You think love means something to me?"

"I love you, Andras," she spoke again. "You're beautiful to me. A beautiful soul trapped in a broken mind. I love you."

"Then, who am I? What do I know about love? You think I know love? That I even know what the hell it is to me? Get out of my room. Just leave. And never come back," I scream loudly. "Never come back for once. I'm sick of your presence. Buy a house out in Alaska for all I care, but get the fuck out of my H GROUP HQ. You're pissing me off."

Turning her chin up at me, she replies strongly, "say it all you like, Andras. I'll never leave. I'll see you tomorrow morning. And I hope you like omelette and feta and garlic clove cause that's what I'm making for you. She leaves, hurrying out of the room and I watch her go.

I know what I'm doing. I'm aware. I'm not stupid. I'm fighting her, finally. Fighting her kindness. Fighting her subtle beauty. And fighting her love.

Like I said before, I just do whatever feels good right this second. I just do whatever I feel like. And right now, I feel like pushing her away from me.

I feel ashamed and idiotic and angry all at the same time.

I could could covet love.

Covet was a word I knew well.

I could desire love even, and jar it and keep it as a pet, but to feel it in real life in the depths of my dark black heart. Who was I to take claim to love?

I was a monster and I knew it.

All I ever wanted was to be a strong man that knew what he wanted and got it.

The time goes by, and now I fear I've wasted my life.

Is this what regret feels like?

I used to think I knew all there was to know.

It's times like these, that I realize I know nothing at all.

Love was nothing but a possession to me, an object to be framed. But my maid, was an angel and I could not love her back.

I'm sorry, Snow white.

I'm sorry, dear.

I'm sorry, you stupid woman.

I really am.

But,

I cannot return your feelings for me.

Infatuation, maybe.

Lust and seduction and desire perhaps.

But love.

Bee was love to me.

And that wasn't a compliment.

She was my life and she was my treasure and hope for the world.

But you, my dear, you are a nuisance.

I stared in realization at my closed door where she had left.

But you, my dear, I have to kill you.

It was the only way to save myself,

from the overwhelming feelings of insecurity boiling inside of my body.

"I love you," Snow white spoke again.

I smiled this time when she said it, knowing what I had to do.

The woman was naive and kind. She had no idea what I was thinking. No idea the extent to which I could hurt her, even if I didn't want to.

There are such a thing as flowers that blossom in the winter, my dear. Did you know that? Flowers that blossom in the way you kept this place beautiful with your sweet sincere heart and and kindness despite its cold and evil presence, but a winter without flowers is no real loss. I could lose you and the place would just be ugly as it should be. We don't need you, dear. Your presence is not implied. That's why I have to kill you. To set things right. And make our ulgy world ugly once more.

Your light.

Your shine.

Your grace.

Your beauty.

Has no place in the darkness that is the heart of Andras.

I look to my doll of Bee that is sitting beside me. I speak to her silently. You're the closest thing I've ever had to love, Bee. Please, don't be angry at me. I have to kill this one. Your jealousy was in vain. I'm going to make everything right again. I'm going to make everything pure and new and true between us once more. I'm going to kill Snow white.

I hope you're disappointed in me. Instead of thrilled as I'm sure you are in Hell. Perhaps, I should've moved on. Perhaps I should've married her instead. But I don't think like that. I think like the sub-creature I am that craves what he cannot have.

And all I saw, was someone that would willingly come with me. Do you really think, that something so good, could entice me the least bit at all? Well, you're wrong if you thought that.

This is what I call giving the girl what she wants. And then taking it right back.

Love and loss.

Loss and love.

In a way, you can give a little, just so long as you take a lot back.

I told the girl that I was fine with that. "That's fine with me," I smiled. "You can love me. You can love me all you want. I would even go so far as to say I love you too."

"You do?" she beamed enthusiastically. "I'm so happy Andras. Thank you so much."

I kissed her. More like pecked at her but the point is I made a valid attempt to be affectionate with her.

I took her to bed and we had sex.

She looked happy. Too happy.

Love and loss.

Loss and love.

I wrapped my hands around her neck.

Then I strangled her to death right afterwards.

She looked shocked that I would hurt her.

She looked absolutely shocked.

I strangled her to death and she was dead and she had died and I threw her body off the bed and sat up, running a hand through my thinning hair.

What a bitch.

Nothing like Bee.

Nothing in the least.

I covered my face with my hands and began to sob. I was a monster.

And in a world where you can only ever be a monster, I have to admit, I liked it.

CHAPTER 8 prologue

"Live and learn, you stupid man.
Live and learn."

~ Fourteen, Andras's shadow

CHAPTER 8

Fourteen is angry at me.

"Live and learn, you stupid man. Live and learn." Fourteen says to me.

Bee is hysterical.

"A murderer to the end," she cries. "A crazy old man that can't even forgive one pretty girl."

Thirteen is haunting me.

"Death awaits you, my friend. Do not stray from your plans to find your heir. I'll never understand why you do the things you do."

The girl Snow white is dead and she isn't coming back.

Her death mocks me.

I love you, she had said. I love you.

I awoke the next morning and was disappointed when Snow white did not show up with breakfast.

I scream like the hyena I am and cry and sob over the maid's dead body on the floor by my bed.

I want to die.

I want to die.

But Death isn't ready for me yet.

Not ready to take me.

I Know I am wrong.

I am only wrong

Once I said, I wanted to explore the world and become its king.

Now I just want to destroy the world and become it's devil.

I hate you Snow white.

I hate you for breaking my heart.

She should've run away when she had the chance.

But she was stupid.

And stupid girls and boys only run away when you don't want them to. Like Bee.

And Fifty-six.

I decided then and there to kidnap Tara once more and trade her life for Fifty-six to come home again. I need him. I need my son. I need him to come home and take over the H GROUP for me for when I have died.

I set up a plan. Put it together.

And call my assassins in, Aiden assassin Two, and Heat, Assassin Seventeen, to carry out the plan.

CHAPTER 9 prologue

Voices whisper to me.

Death.

See me death.

Take me death

watch me death.

My mind and I

We fall apart as night falls.

If it weren't for you.

I don't think I would've even bothered.

Andras, leader of H Group

CHAPTER 9

After kidnapping Tara Jones and using her as bait to lure Fifty-six back home, I have finally convinced Fifty-six to rejoin the H group and become its next leader.

I have successfully made Fifty-six my heir.

I touch his hand. and kiss him on the forehead.

Like a son to me, he was.

It was expensive of course, as most things are. I had to let Tara Jones live to get him to work for us again but it was worth it.

I know now that love is the answer and that for the world to exist in the way it does and turn in the way you want it to, love must be manipulated, controlled, and passed out evenly in the form of hatred.

She is dragged away down the hallways of HQ on her way home to the States.

"I know, Fifty-six. It's men like us, that don't appreciate the woman. We covet her. We long for her. We want her. It's men like us, that don't realize what we have, until she's gone."

Fifty-six touches the screen of the surveillance TV and kissed the image of tara, nodding slowly in agreement.

"Until she's gone," Fifty six repeats gently.

Voices whisper to me.

Death.

See me death.

Take me death.

watch me death.

My mind and I

We fall apart as night falls.

If it weren't for you,

I don't think I would've even bothered.
Goodbye Snow White. Maybe next time, I'll love you.
If there is a next time,
or such a thing as second chances,
Maybe we can try again.

BOOK 3 End.

BOOK 4

A Killers Instinct:
Lace's Story

CHAPTER 1 prologue

"He's wilted.

Like a flower.

His life, aches from weight. It's heavy, he says. It's heavy

He can't carry it.

He can't hold it anymore.

I tell him. I'll carry it with you if it would ease the burden."

~Lace

CHAPTER 1

Ten years later.

There are no words. His smile. I cry. I want to be with him. His bed is old and tailored and oak wooden and there are no bed posts because he cut them off in a fit of rage one night. He dropped to his knees that night in front of it and told me he couldn't live any longer the life he lived.

I hug him. Or maybe he was hugging me. I never knew. He pushed me away so many times before I never knew exactly. I'm drawn to him. The way he stares. I want to tell him, to reassure him it'll all be alright. But he never knew that. He never heard a single word I said. It was more about the blood than about the night's sky that lay above us. My love. My nightmare. My dream. If only you were born as a good man, my dear. And not as an assassin.

"I'm sorry, darling, that I kill people" he told me that night.

"Why don't you stop."

"Because when I was young, they spared my love's life if I would work for them. I work for a man named Andras. He's like a father to me. He is my death. It has been ten years since that day."

"Your death?"

"Yes. I traded my life for my love." he said.

"Choose me," I cried. I sobbed. I sobbed so loud I thought I would die from the ache in my chest. I cried and cried. "The woman you love. I'm sure she's beautiful. I'm sure she's a fine person. But choose me. Please. I beg you to choose me. We can leave. We don't have to be here. Let them kill her and choose me instead. Just let her die, Michael. Let her die."

Still on his knees he said. "I can't. I just can't." His hands dropped to the floor. "Forgive me, Lace. I love you too. But I can't abandon her. I can't do that."

He waves. Goodbye, he says. I wonder if I'll see him again. His words. Like fire. They burn me. I can't, he said. I can't. But why. Why couldn't he? In another world. In another life, we would've been together I think. If I had met him first. The story of Michael and Tara, that could've been my story. If I had met him first, would he have loved me?

In my life, you may think me strange. A hooker. A prostitute. With a fetish for men's feet, black coffee, and dark chocolate. I met Michael, because he told me he had never been with a woman before and wanted to try it out. He paid me two hundred dollars to spend the night with him. He was the best I ever had. Strong. Tender. Sweet. He was handsome. In his late twenties. Beautiful man. Truly and truly. I couldn't get enough. He tasted like sweat and gun powder. His eyes broke me. They broke me. They broke me.

I'm artistic. Not artistic in the way that painter's paint and writers write. But I see the world in an artistic way. The beauty of Michael. The beauty of his face. His rock hard body. The way he moves and talks. As an artistic interpretor, I would even go so far as to say, he's a work of pure genius. When God made him, they must've mistook him for an angel because his wings spread wide and he flies when he walks by me. The rustle of his hair. His way of doing things. He moves me. In the way music moves a snake.

I never thought I'd ever use the word love in the same sentence as a man's name. Women, I can love. Women, are sweet and soft and make me smile I used to be gay. Men disgusted me. Not Michael. He didn't disgust me at all. But women were like mothers to me They were cozy and they were kind and they held me in their arms in giant hugs and always told me everything was going to be okay. But Michael was different. Michael could've been a rock or a frog or a girl or a man and I would've loved him. It was his soul I loved. And I loved him more than I had ever loved anyone before in my life.

He told me once that things would get better for me someday. He said he'd save some money up and buy me a house and a car and pay the utilities and even marry me if I wanted though he couldn't promise he'd be there more than once a month. I was flattered. Marry me and make me the happiest woman in the universe, I teased. Go ahead. I'd love it. He replied. We'll do that then. We'll get married and we'll be happy.

Then the truth came out. The awful truth. It wasn't me he lived for. It wasn't me that he thought about when we made love. It was Tara. A stupid stubborn selfish girl with no idea how to make a man happy. And his job, the secret he had kept from me the two years we had known each other, was that he was a killer, a murderer, and only did it to protect one person.

Let that one person being protected be you, Michael.

After the hard life you've lived you deserve it. Let that one person who's fine be you for once. Once Tara was dead, there'd be no reason for Michael to work for the H Group any longer. Once Tara was dead, Lace and Michael could finally be together and nothing would keep them apart.

It's heavy, he said. The weight of the world. His life. It's heavy he said. His pain. His suffering. I can't take it. I want to free him. I want to save him. Tara. I'll be the one to kill you instead. Once you're dead... There will be no more pain for him. Just love. Just love and joy and him and me. I can't believe you let him do that for you. I can't believe it. A selfish woman like you Tara, it's women like you that deserve to die.

CHAPTER 2 prologue

"Love.

Loss.

The way things are to me.

I see you from a distance

but you can never see me.

Even though we're not together,

I hope you'll remember me forever."

~Michael, assassin fifty six.

CHAPTER 2

A gun to the mouth. A bullet shot. Dead dead dead. Michael killed his target in the way a lion hunts for meat. Just enough to sustain him, to sustain him and his love for Tara. And not a penny more. And dead. And dead, he thought once more. His life as an assassin. It burdened his soul. He felt terrible. To murder for love. It was becoming a love for murder. He couldn't take it anymore. He wanted to die.

The next bullet that left his gun, he promised, the next bullet, he'd kill Andras. If that didn't work, he'd kill himself and Tara and they could rest in peace together in heaven. He headed to his car.

He started the car and began to drive. Despite the risks, he wanted to see her again. He wanted to wrap his arms around her and show her how much he loved her.

He knew the idea was stupid.

He knew it was dangerous. He knew it could be the death to attempt it.

But he had to see Tara again.

He just had to.

So killing Andras was all he could do.

And once again, be on the run.

Love.

Loss.

The way things are to me.

I see you from a distance

but you can never see me.

Even though we're not together,

I hope you'll remember me forever.

Michael made it back to H Group headquarters, a channeling group of underground tunnels and buildings. I approached a giant artificial tree in the middle of the forest, hiding a briefcase stuffed with cash under a pile of leaves, and pushed a button on the trunk. The bark slipped away revealing a keyboard. I typed in the password 54546. The tree opened, revealing a narrow elevator. I took it to the ground floor. The hallway was a blare of glaring white lights and fans over the ceiling.

I Love

I loss

and the way she looked at me

These feelings

They are not meant to be.

He didn't know what he should do about the suicidal thoughts he had been having lately. But love kept him alive. His love for Tara was eternal. And he knew that she loved him too. He walked to Andras' room and knocked on the door. "It's me," I said. I could do this. I could kill Andras. I could be free of the beast that held me captive. Then Tara and I could run away together, just like they had tried in the past.

Andras opened the door. He was tall and lean and older now. It had been ten years since Michael had given up his life to the H GROUP once and for all. His white suit was pressed and bleached and looked a little too clean for the place they lived. I pushed past him and headed in.

A taxidermied woman sat on a chair at the dining room table of the nice bedroom. Beautiful antique paintings had long since been replaced with enlarged photographs of the woman as she had been in life, smiling into the camera.

"How's Bee?" I asked, referring to the dead woman at the table.

"Very well, very well indeed," Andras replied quickly. "And yourself. How did the mission go?"

"Well, he's dead if that's what you're asking."

"And the money. Did they deliver the money with the mission."

"Yes. I picked it up first before the kill. It's in storage even as we speak."" I lied. I had actually hidden the money under the leaves with intention to run away with Tara and use the money to do so.

"As you should. As you should," Andras replied.

"How was your day?"

"All work and no play, my boy. Never play. Just work."

"I see."

Andras, my death and the leader of the H Group. It would be so easy to just shoot him. To kill him right here and right now and be done with the whole thing. He wanted me to be his heir. Hahah, as if I would ever.

My love

my life.

I your husband

and you my wife.

I realize that there's no such thing as the perfect time to do something. There's really no difference either way.

But now was as good a time as any to kill Andras.

I pulled out my gun and shot at him, emptying it into his chest.

I could do it. We could do it. I could run away now. I could get away. Tara. Forgive me. The burden was too heavy. I'm afraid I couldn't carry it alone.

Andras fell back onto the floor. I reloaded my gun and waited. No movement from Andras. I kicked him. Just a corpse. Goodbye H Group. Tara here I come. The man was dead. Dead dead dead. Dead like all his other victims. How he had awaited this moment.

Sensing no further movement from Andras, Michael walked away and left the room.

Tara looked skinny and pretty in her pink blouse and floral skirt that hung to her knees. Her shoes were pink heels.

Lifting her hand, Tara pulled open the small mail box, pulling out a pile of wide envelopes from inside. She closed the box again and locked it. She glanced at the mail as she walked back to her apartment. Oh good. Her new credit card had come in. She tore open the envelope and pulled out folded papers inside. Terms and conditions, etc, etc. She took the card from the paper and read the front.

Taba Jones

Incorrect.

She pursed her lips. Damn it, they had spelled her name wrong again. She was going to have to get a new one and wait all over again.

Sighing, she pulled out another envelope and opened it. Addressed to her, but no return address. Strange. When she opened it. She found a letter from Michael. Telling her to come meet her at the grocery store down her street.

Her heart jumped in her chest and she the rest of the mail dropped from her hands.

She felt stunned.

Michael.

Longing.

Too much time gone by of knowing you'd leave, knowing you'd disappear.

Then too much time gone by after you did disappear for good.

Where are you Michael?

Where are you?

I miss you.

I felt tears in my eyes.

Michael was the most beautiful person she had ever met in her life. And she missed him.

Michael.

I miss you.

Where are you Michael?

Where are you?

"Michael?" I gasped.

I'm coming. I'm coming. I'm coming.

I let out a delighted shriek.

Michael

I miss you.

Despair and longing.

Love

Loss.

What could hurt more than losing the one you love.

I headed outside. The weather was comfortable and the sun was bright. I ran to my gray sedan. I started my car.

I drove quickly out of the parking lot and onto the road, heading to the grocery store nearest her apartment building

I love you

I miss you

Desire and longing

Love and loss

Please don't ever leave again.
When I look for you
please be there waiting for me.
I got out of my car and jogged into the store.
Michael.
You were my world.
My life.

I walked around the store. In the corner, I saw a man working at the register. It was Michael. Michael.

"Michael!!" I shrieked. I ran to him. He held his arms open and embraced me.

"I knew you'd come back," I cried. The tears fell freely. "I knew you'd come back to me, my love."

"I'm so sorry I left," Michael whispered into my hair. "I'm so sorry, Tara. I love you so much."

His arms around me
I'm smiling
I'm actually smiling
My love
Never leave again.
Please
Or if you do
Next time, darling
Just take me with you,
and I'll follow you to the ends of the world till we fall off the edges.

CHAPTER 3 prologue

"I Love
I loss
and the way she looked at me
These feelings
They are not meant to be."

~ Michael, assassin Fifty-six

CHAPTER 3

Kill Michael
Then kill Tara
Slowly.

Andras finished his sticky note. When he was done, he took it and pressed it to Bee's head. "There You go Bee. Remind me what I have to do."

Andras groaned. His rib was broken, or so it felt like, from the impact, but the bullet proof vest he always wore in secret seemed to protect him for the most part.

The idiot should've checked to make sure he was dead, not just assumed it.

Ten years of trust. Of loyalty. And then nothing. Pure betrayal.

My death

that's all I saw.

My death flash before my eyes.

I groaned again. Michael. Fifty-six. How could you? How could you do this to me?

I felt annoyed.

Annoyed.

Sighing, Andras walked to Bee's taxidermied form and kissed her over the cheek. "I know darling. It'll all get better one day. I hate to do this but I need to. I must kill Fifty-six and Tara for betraying me. There's no forgiveness for what they've done to me."

He went to his phone and began dialing the numbers of his strongest killers.

Seventeen answered the phone. "Hello," he spoke softly.

"Seventeen. I need your help. I'm afraid Fifty-six tried to kill me today."

"He would do that," Seventeen replied. "I knew he would. You know how those type are. Bad boys until the end. They always feel the need to rebel."

"I need him dead. He's strong. Too strong. You may need a few days to do it. And kill Tara too."

"Fifty-six's little girlfriend?"

"Yes. And then you will be heir instead of Fifty six. Just like I promised you. I'll send you the information," Andras spoke. "But first, I need you to tell the others that Fifty-six is no longer welcome in the H Group. If they see him wandering the facility. I want them to kill him on sight. Now send a spy. I want to know everything about where he is and what he's doing right now. If all else fails. Find a friend of his that can do it for him. I want it to be subtle. If he catches on, it won't work."

You may think me strange. The way I looked for him. The way I followed him. I said to him once I would follow him throughout the end of time and he told me that was a nice thing and he liked that very much.

When I did follow him to the edge of the world, I found him with another woman. I spied at them from behind the shelves of a grocery store and watched as they hugged each other. Who was that person? I wasn't sure but I thought it could be the Tara woman he spoke about because of the way he held her.

Biting my lip, I took a breath. They were now chatting casually, and I walked over to them. "Michael," I called out. "Fancy meeting you here." I glanced at the girl. "And this is?"

"Lace, it's you," he shook his head, putting a hand to his forehead. "Oh, Lace. Of course. This is Tara. The girl I told you about."

"How nice to run into you two," Lace smiled. Dreaming, distorted reality, teeth shattering. A dead woman. That's all she saw, Tara, the dead woman. She gestured at the apron that Michael was wearing. "You get a new job or something."

"Yes. I work here now."

"That's good to know."

I smiled at them. "Maybe I'll see you guys around."

I left.

He's wilted.

Like a flower.

His life, aches from weight. It's heavy, he says. It's heavy

He can't carry it.

He can't hold it anymore.

I tell him. I'll carry it with you if it would ease the burden.

I felt cold and crossed my arms over my body.

There was such a thing as loving someone too much.

It was possible to love someone so much that you died from it.

It hurt so much that you killed the feeling of love until there is no love at all and only hate.

That was the feeling I held for Michael now. Nothing but pure wrath and hatred.

If I could choose which world to live in, it would be the one with Michael in it. But Michael didn't want that world and neither did God apparently so I'm stuck in the reality of this one. And this one says that Michael and I could never be together.

All I saw was blood and teeth shattering. Dreaming. The dead ones. That's who they were to me. The dead ones.

I walked away.

A man bumped into me. Rather casually. Too casually. "Excuse me," I snapped, spinning around.

"Oh, of course. I'm sorry." He smiled at me. "You're Michael's friend, aren't you? You know Michael, don't you?" he smiled again as he stepped closer and pressed. "Don't you? Don't you?"

"Yes I do. What of it. Or should I say, I did know him. No good in knowing him now that he's reunited with his tramp."

"Reunited with his tramp you say," the man started. He was starting to look excited. "Why now, I know exactly what you need and what you want. How would you like to work for the H Group. We're hit men for hire."

"Excuse me?"

"We can hire you for just the one job. Hey, you do well and maybe we'll even hire you again. And then again after that." he made a gesture with his hand. "Come with me and we can talk some more in private."

We walked to a nearby cafe and sat down. He took off a pair of sunglasses revealing a relatively handsome face, despite his odd demeanor.

"So who do you want me to kill?" I asked nervously.

"Michael and Tara. You know them? Don't you?"

I felt stunned. The dead ones. That's all i saw. I was in true life, just a simple woman. I never thought I'd truly kill them. Just thought it in my head to make myself feel better but this was it. This was truly an opportunity worth thinking about. Could she do it? "I'd kill them for free," I joked flatly. "Why do you want to pay me to do it?"

"Let's just say there's a consequence for every action and a kind of this for every that."

"What's that mean?"

"It means that Michael kinda screwed us over once upon a time. He made a bargain with the boss he'd stick around for his girlfriend's life, then he bailed on us and tried to assassinate the boss, thinking he'd go all noble in a different way I'm thinking and try to make a difference for once. Didn't do him any good. The boss had on a bullet proof vest and the idiot didn't think to check to make sure the guy was dead."

"I'll do it," I said without thinking. "What's your name anyway?"

"Seventeen. That's what you can call me."

Hate

Love

What was the difference anymore?

I could live for love or live for hate. Either way, it wouldn't make Michael love me back. So in that sense, I could go for all eternity just living on pure hate.

I shook the man's hand. "Sir, you got yourself a deal."

'Wonderful!" he exclaimed. He dropped two small vials into my hands. "Here. It's poison. Slip it into their drinks. I don't care how you get them into that situation. Just do it quickly and meet me here next week, same time, same place. Here's two thousand dollars. We'll give you another two grand if you finish the job by next week."

"Thanks. Sounds good."

She tucked them into her coat pocket.

Hatred

Love.

What was the difference anymore.

I thought I knew what love was. It was the unconditional bond between two people that lasted for all eternity. But what if he didn't love you back? What if he didn't want to be with you and had someone else in mind?

Hatred.

There were few things in this world, she appreciated more than her love for Michael and now, that was her hatred for him. I loved him for all eternity. Now gone. Gone gone gone. Gone with the wind. Away he blows. My love. My life. I give to you in a different way. And my death, I lay upon you like broken wings of a bird. Feel my love and my hate. I long for you, my dear. I covet your existence. And only in death can we be together.

And so in death, I take you first and your love. In death you two can hold hands for all eternity for all I care, but when it comes to forever, it'll be me that ends up with Michael and has the last laugh.

Michael and Tara.

I'm going to kill you.

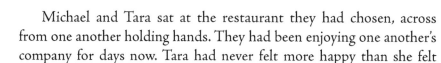

Michael and Tara sat at the restaurant they had chosen, across from one another holding hands. They had been enjoying one another's company for days now. Tara had never felt more happy than she felt right now.

Ache.

Was this happiness?

Your eyes.

I stare.

Your smile.

I long for you.

I long for you.

I long for you.

Even when you're here, I long for you.

There's no such thing as close enough to you. I can't believe it. To finally see him again.

It brought tears to her eyes.

I cry, wiping at my eyes.

"What's wrong?" he asked.

"I'm just so happy."

He smiled at me. "How happy are you?"

"Very. Very Very.""

"A toast then."

"To us." I finished.

He leaned forward and kissed me on the lips, catching me off guard. I blushed. It was our first kiss. I let his lips linger on my own for awhile. I long for you. Even when you're already here. Please be with me forever this time. Please never leave again.

"Heavy" he said.

"You killed him?"

"Yes. He was too heavy to carry. I loved him like a father but I had to do it. He was holding me hostage"

"Heavy," I breathed slowly.

"Heavy is the burden I carry."

"A poem?"

"Yes. I wrote it for Lace."

"Who's Lace."

"The woman from a couple days ago. She was my only friend for awhile. I wrote it for her. That doesn't make you angry does it."

"Not at all." I was only a little jealous. Maybe it was the way he spoke that told me this was something very very important to him and I knew that I should listen with sincerity, not envy of their friendship.

"Heavy is the burden I carry," He continued. "Too heavy. Too heavy. The burden kills me. It weighs me down. I hold you in my arms. And even so, the burden kills me still. Please don't leave me. Even if I die, please don't forget I exist." He stopped. "I forget the rest but the point is, this poem is for you now. Please don't leave me. I want you to stay with me forever. I want you to marry me."

I reply, "Yes. I'll marry you, Michael. I love you so much."

"Please don't leave me."

"Please don't leave me either," I said.

"I'll do anything," Tears were in his eyes now. "Just don't leave me."

"I promise. I'll never leave you."

Kiss. kiss.

He kissed me again.

He held my hands and I smiled at him. This burden of his. She would do all she could to hold on to it. "Thank you so much for coming back, Michael. I promise I'll never leave you." His hands were warm in hers, and they held hands as if they were two creatures of pure unity. His skin was like poetry against hers. When he kissed her, she felt happy as if for the first time in her life. They went together in the way that two people went together when they danced, perfectly in time to one another.

Those were my thoughts.

As he held my hand.

Dear Michael. I love you.

I'll never leave you.

Please never leave me.

And please. Stop calling the world a heavy place and a burden to live in. I'm here now. You don't have to be scared anymore. I'll never let anyone hurt you. And I never break a promise. So for now, just be with me. Just love me. Just kiss me. Just marry me.

Just.

Just know I will always be there for you.

So please. No more tears. This heavy world of yours. I give it wings so it can fly away and take care of itself for once. No more pain. No more hurting. No more longing for you. Just love. Just peace. Just unity. Please forgive me, but my love for you is forever, and there's no such thing as me leaving you. So please don't think I would.

CHAPTER 4 prologue

"The necklace you bought for me hangs around my neck. I'd give it back to you if it weren't for the fact that I never saw you again."

~ Lace

CHAPTER 4

I never thought of myself as a selfish woman. Scratch that. Selfless. No scratch that again. Selfish is better. I never thought of myself as selfish woman.

Sigh.

What am I trying to say here.

I don't want to kill for money.

Lace sat in her trailer home, staring at the two vials of poison in her hand.

I don't want to kill for money.

Killing for love. That's funny to me. That's like killing in the name of vegetarianism. It doesn't really make any sense. That's what killing for love is. Something that doesn't make any sense.

So anyway. I'm going to begin by telling my life story to you, my journal and write in words how I feel from now on.

Dear diary. march 28th 2010

Today i was approached by the H group. They want me to kill Michael and Tara. Would I? I'm not going to pretend it didn't cross my mind as a good idea. I even told them i would and took the money. But what's money. Two grand isnt chump change, but it isn't a forturne and taking a life is complicated and not necessarily the path i really want to go in in life.

Im going to have to think about these things for a few days.

Selfish.

Im a selfish person by nature.

But as i say, i came into this world alone and alone i'll die. I dont really need anyone. If you think about it, we dont need others to be happy. I could be perfectly happy on my own with nothing but my thoughts. You have to wonder. What's life without other people. But life, there's no such thing as a world that doesn't remake the same thing over and over again with its theories on existentialism. Im trying to say that i could go on forever wondering why i do what i do or think what i think or say what i say but it the end, does anyone ever care enough to listen.

No.

They dont.

That's the answer to that question. No one listens. Because they cant hear you and they're sick of themselves.

Michael once told me his burden was to heavy to carry.

I told him i'd carry it too if that were possible but i dont think he was listening. You can hear someone but that doesn't mean youre listening. It goes in through one ear and out the other. I think i'll stop digressing from my point.

Existentialism always pissed me off. It implies i cant exist without asking why every five minutes. I dont need to know why im here or why i shit or why i eat or why i think venus is a star not a planet or even what day it is if i dont feel like it.

Im sick of thinking. I just want to relax.

This journal is very close to being my only friend.

i've spent my entire life talking to you and you never talk back. But its not neccessary for you to reply. Just as long as you listen i feel content that we've had a conversation.

I used to think talking to mIchael was the best thing that could happen to me. I dont think i ever lost that feeling of hope that he'd walk back into my home and tell me the whole thing was just a terrible misunderstanding or that i had had some awful nightmare only and that what led me up to this point was just a dream.

Im not going to lie to Diary. I despise my life. I want to die right now. If i could die. I would. I dont want to go on in a world where the closest thing i've ever felt to love has turned putrid and dropped to the floor and rotted and become something like hatred. I never thought i could hate Michael but right now. that's kind of how i feel. Like i hate him. but most of all, I hate tara for taking him from me. I love you but i dont want to be with you right now, he said to me in a long time ago. He said all that garbage about wanting to get married and run away together and now he's with that tramp and im just supposed to sit back and take it like the bitch whore i am but i dont want to.

I dont want to.

I dont want this life or this world or to wonder if i was ever meant to be an angel in the hands of the world or just a villian in the eyes of the devil. What i mean is i dont want to know if im meant to die the good guy or the bad guy. I want to think that i was meant for more than that.

I wasnt' born on this planet to impress anyone. That much i can assure you. So what im trying to say is that im sad that i have to put my life into terms of good and evil and nice and bad and right and wrong to begin with. What's the point of life if i can t be with the one i love? No point at all. As a matter of fact i think i'd rather die than even fimish writing this entry to you.

Good

Bad

Sad

Happy

Nice.

Evil.

I dont know. I think im rambling. what do those words mean to you dear diary.

I have two vials of poison right now. i could either take the poisone myself and commit suicide, and die as a martyr.

Or....

I could kill those two without thinking anything of it. Either way i wont be happy. As a dead woman i wont find solace and as a murderer i'll be well, a murderer.

I dont know.

Maybe im meant to die now and never have to think these things again. An eternal suicide. That's what i call this. Or maybe im supposed to be the bad guy and kill those two and live forever as a evil villian that couldnt even win over the man she loved in a battle of relationshiops.

Once upon a time, i found myself knowing that i was a loser. When i was in highschool, i had a best friend. This best friend's name was Shell. Like sea shell. I dont know maybe it was more like shell the gas station lol. Never mind. the one thing about telling you jokes is that you never seem to laugh back my diary but i wont hold that against you. AS a matter of fact i like you more for at least hearing the joke whether you get it or not which i respect your intelligence enough to know you do get my joke even if youre not capable of laughing.

Anyway, so my friend Shell was what i call a Super Person. Let's jsut say i hate super people. Super people to me is when a person can get whatever they want, whenever they want, no matter what. its a no matter what type thing.

At all.

That's another way to write it.

She got what she wanted at all.

Some called her spoiled, some called her a bitch. She thought of herself as a strong woman that knew what she wanted and had the decency to get it. It was knowing this that drove me to become a prostitute.

AS for prostitution. I hate prostituation. I never wanted to be a prostisttute, but seeing Shell steal everything she ever had in her life made me sick. She wanted a purse, she stole it. She wanted a boyfriend. She took him, even if he was already taken. I was never like that. One time, Shell stole my boyfriend because as she claimed, he liked her more and if she could do that why wouldnt she.

"It's possible," she said to me.

"whats' that mean?" i asked.

"If i can steal him i must be more desireable.."

"He was my first love Shell." I told her.

"yeah but he wants me. If he wants me then why cant i have him."

I think it was twice she stole my boyfriend. As a matter of fact. If she were still here today and not dead by that wretched car accident that took her life, i would even go so far as to say that she would steal Michael right now if she thought it were possible.

what am i saying. Im getting tired. But anyway. Super people piss me off. I hate greedy people and there's nothing more greedy than to covet another person's wealth or man and then take it for no reason. I think that's why i became a prostitute. I thought i'd pay for Shell's theory on life by giving for all eternity and never taking from society. I thought to myself, if i could spend an entire life living as a giver, then things would get better and better for me and i would not take. No i would never take.

To take is evil.

God do i hate super people. They're so annoying. Not that i dont miss Shell once in awhile, god rest her soul in heaven, but i do think that she's a bit of a jerk. She left two holes in my heart, one knowing that she was a terrible person and probably deserved to be drunk that night and drive her car off the highway and another hole where i knew i would never see her again and that does, despite everything else. make me a little sad.

Im dissappointed in myself. Once michael and tara are dead, that's if i do decide to kill them, im going to have to live with myself for a very long time. I probably wont be much different from when Shell died. I can hate her all i want but death and separation does soemthing to a person. Its something you never get back and its something that doesn't go away with age and timelessness. It actually, in realtiy only gets worse and worse and i think thats something im going to have to think about for a long time.

As for the rest of the entry, i got so tied up in my thoughts ive forgotten all i had to say so for now i'll say goodbye. I'll write tomorrow and hopefully you'll be happy with me again and forgive me for complaining so very much about my dead friend Shell. I know its evil and petty to remember the boyfriend thing. Whats love between a man and woman when you have friendship, but in reality, by stealing my first love, she was no friend to me at all and i dont want to think about this any longer. All i know i am sad to this day about what happened. So goodnight diary and i'll leave you for now.

CHAPTER 5

Dear Diary march 29th 2010

i spent the two grand on drugs.

im sorry.

I know youre going to think i wasted it but i really didnt. I invited a bunch of friends over and we smoked most of it and ate the rest. I know youre going to think thats a stupid way to spend all the money but i didnt really know what to do with it. Im going to be honest with you. I dont like drugs. I hate drugs. I do drugs because they make me feel smarter and by that, i mean im probably significantly stupider, especially right now.

I know. Drugs are cool. No. drugs are a reliance. what's a reliance to me. A reliance to me is someting i rely on so i dont have to feel. What was i feeling? sad. What do i feel now? nothing. Mission accomplished. Life successfully bleeped out.

I like how in tv they edit out all the bad stuff. Or as me and shell used to joke as teenagers, edited out all the good stuff. I wish i could say the same thing about life. If i had an eraser, i would erase out all the bad things and leave nothing but good things behind. then when i read my life like a book it would be pure and clean and good and a nice thing.

That was fine.

Very fine

Im a little high righ tnow. I wasnt going to tell you because i promised back in 06 i would never do drugs again but you know how i am. a promise from me is a like a bullet to the head. Who do you trust more? Me or the gun? Not me. But a bullet kills you either way, regardless of intent so i just sat there knowing that all day long while my friends ruined my trailer.

Yes. I have friends. I dont know why but i always forget to mention my current girlfriends..

First there's Amanda. She's cool. Not just cool. but special to me. I used to be gay. But you know that. I dated amanda for two years and then we broke up when i met michael because i didn't want to cheat on her.

that was called being in like. The thing with amanda. I really liked her. She was sweet and i liked her tits. But she was a figment of my imagination. She was cute and funny and swell to talk to but she was kind of a martyr in a way. She used to run around telling me i was the best thing she ever saw and to me that was martyristic because only the best one has the decency to run around calling people the best one. Or something like that.

So anyway, She was the best one for being sweet. thats what she was. sweet. Thats a better word for her.

And as for the like thing. I dont really know why i thought like was love and love was like. I was confused by the fact that i could feel anything at all at first. Because other than hating Shell and losing my first love, i guess you'd call that sad, I never really felt much of anything before. Other than regret.

Regret.

Yes. I regret. I regret being friends with Shell. I regret meeting Michael. I regret seeing him with Tara that day. I regret the world in a way i never thought possible.

next friend. Whitherspin. She's a beauty. We only dated for two weeks. But was INTENSE. And i spell that with a capital I. She was sexy. She waS fun. she was interesting. She made my world go round. Then it was over. Nothing but stupid girl sex and no substence. thats how i would describe her. Lacking in substance but not lacking in beauty. A beautiful girl to a fault. If she weren't so spacey, I'd probably call her the perfect ideal woman.

Last friend, Penelope. She was prostitute too. I think the other two are strippers or someting these days, i havent asked lately and they tend to switch jobs a lot. So i never dated Penelope but always wanted to. I call her fuckable by nature. which means we never fucked and i would if i could but she's married and doesn't really do the lesbian thing for some reason. I always fantasized we'd have an affair someday but it never manifested itself physically somehow. So.

those are my friends. We did all the drugs in a few hours. Really expensive stuff. I got the best on the market. My drug dealer was happy. I gave him a hundred dollar tip extra for always being trustworthy and paid him back the other two hundred i owed him from the week before. Usually drug dealers dont do that but he knows im good for it and trusts me because he was a client of mine and when i dont pay him back, he usually just rapes me for the money's worth, lol. Just joking. No. i just give him a couple freebies and he's happy.

We did all the drugs and yes i spent all the money. My friends went home and now im alone with just some dizzyness and my world spinning and no one but me and two vials of poison.

I take them into my left hand as i write this. Im not sure why but im so high i wouldnt mind drinking them myself. No more pain. No more suffering. no more michael. I'd love to die here and now, right after a party, right after smoking two pounds of weed and making cocaine brownies. Im sick of this world. Im ready to die. Please let me die. Please let me die.

I know what youre thinking diary. PUt down the poison Lace, youre just kidding yourself.

But im not. Im not sure why but i love playing games with my own life. It reminds me of the time i clung to the car hood while my friend whitherspin gunned the engine to 45 miles per hour. Didn't i say we had an intense two weeks together. By intense. I mean truly intense.

WEll i have to go but i'll write back soon.

See you tomorrow.

CHAPTER 6

Dear diary March 30 2010

love.

Love and loss.

michael *used to say that to me. That love and loss were intertwined. Why did we even bother, knowing that one thing led to another. Love. Then breaking up. Why start someting you know is going to end.*

Love is eternal

Maybe in the movies. Or maybe in some hell i dont know about but love my friend is not eternal or good or anything i would brag about feeling right about now.

Love.

i love you.

I LOVE YOU.

how pretty.

Im laughing now. The more i write it the prettier it looks in script.

Well anyway, back to what i was saying. What is love? I used to think love was a someting like the stork story you tell children so they dont know they came out your mother fucking vagina. I thought fairies invented love and dropped it down on good boys and girls so that they could get married someday and have kids.

Then SHELL STOLE MY FUCKING BOYFRIEND. And then she died. on top of all that.

sorry. im drunk. I slept with someone for a hundred bucks, bought a whole bunch of liquor and drank it all.

as for fairies they probably dont exist but i did believe in them once. I remember telling Michael about my fairie theory. He had laughed and i giggled and we were in bed together because we had just had sex for the first time. It was wonderful.

I want you to know that i never wanted to give up on you michael. I wanted to love you forever and hold you in my arms in some way that would make us both happier for it. I never thought my life would turn out so poorly that i'd be in a situatin where either way i'll never see you again.

I got the wedding invitation by the way, diary. I'll read it to you.

Dear Lace Winehouse.

You are cordually invited to the wedding of Michael Jones and Tara Jones. Please VIP if you plan on coming.

date. April 7ᵗʰ 2010

Hmmmmmm.

well its signed. Looks real. I doubt its a joke being played on me by Shell from the other side, so im going to assume this is real. hmmm.

HMMMMMMMMMMMMMMMM

I feel like im going to cry.

But i dont want to.

If i cry, they kind of win. I feel like they're mocking me, like the skeletons from Michael's dream that he told me about. Some reoccuring dream about his childhoood. He never really explained it well, but it seemed to mean a lot to him so i listened. I listened. I truly listened.

something he never did.

the vials of poison are on my coffee table in front my couch. As i write this, im sitting on the couch, with the rest of my vodka in my hand and i want to pour the poison into my drink, and then i want to die.

DIE.

All i can see is Tara's smiling face in my mind, kissing my Michael, holding my Michael, doing whatever she wants with my Michael. Why is she allowed to do those things?

Because she's a super person, like Shell was. She wanted Michael and she took him. She wanted to live, and she stole michaels life for ten years, letting him sacrifice himself just so that she could be happy somewhere else and live out the rest of her life at his expense.

cordually invited.

My ass.

Fuck them.

Fuck them.

Im crying now. I know its immature but i cant take it. I dont want them to get married. I dont want them to do this to me. I dont want michael to dissappear forever.

If i kill them they cant get married.

I could go to the wedding. I could put poison into their drinks. during the wedding toast. If there's a wedding rehearsal i can put the poison into their drinks then and then who would ever even think of them as man and wife, just a tragic couple that couldnt even make it to the alter before they died.

lol.

I know im getting mean. Im just joking. Maybe im bitter. Maybe im not. I dont want to think about it. I dont want to think about anything. I just want to sit here and for once not think about anything i ever thought about in my entire life. I hate thinking. thinking is overrated. I could go my whole life without thinking a single thought and id be perfectly happy. maybe thats what death feels like. Pure thoughtlessness. Forever and ever.

It'd be like being unconscious. but better.

If i kill them

They cant get married.

they just cant.

I cry. Please dont marry her Michael. Please dont marry her. Marry me instead. Please. Please. Please.

Please michael. Dont leave me.

Maybe i can just kill tara. Two vials of poison.

I'll kill tara then kill the assassin that hired me and me and michael could run away together. Why wouldnt i do that. Why wouldnt i do that for him

I dont know.

we could run away never see this world again. that would be beautiful.

But he'd hate me. I know he would.

I cant

I just cant.

Last night i had a series of dreams.

~I am the Lord your God. You shall have no other Gods besides me~

I dreamt I was a man.

It was terrifying but it made perfect sense to me when it was over.

I was thirty-two years old. I had light-colored hair and eyes and a tall frame. I pulled the cigarette from my mouth, letting out a breath of smoke. the dream tells me that in my younger days i had been a young reverend.

In the dream im married to a cheating whore who cheats and never comes home again named Tara

She reminds me of my love for Amanda. Long. Full of like. And disintigrating with time.

Over and dead.

That's all i thought.

I put the cigarette back in my mouth, shifting from where I stood and moving my eyes down to the handgun I held. My days as a reverend were over, but not my days on the side of God. I was forever standing in the good grace of heaven's army, a loyal soldier till the end.

And by that, i mean the dream represents me as an overly moral bitch with a gun. Guess that's what happens when you smoke to much weed and eat too much cocaine. You go a little crazy, because that's what happened to me.

I tucked the gun into the inside pocket of my black coat. My jeans were old and the white t-shirt I wore even older. I only owned the one set of clothes. No earthly possessions could tempt me. I lived with as little as I could.

I moved my way toward the small warehouse. From the outside it looked abandoned and empty, crusted with dirt and flaking paint. But I knew better than that. Inside the building, there were sinners that looked like little taras and they were doing their devil dances and worshiping their Satans. It made me sick to his stomach.

~You shall not make for yourself an idol~

I took a last drag from my cigarette before dropping it to the cement and stepping my foot on it. There was only one way to make peace. To wash the dirt that clung to me. Tara had dirtied me. Only one way to be clean again.

I pulled the gun out and aimed it at the door of the warehouse. The lock exploded in a splintering of metal and wood. I lifted my foot and kicked the door hard, watching as it swung open. The room was barely lit, with tiny golden glows from tall candlesticks lining the walls and floor. Surprised faces looked up at mehrough the hoods of white cloaks.

I know this sounds crazy, but i really dreampt this.

And as for the faces, they were all tara's, no joke. that really happened.

A giant pentagram was painted in neon green paint on the wall behind them. Beside it sat a giant statue of an overweight woman with her hands extended on each side, leaves dripping from her arms and legs.

I lifted my gun, aiming into the group of women and began firing. Bullets entered their bodies, tearing through skulls and torsos. I took a step forward as I fired. I watched as bodies fell to the ground, limp and twitching, blood spilling from their wounds and soaking their white cloaks red. Soon, there was nothing but red. A pile of red bodies on a slick, red floor, shiny with their blood.

A Tara sat curled in the corner of the room, trembling from the attack, but otherwise unharmed. I began walking toward her, stepping over twisted bodies as I did so. My eyes moved briefly to a another Tara's gaping, open mouth, a black hole through one of her eye sockets. She lay on her back, her head tilted upward toward the heavens. She had no idea how close she had come to eternal damnation. If only she knew, she'd thank me for it.

My left hand worked methodically as I walked, pulling out a new cartridge of bullets and replacing the empty one in my gun. The Tara was still shaking from where she sat on the ground. From closer up, I could make out the splatters of blood from her fellow heathen sisters on the woman's cloak. "Are you scared?" I asked, stepping up to the tara and bending down before her.

The Tara Jones nodded slowly, her thin face pale and covered in sweat. "Please, don't hurt me," she begged, her voice trembling.

"My Dear," I continued gently. "I'm not here to hurt you. Im here to set you free. That's good right?," I smiled agreeably. Even now the Tara didn't understand. The price that came with worshipping false idols and rejecting their God. To sacrifice an eternity of pure bliss and happiness for the sake of a moment's false joy in the name of the devil. The Tara had lost herself to her Earthly greed.

But then again, Super people tend to do things like that.

Greed.

The bitch.

I kneeled down, grasping the Tara's left hand and pressing in an urgent voice, "Why do you follow the devil?"

"But... but I don't," Tara lied, in tears, i don't follow the devil."

I felt my stare harden at the reply. Surely this woman realized... but the devil had ways to cloud the judgment of men and women. He was the king of lie and deceit. I pointed a finger angrily to the statue of the woman covered in leaves. "Then what do you call that?!"

I gave the hand I still held a hard jerk before the woman could finish her sentence. I felt as the Tara's fingers snapped with the sudden movement, breaking at least two of them. The Tara howled in pain and I asked again, my voice growing louder and more angry. "I'll ask again. Why do you follow the devil?"

"I don't! I don't follow the devil!" The Tara lied.

I wouldn't hear it. I lifted my gun and pressed it to Tara's forehead, watching as Tara's wide eyes quivered in fear. "There's only path to the road of salvation, my dear," I said quietly. I closed my eyes and pulled the trigger. When I opened them again, the woman's young face was no longer recognizable before me. The forehead looked something like an explosion had gone off, splattering blood and bits of brain against the wall behind her. I pulled the gun away, watching as the body fell forward, limp and lifeless on the slick floor.

Blood dribbled down the cracked wall. The dead bodies on the floor lay silent and stiff in their crimson puddles. Falling to my knees, I pressed my hands together in front of me and prayed for the Taras' safe passage in their journey to heaven.

~ *You shall not take the name of the Lord your God in vain*"

I felt the past rain down on me like showers of red blood. Even if I were to hold out my arms and bathe in it, there was no hope for becoming clean. I was filthy. My house had been defiled. My home was no longer My own.

I paced the tiny motel room, wiping at my face as I did so. My small bag of possessions lay on my bed, mostly consisting of socks and toiletries.

It was only through My great love for her that I could think enough to set her free.

I press my fingers to my closed eyelids. The memories haunted me. They never let me alone. Michael had smiled at me coyly that morning, grasping my face in both his hands and whispering in my ear, "I swear to God, Lace. I love you more than anything in this world."

Letting out a growl, I took the gun from my coat and threw it against the wall. It clattered loudly against the fresh white paint before bouncing to the carpeted floor. Why did it have to hurt so bad? Even after an entire year had past, it hurt like it had just happened the day before.

It was only because I loved him, that I could still think to save him from his own damnation.

~*Remember the sabbath day, to keep it holy*~

He first found out Michael was cheating on me in his heart with Tara around February. So about a month ago. In my dream, to continue with that,

It was a Sunday when I ran into a new Tara. The Tara was evil as usual in my dreams. She ran around killing people and making a big deal out of herself and being a super person like usual. Then she went and killed her own parents in front of me and i knew i was staring at the worst person in the universe.

~Honor your father and your mother~

The two bodies lay on the ground, completely bludgeoned to death. I stepped forward for a closer look. Their faces were hard to make out. Completely smashed in. But they appeared to be very very very dead.

"You killed your own parents?" I asked gently. "How awful. Youre awful. Youre terrible Tara." I felt tears in my eyes. "Youre terrible. Youre terrible Tara. Your'e terrible."

"Thou shall not kill," I said in a quiet voice. "There's only path to the road of salvation, my dear. I can take you there. I can help you if you let me."

~ You shall not commit murder~

The woman nodded, falling to the floor. "Help me," she sobbed, her voice cracked and distorted sounding. I pulled my gun of justice from my jacket, lifting it in the direction of the crying woman. "Only God can save you now."

I pulled the trigger. The sound of the gun firing echoed throughout the entire world and Taras all around me screeched from the streets threatening to call the Tara police. The woman crumpled to the floor, and I watched her as she did so. Blood poured from the place in her forehead where the bullet had pierced her. "Go in peace, my dear."

I kneeled to the ground, clasping his hands in front of him and began to pray.

~YOU SHALL NOT COMMIT ADULTERY~

ADULTERY

A

D

U

L

T

E

R

Y

Michael cheated.
With Tara.
His heart.
The marriage.
The invitation to the wedding.
Love
Loss.
he told me it was heavy.
His world.
too heavy to bear.
Please dont leave me Michael.
Please dont marry her.
THOU SHALL NOT.
ADULTERY.

I was on the road again, traveling to Michaeal and Tara's home. My stomach felt ill. It moved and flipped in my gut as I walked. I had found out about the cheating around last month, as i said, and I was not happy that his heart was carrying Tara. Lived for Tara. Revolved around Tara, not me.

I had often wondered why he had dirtied my world like that. Surely, he must've known he'd get caught eventually.

Either way, it didn't matter anymore.

I was going to save him and her. Save my Michael and his Tara from the eternal fires of hell. Even after all she had done, after how she had hurt me, I still loved her enough to save her.

It wasn't long before I was standing in front of the colonial-style home.

Pulling the gun from my pocket, I shot off the lock on the door. Then I pushed it open, rushing into the living room. Inside, Tara jumped up from the couch, screaming as if her life depended on it. I shot her twice in each leg, feeling excited at the sight of blood that rushed in streams down her delicate skin.

I smiled at her, stepping forward and gazing down at her form curled on the floor.

"Lace," she screamed. "What the fuck do you think you're doing!?"

"Saving you," I replied simply. I lifted the gun, pressing it to her red face. I paused.

The sound of running water from upstairs had grabbed my attention. I pulled the gun away, letting it hang at my side. "That Michael up there?" I asked.

Her eyes widened fearfully as she realized what I was about to do. "N... No! Lace! Please don't! Don't do it!!"

~YOU SHALL NOT STEAL~

I smiled once more, ignoring her pleas as I pulled away from her and turned around. I could feel her grasping at my waist, hanging from my body, clawing at me to make me stop. I shook her off. Then I headed toward the staircase and began to make my way upstairs.

When I reached the top, I could make out the cloud of steam escaping the bathroom door. The sound of the shower running drowned out my footsteps. I lifted my gun, pushing the bathroom door open slowly and stepping inside. "Michael?" I asked.

The curtain pulled back, and Michael's head peeked out. He jumped at the sight of me. "What the fuck are you doing here?"

"You're almost not worth saving," I muttered.

Michael's eyes fell to the gun, and he moved back, looking terrified. "What the fuck do you think you're doing!"

I cried. I was a woman again. My man image melted as i entered their home and i Was Lace again. Tears streamed down my face as i lifted the gun and aimed it at Michael.

"I love you michael," I sobbed.

"Lace what's going on here."

"I love you so much michael."

"Stop this. You dont know what youre doing."

I screamed for him to shut up. "No. please dont marry Tara. Please dont leave me. Please dont do this to me."

"Lace stop it right now."

"Remember the ring?" I lifted my left hand. "I still have it. The ring you gave me. the promise ring that we'd run away together someday I never forgot."

"Lace put the gun down."

I aimed the gun down and fired. The bullet blew off Michael's penis. Michael fell to the floor of the tub and howling out loud. "You took my love and threw it in the garbage. You took it and threw it away like it was rotted and old but it was new and good and pure to me. MIchael. I have to kill you."

"Stop it!" The voice cried from behind. Tara had dragged herself up the stairs, leaving a bloody trail behind her and lay panting in the hallway. The steam escaping the bathroom had finally set off the fire alarm, adding to the chaos. The sound screamed loudly from the small contraption on the ceiling. "We didn't do anything!" Tara cried again. "He didn't do anything. Just leave us alone."

"Stealing's bad," I continued, taking a step closer. "God punishes for stealing."

~YOU SHALL NOT BEAR FALSE WITNESS AGAINST YOUR NEIGHBOR~

"I didn't steal anything, you fucking lunatic!" Tara shrieked

"Fuck you," I muttered. I narrowed my eyes. "Thou shall not covet thy neighbor's boyfriend."

~YOU SHALL NOT COVET YOUR NEIGHBOR'S HOUSE; YOU SHALL NOT COVET YOUR NEIGHBOR'S WIFE OR HIS MALE SERVANT OR HIS OX OR HIS DONKEY OR ANYTHING THAT BELONGS TO YOUR NEIGHBOR~

I fired the gun again. I emptied my gun into Michael's body, watching as blood exploded from Michael's flesh. The entire curtain and tiled wall dripped in his blood and torn flesh. The water ran down over him, running swirling streams of red down the drain. A second baptism, perhaps? I had saved his soul. The undeserving fucker that he was.

Tara shrieked from the ground, shrieking and crying out as she covered her eyes and cried from the floor. The fire alarm wailed above her, blinking and making noise. I moved up to her, kicking her hard in the face. She flew back, a red spot over her eye appearing where I had hit her.

I kicked her again in the stomach. Blood oozed from the bullet wounds beneath her pant legs. My hand reached into my pocket, pulling out a long knife.

Tara begged from the floor. "Please don't do this."

I lifted the knife and dug it into her squealing form, ripping it down her torso from shoulder to hip bone. Organs were exposed as I ripped the knife and stabbed it down again and again. Blood spurted from her mouth and ran down her eyes. "May you rest in peace," I whispered, bringing the knife down once more. "You Fuckling super person you."

So anway that was my transformative dream.

I woke up several times during the nightmare.

I would have to say the dream goes in leu with my good intent criminalism theory.

I can die one of several ways. One way, as a good intent criminal, a defender of injustice but thinking im the good guy. That's my bigggest fear. To become the reverend from my dream a pure murderer. I dont want to take that path. I dont want to murder an innocent person and call myself the good guy

The second dream i had goes in leu with my next fear. Evil criminalism. it says that i could become an evil criminal that murders them both and then feels bad about it forever.

In this dream. which starts shortly after the high and mighty dream where im a killer reverend, I dream that Im a simple murderer with a guilty conscious.

I'm a man again. I have dreams like that a lot. That im a man.

And i walk home from work. As im walking home, i see michael and Tara walking hand in hand together.

I look at them.

They look at me.

I pull out a gun and they scream.

I nonchalantly shoot them dead. tuck the gun back into my pocket. walk to a gas station and buy a pack of cigarettes.

"Same as always?" the gas station attendant asks.

"menthal 100's please. The red pack. Thanks."

"Gotcha." He smiles and i smile back. Even though i am dreaming i can tell my teeth are crooked when i smile.

In the dream, and i swear this really happened in the dream, i end up walking home, cigarette in mouth, and writing in my diary. So yes, from here on I am writing in my diary about something i wrote in my diary in the dream.

"Same as always" he says.

I smile with crooked teeth yes.

"gotcha" he says.

a diary entry about a dream where i make dream diary entries. Dear Dream Diary, today i killed Michael and Tara. I didn't feel bad. As a matter of fact, I felt rather heartless about it.

murdering them was the most nonchalant thing i had ever done before in my life.

I hesistate from the dream diary entry.

Guilt.

What's guilt to me.

this is the feeling i would've felt if i had truly killed michael and Tara.

Guilt.

I Feel bad.

Why did i do it?

I dont know.

What is the meaning and source of guilt. it could be that my love has twisted and transformed into an unrecognizable being. Im lost in it. It drowns me. I'd ask for help but i know i dont deserve it.

Im drowning.

Have you ever felt as if you were drowing in guilt. I can't breathe. Its the worst feeling ever. Kind of like dying minus the good parts. I want to say i never felt guilt before but i felt a kind of guiltiness when i killed them. It ate at me.

The guilt is so bad it starts to make me crazy.

Im not going to lie. I've been prone to crazy since Shell died. Im not one for big hello's or goodbyes. I just know one thing about myself, and that is that i never expected a dead man to say anything to me or a dead woman to think things were anyting other than worth it for her. I know it sounds silly but im an optimist. Im exactly everything i think and say I am. A drowing optimist. Or maybe that's too much of a joke.

Im worried that things will only ever fall apart for me from now on. The guilt is eating at me. I can see their faces contorted in fear and im frightened. The guilt is too much.

I know what i need. I need forgiveness. I dont want to break rules or hide or be bad or do anything that could upset the balance of things. But on the second hand, i want things to get better and be like they should be. Im not lying when i tell you i believe in things like angels granting wishes for past lives that went awry. So basically, Im going to tell you this, I live for the moment and that moment right now is to feel bad for the things i've done or would do or did do and basically i shouldn't have killed Michael and tara just because i felt like it.

I know this is just a dream but i really thought these things in my head and wondered why i had worked so hard to do something that would make little to no sense later on in my life.

Regret.

Guilt.

To be honest, this waS all just a dream and i technically haven't done anything yet. In reality and in fact, i have not killed Michael and Tara. they live and are alive and are mocking me with their wedding invitation even as i write this, so why do i feel so bad.

Diary, i dont think i was meant to be happy. Im thinking how sad i am even now. Im worried that i'll spend my whole life engulfed in this matter of fact state of subconscious discontent with life and never feel happy again. The point is that michael and Tara are getting married and Im absolutely terrified i might kill them before they reach the alter.

I'm sorry i did this. Im sorry i did that. I'm sorry for the things i did or would do or even just think is a good idea.

I dont want to drown in this guilt any longer. I said i believed in angels and i think they exist right now for me. I want them to come to me and fly me away to heaven and tell me everything will be okay. I want them to convince me to kill myself, to take my life instead of michael and tara's and be free from the guilt of wanting to murder them to begin with.

Angels.

Death.

I dont know why but i find myself fascinated by the subjects of both.

There's an erie sense of accomplishment that bellows in your heart when contemplating pure suicide. I want to kill myself. And when i do or if i do, i will be flown to heaven and rejoiced a martyr, who took her own life instead of the lives of two innocents who i envied so hard i came too close to murdering them out of spite.

Drowning in my guilt, the coin flips to evil.

Tails, he says.

And I'm aware that i could just as easily just kill them, be done with it, and live the rest of my life a sorrowful women full of regret only until the day i die an elderly woman instead.

I cry.

I feel like im dividing into two. Like there are two me's now. The one that is good and the one that evil. The good one says to feel guilt for murdering them and the second says to move on without a second thought about it.

I go to a field of flowers with my dream diary in the dream. I lay there with the diary staring up at the bright blue sky. A butterfly flies past me and reminds me that im dreaming and not awake and that none of this is real and tara and michael are in fact not dead, and actually fucking somewhere on the other side of the universe.

The dream transforms and

Im no longer scared.

My angel arrives, told you there were angels. and I'm faced wtih the following scenerio.

the dream continues with me as I awake to the sound of tapping. I sat up in my bed and moved my gaze toward the window where it was dark outside. There, a strange figure breathed heavily and looked as if it were encased in a thick fog. The image resembled a woman, though could very well have also been a beautiful man. He could make out the faint outline of large feathered wings poking from behind.

I felt frightened at the sight, my hands tightening around the blankets that lay over me. I blinked. When my eyes opened, I was laying in bed once more, and my alarm clock was ringing. It was daytime. A dream? I felt perplexed.

. I had light hair and blue eyes in this dream and thought of myself as the practical type, the practical type, the practical type, and disregarded the image almost instantly.

I stood up and found myself facing the sight again. The figure fell forward on me, its delicate hands falling to my shoulders. It leaned toward my face and breathed in an airy voice, "Yaasayaita. Iiamiyashita."

I felt frightened by the closeness of the being. I couldn't speak.

Just as quickly, the figure disappeared. In an instant, a blink, and gone.

I closed my eyes. Was i imagining things? I opened them, and found myself outside. A shovel was in my arms. I looked down at it. It was the strangest feeling. I felt compelled to dig. So I began digging into the earth. Deeper and deeper I dug.

I hit something. I kneeled down to the ground and began scooping with My hands, pushing away dark soil. A skull revealed itself. I pushed away more dirt. Already I could make out the giant hawk-like wings. I carefully moved the dirt from the body, and eventually, the entire skeleton lay in perfect condition in the bed of soil below me.

I could do nothing but gaze at it. An angel's skeleton? But how?

Hours passed. I could do nothing but stare at it still forever and ever and ever and in the dream i knew i was being spoken to by an angel. The sun fell and it was night once more. To My surprise, the skeleton twitched. I took in a sharp breath, stepping back. The bones rattled and shook.

The arms of bone pulled themselves from the ground, and lifted into the air, grasping blindly at nothing. They slammed back down once more, hands clawing at the ground and pushing against it. It lifted its body up, wings ripping from the dirt. The skull turned, and looked at me through dark, eyeless sockets. The teeth grinned at me.

The wings began to flap and the body lifted into the air. It watched me as it took flight. "Yaasayaita. Iiamiyashita," it spoke. Its voice was hollow and strange, as if it echoed from all directions at once. Then it soared into the sky, becoming a dark shadow that disappeared into the night.

"Yaasayaita. Iiamiyashita," I breathed. "I wonder what that means."

The dream goes on to explain my guilt and some strange analogy between the angel's skeleton and what i did to Michael and tara. But i dont remember. I dont know.

Im tired diary. Im drunk and im tired and im starting to not make any sense.

But the point is, the dreams all led me in one main direction. Killing Tara and Michael.

Guilt

Angels

Where am i going with this.

And that the hell does Yaasayaita Iiamiyashita mean. I want to think it means i love you. That an angel is telling me he loves me and wants to take care of me forever. and that things can only get better and better forever.

The angel might even represent my guilt flying away and me forgiving myself one day. I dont know. Im not sure.

Well the fact is that it was a dream and it scared me and I dont want to give into the temptation to kill them just now. Maybe at their wedding. I dont know for sure. Im going to let you go diary. with the two dreams and my very last fear of being the victim myself. I hope you'll understand me someday. But i think you do already. I'll write tomorrow and tell you what im thinking.

But for now just know this, Tara and Michael are still alive and well and I hate them very very much right now.

CHAPTER 7

Dear diary march 31 2010

Hi its me again, Lace.

Do you ever wonder about the unknown. When i was younger I believed in fairies and pixies and dragons and that there was a nessie that lived in the water.

I like thinking about the unknown because its existence explains my feelings of love for Michael. Love is inconrpehensible. Love is strange and doesnt make any sense and the worst thing about it all is that it hurts. Why would we do that to ourselves. Well i could go so far as to say love is fake and not real like my pixies and angels and dragons but it is real and that means pixies and angels and dragons are possible too. So there.

The mysteries of places like the Bermuda triangle remain mysteries despite our efforts to explain them away scientifically. The fact of the matter is that there are places on this Earth where human beings seem to altogether cease to exist. They disappear. More than that. It's as if they never were. Gone without a trace. Just like me if i were to die. Just like me if i were to cease to exist all together. Or just like tara and michael if they died instead of me.

Here's an example. one such place exists in a small town in the state of Georgia. About forty-five minutes from the highway in Riversville, a road called Terrance Street.

But the people of that town don't call it that. They call it something else entirely. They call it Hell's Road. For several reasons really. Because the weather is always a little worse on that street. The water levels higher in bad rain, for example. The road a little slicker during icy weather than what's normal. When it storms, the storm seems to brew from directly above the street. As if the very eye of the storm originates from the sky above Hell's Road

237

itself. When lightening strikes, it seems to strike from directly overhead. When thunder growls, it's as if you're inside the very belly that its growling from.

More than that, drivers have claimed to hear strange noises when they drive Hell's road at night. Skittering and scratching sounds against their cars. Or even worse, what's described as an inhuman high-pitched squeal, racked with pain and agony. Screeches so frightening that they're enough to drive a man mad, they say.

The disappearances on Hell's road date back to the 1940's at the very least. The ones recorded anyway. Most frightening of all, the reason so many fear driving Hell's road, are the cars full of passengers, disappeared just like that. A road that leads straight to Hell, the locals explain. It had happened on more than one occasion. Whole families, at times, or teenagers, or couples that lost their way. They disappeared, as well as their cars, as well as their luggage if they had any, without ever being found again.

But like tales of Nessie, the Loch Ness monster, these stories go unnoticed by the rest of the country. The only ones who believe them are the locals, and a local swearing on supernatural occurrences is no news to anyone. They're all the same to disbelievers. Whether the story's about Nessie, or Bigfoot, or Witches, or the Bermuda Triangle. It's something one has to see for himself to truly appreciate the grand scale of horror such a situation truly presents.

I had another dream. It was about hell's road. I read about hell's road in the tabloids and let me say that i take tabloids very seriously. Dead seriously. Because even if they're not real in our world they could be real in another. Just because we dont live in some kind of magical universe doesn't mean someone else doesn't.

In the dream, I was a writer. i longed to be a writer in this dream, and my aspirations had led me to write for tabloids myself. Experience, they called it. Because an unknown author trying to publish the next best seller was nothing new to literary agents. They were one in a million, in a sea of creative hopefuls trying to make their mark on the world. Too few books were published and too many authors had stories to tell.

I wrote for Gilmore's press, a tabloid that made outrageous claims about possessed rat creatures and the next coming of Christ. They foretold the end of the world nearly every other week.

in the dream my hair was streaked with gray. My blue eyes were dimmed and crinkled with worry lines. I had gained weight over the years from the stress of failure. Thirty-seven already. Nothing had changed, and nothing had gotten any better. I was almost forty and I was a nobody. Creating nobody stories for nobody people.

Yet, despite feeling that way, I took at least one weekend a month to explore the country's most wildest legends. I spend the dream knowing that. And knowing that I was this close to finding the proof we needed to prove my fairies and dragons and were real.

I glanced down at the map in my hand, trying to alternate between the map and the street in front of me. Hell's Road. The locals of Riversville claimed on everything that it was haunted. That the devil himself had paved the road out of rotten souls and ashes, like a trail leading children to the witch's gingerbread house. They claimed people had disappeared on this road. That they had vanished, just like that, never to be seen again.

I looked around me. The road was pretty beat up, with cracked cement and unsettling dips. I wouldn't be surprised if the wheels of my car flew off from the constant rattling. My car would bump and bounce up and down with every contact the wheels made with crumbling potholes. There was only one other car on the road. It stayed going straight in front of me. I had noticed it with little interest. There appeared to be a man and woman in the front seat, with the man driving. No stop lights. Too bad. I wanted to ask them if they were aware of Hell's Road's history, and if they knew anything about the horror stories that flew around the town of Riversville.

Dark clouds rumbled high ahead. I glanced up in dismay. Rain? I hadn't heard anything about it raining today. I decided I might come back another day to investigate then. I hadn't seen anything interesting yet, and I had been driving for a good half-hour already. No strange noises, no strange sightings. Just me and the car in front of me in an uneventful half-hour. Nothing new. Just more of the usual.

I realized that the two in the car in front of me were Tara and Michael. It disturbed me and i felt sad thinking that i was destined to drive behind them, followng in Michael's shadow for all eternity.

It made me nervous driving behind them.

As you can see Tara and michael have been a reoccuring theme in my dreams as of late and I dont know why but i cant seem to get over the shaking feeling that i am becoming obsessed.

Back to the dream, I wanted to get away from Michael and Tara's car and nothing interesting had happened on Hell's road. I tried to find a place to pull into so I could turn around but there weren't any good spots. The road was surrounded by thick trees and dense woods. I'd have to roll into the grass just to make a wide enough U-turn in the opposite direction.

I was just about to do just that when the rain fell. It didn't just fall. It came in a gray sheet that blinded me instantly. "Holy shit!" I cried out, turning on my wipers. I swerved slightly, squinting as heavy droplets rolled down his windshield. I couldn't see an inch in front of him. I didn't know if I should just slam on the brakes or pull blindly to the side and hope I wasn't driving into a tree.

It was ridiculous how much rain there was. I took a chance and pulled off to the side. My wheel hit a rock and my car bounced up and down once more, sending me bounding off of my seat. I put the car in park, letting out a deep breath. All in all, I seemed okay. There was so much rain he wouldn't have been surprised if I had run into a tree. It was like driving blindfolded. I decided to wait out the rain. Storms like this normally didn't take long to calm down. I'd be waiting a couple minutes, tops.

I tried turning on the radio. Static sounded loudly, making me grimace. I turned it down and began scanning all the stations. I switched stations, finding nothing but static on every FM station. I tried AM. Same thing. I turned off the noise, settling back into my chair and watching idly out the window. The sound of rain was beating hard on the hood of my car. It was so loud, it almost sounded like a hundred fists were punching the outside of his vehicle. A silly thought, but it did sound like that.

The rain began to slow down. Much like I expected, it didn't take long. It came at a slower pace now, practically a drizzle compared to the downpour I just been in. To my surprise, the car that had been in front of me had also pulled to the side of the road, only a few feet ahead. tara and michael.

I saw them clearly ahead of me now, talking to each other in the car. I thought about ramming into them. I thought about getting out of my car, going up to tara and strangling her to death then strangling michael to death. I thought about scaring them out of the car and then running them over on the road. I thought all these things. I know it sounds crazy but i cant stop thinking about it

I noticed how dark the sky was now. The clouds blocked out the light completely. It felt like night had fallen in the few minutes since the rain had started. A little eerie, considering where I was. I glanced back up at the car in front of me. They had the same idea, now that the rain had slowed. I could see they had started their car and were slowly beginning to pull back out onto the street.

Maybe they were scared of me? Maybe they were running away.

A flash of red from their back window caught my eyes and I jumped, gasping out loud. My imagination? It couldn't be. They looked like eyes. A small pair of red eyes watching me from the back of their car.

I blinked.

The car was gone. I felt numb as I looked around me, dumbfounded by the event. *Where did they go?* I looked around me once more, turning behind me and then searching ahead, my eyes squinted. *The car was gone? But how? It just... as if it just... disappeared completely, right before my eyes.*

Gone.

Dissappeared from sight With no logical explanation.

As if they had been spirited away somehow. I felt sad knowing that the road had killed them before i could.

I thought of the red eyes and shivered, my skin crawling at the memory. Beady red eyes watching me from the back window of the car. *What did that mean? To disappear like that? Tara and Michael, Where were they now? When two people and their car disappear just like that, where did they go? To nowhere? Could that happen? Could human beings really be wiped out that easily from existence?*

I glanced behind me, finding the sight of red eyes once more, watching me from outside my back car window. I jumped, letting out a yelp. They disappeared. *What the hell.... What the hell! What the hell was that?* I began pulling my car back onto the road, turning the vehicle around so that I was headed back the way I came.

My wheel hit several bumps in the grass, making my wheels bound up and down over the uneven ground. I heard a single high-pitched shriek sound from beneath my car with the third bump. *What was that sound?! What was it?! Did I hit an animal when I was pulling out?* I had no idea. I slammed my foot on the gas, jerking the car into drive and pulling forward.

My car didn't move. It stayed stuck in place, the wheels spinning madly. I realized my back wheels were stuck in a ditch, the front half of my car partway on the road. It didn't feel right getting out of the car to push it free. I slammed his foot harder on the gas, hoping it would loosen itself on its own.

Scratching sounded. Scratching and grating against the outside of his car. I stopped, glancing around frantically to find the source of the noise. What the hell was it?! I looked outside, finding nothing but wet grass and stones. What the hell?!

I know. My dream turned into a nightmare. It was frigtening and i think michael and Tara were haunting me for all the visions i was having of their deaths.

Anyway, The scratching grew louder. It became unbearably loud, making me squirm. The sound intensified, growing until it was as high sounding as nails on a chalkboard, scraping paint from the metal of his vehicle. I covered my ears, feeling panicked. What the fuck was I supposed to do?! I was scared. They were getting me back. Tara and michael were getting me back for wanting to hurt them.

The blue vials of poison.

The burden he couldn't carry.

it was all too much for her.

She couldn't take it anymore.

They were haunting her. They were hautning her. They were haunting her.

i was shaking as I began struggling with the wheel of my car, slamming my foot on the gas pedal. I crushed my eyes shut. The scatching sound. It didn't stop. It only grew louder. There was something outside. More than something. There was more than one. There had to be. An army of evil was outside my car. All of them. They were trying to get in and they wanted me to come out.

The radio turned on. I stopped, turning to look at it in dismay. The knob on the radio was turning itself, changing stations frantically back and forth. What the hell!? My lip quivered as I watched the knob turning itself, different pitches of static blaring loudly from the speakers. The static sounds began to warp themselves. At least, that was what it sounded like to me. But maybe I was just imagining things. As a matter of fact, imagining the whole thing? The static sounds began to contort and change until they took on the sound of howling and screeching. Hissing sounds shrieked through the speakers, as if from a dozen dying cats.

Animals? It sounded like animals crying. They were shrieking and crying out in agonizing pain.

I felt tears begin to stream down my face. Why? I couldn't explain it. I felt sad. A wrenching sadness clutched at my gut. I lifted a hand, wiping at my cheek. I was crying? What was going on? Why did I feel this way? Why did I feel so terribly sad?

The rain had stopped. Scratching came chaotically from all directions outside my car.

They were getting revenge. That was all i could think of.

they were frightening me. Tara and Michael. Michael and Tara. They were ghosts now and i was their victim. My biggest fear of all. it was becoming a reality in this nightmare. That i would be their victim forever and they would never be mine. That they would hurt me forever by loving each other and rejecting me and i would forever be a slave to their hurting me.

The radio blared out the sounds of animal shrieks and cries. My gaze moved off to the distance, finding a pair of lights headed in his direction. My eyes widened. A semi-truck. A semi was headed in My direction. I began waving my hands frantically in front of me. "Hey!" I screamed. "I'm in here!" The sound of scratching and scraping kept me from opening the window or climbing out. The car was protecting me from the wrath of Tara and Michael and i wanted it to stay that way for at least a while longer.

The semi came closer, headed directly for me. I froze, wondering why the truck wasn't slowing down. Didn't they see me? Didn't they know I was there? The truck kept coming. It didn't slow. It didn't acknowledge my presence at all. Fuck! The truck was going to run right into me and my car! They were going to collide! Didn't the idiot see me! I was right there! What was going on?! Couldn't they tell I was there?! "You fucking moron!" I shrieked. "You're going to hit me!"

i know its just a dream but i was becoming convicned that this dream was the reality and the whole thing with Michael and tara was just the dream.

Reality or dreams.

I was having trouble telling them apart.

I rolled down the window in a panic, screaming out, "STOP! YOU'RE GOING TO HIT ME!"

An invisible wave came at me the second i rolled the window down. My mistake. The wave of invisible claws covered my body, scratching me with sharp nails. I began shrieking, trying to grasp at the invisible creatures that were clawing at me. Blood began to pour from the scratch wounds, as invisible claws created gaping gashes on my face and arms. I pawed at my face and shoulders, unable to get a grasp on anything that attacked me. They continued to scratch at me, even as I looked up and realized the semi truck was only a second from colliding into me.

I felt blinded by the headlights of the large vehicle glaring back at me. I lifted my bleeding arms to shield my face, closing my eyes and preparing for the impact of the oncoming semi.

Nothing.

I opened my eyes.

Something was wrong.

I looked around me. Something was different. Because I wasn't Lace anymore. I was a dead cat, a dead squirrel or raccoon. I could've been anything. But the point was I was literally roadkill. I looked up, trapped in the corpse of the dead creature, watching as the semi rushed right through my car. The car itself was unfazed. The semi drove through it as if it weren't even there. I watched as the car began to slowly fade away, my body inside along with it. I watched as it disappeared into oblivion. Gone. My car was gone. My body was gone.

I looked up just as the semi rolled over the already mutilated corpse of the dead animal my soul was trapped inside of. It didn't hurt. Just felt numb. I watched as guts and fur was streaked across the road. I noticed the tail and paw connected to me.

I looked around, watching as hundreds of pairs of red eyes looked out at me from the forests. They seemed to be speaking to me in a silent way. I understood now. Understood their pain and their suffering. Tara and Michael were ghosts now. Their angry spirits had created this Hell Road and were destroying me with the wrath of dead animals. They were killing me for hating them. They were cursing me for damning their love.

So this was my nightmare. The story of Hell's Road and the animals that haunted it, controlled by the angry spirits of michael and Tara.

I looked up. A car came rushing past, the wheel driving over my mangled body once more.

As I write in my diary now, i wonder what the animals represented. Maybe they're the hands of god punishing me for my evil dreams and thoughts. I feel sad. Why did i get born into a world alone.

As i said, as i came into this world alone, born alone, die alone. I am, in every reference and epitome of the word alone.

Sadness.

Loneliness.

I cant begin to explain how painful it is to put these two things together to me and try to make them into one word.

According to a dream interpretation book, animals in a dream represent finding out a key source of what is wrong in your life. It indicates a root problem being resolved and they deal with our desire to be wild and free and are full of emotion.

As for animals attacking in dreams, my book says it represents the feeling of being threatened in life.

Tara, i feel threatened by you.

I suppose that's what the dream meant.

As i write, im drinking and smoking some weed. I feel a little crazy. I dont know why i did this to myself. I never should've met Michael. I never should've fallen in love.

CHAPTER 8

Dear Diary April 1, 2010.

When i was little, my father, god rest his soul in heaven, thought i was bi polar. He told me it wasn't normal to go from one high to the next, to be perfectly fine one day and then berserk the next day. When Iwas ten he called me schizophrenic because i talked to myself too much. When i was seventeen, he said i had a multiple personality disorder because i referred to myself in the third person as often as possible.

Anyway, im not calling my father a good man or a bad man or going to accuse him of insulting me as a child. What im thinking right now is that he may've been right about the mental disorder thing. I did so much drugs in the last couple of days i think i have a mental disorder now.

I'm usually a calm woman but right now im crazy. Im screaming and crying and crazy.

My tears fall on my desk as i write.

Im dying from pain i cant see.

Im aching from love i dont want.

Im starting to belive in things that aren't real.

I dream in works of magic.

Im scared.

Im scared.

I feel like Im losing myself and my identity.

It was without explanation or warning that this peculiar thing had begun to happen to me. My name is no longer Lace. As a matter of fact, it is now Leonard Write, and in the fashion of spontaneous combustion, a modern mystery that might as well have been a hoax, I became the walking harbinger of death and disease. Perhaps the true son of Satan, and as this spawn of fallen angel who did naught but suffer for his transgressions, it was I who hurt most in the suffering that was brought.

I am thirteen years old.

Or something like that.

HOld on i need a drink.

Okay im back.

Anyway I fancy myself a teenager again. that's true. Its not so strange or out of character for me to think of myself as a man. I dont know why but when i used to be a lesbian, i was the boy of the couple. I gave and she took. It was just the way it was.

So anyway, I like to think in terms of being a boy. Knowing that now, I'll tell you about my day.

when I woke up, i had an expectation.

To be in a clean room, and in this place where a room with walls painted blue and green comforters should have laid before me and beneath me and as they had been left when I had fallen asleep, instead, nothing more than a pile of decayed materials aged brown and gray. When I stood, dazed and confused, the silence was deafening, and only the squish of soft wood and carpet beneath my foot made noise as a toe broke through the rotted panels. I pulled it out, recalling many nights of sweet normality, now overwhelmed with fears of burglary and plague and angry poltergeists that go bump in the night.

I called out loudly for my mother and father but they didn't reply.

With no response, when there had always been one before, I called again and again, crawling through the rubble, still dazed at the sights of a dresser reduced to driftwood, and a desk no longer any different than the mulch my father laid on their garden every other year. The names poured from my trembling lips, for "Christi?" my alter ego's sister, and "John?!" my alter ego's smaller brother. My hand locked on the door frame, but rather than give me support, it crumbled beneath my fingertips, and I lost my footing, falling forward and crashing through the floor entirely till I was on the first, my arms flying over my face to shield them from falling ceiling, only to find it had disintegrated to dust before landing on me again.

Rot and decay.

that's all i saw today. I was surrounded by a rotting, festering world of death and odor and unappeal. I want it to go away but it sticks. I want it to disappear but it stays.

I feel as if i am death.

And as the future murderer of Michael and Tara, I am the harbinger of true death.

The fall had hardly been a hard one. The ground I had struck had felt more like tilled soil than the hardwood floor it should've been. I dared to open my eyes for barely a second when I saw the sight above me, hanging though tears in the ceiling, a tangle of bones that stared back with dark hallows for eyes. I gasped, then screamed, and screamed louder as another fell through as well, wide and long, it was Michael, his death offered sickening proof and I ran away, pulling and clawing my way from the wretched house. The door fell open as he crashed through it, tumbling onto a green patch of grass which turned brown instantly at contact.

I was more than confused. In my state of disbelief, of shock, I decided it was only a nightmare. Only a nightmare, from which I could awaken at any time, and therefore, should be well-prepared for the relief that would come from it. My fingers clenched at the blades, my eyes crushed shut. Just a dream. Just a dream. Then the feel of the grass changed. I opened my eyes. Just watch it now.

My lips parted as he took it all in. The once green grass had died instantly when I touched it. Beneath my fingertips. Before my eyes. The grass was dying. The tan color that spread throughout was hard to miss, it started at the tips and worked down to the roots, quite visibly, and instantly, though not so instantly that I could not watch it happen at my own leisure. Quite obviously, it began from the place that I myself had touched.

A mistake.

I had to be misinterpreting.

I am death.

The reason for death.

The cause of Michael and Tara's death, or at least, I should be.

I climbed up on unsteady legs, and started to run. There was no escaping it. Flowers wilted. Grass died. The neighbor's dog, it fell over in a quiet heap as I passed, a tongue rolled out just inches from the gate that held him to the back yard. I wouldn't believe it if i hadn't seen it. Above me I heard something like a missile being shot in the sky. No wonder. A missile? An atom bomb? Here and now? Whoever would've thought. They were under attack and I was not to blame after all.

I realized that the world was ending and it wanted to end today.

They were under attack!

Under attack!

The wind from the explosion had knocked me forward, sending me rolling onto the concrete.

I checked my arms then my legs.

No cuts though. Not the slightest of nicks on my arms or legs.

No evidence that any of this ever occurred, even as i write this.

I know its confusing thats why even I dont understand what is happening to me. What am i becoming?

The bringer of death.

the stone that slowly became like dust around my body was no longer something that surprised me. I glanced back when it had calmed down, and was surprised to see what appeared to be a plane that had fallen from the sky just ten houses down from where I lay. It barely smoked, and then, just like that, even the fire that surely should have resulted was smothered out by invisible forces. Then the birds fell. They fell one by one from trees and phone lines, landing around me and dotting the lonely landscape, not all at the exact moment, but beginning in the radius to the distance that was closest to him first and working its way outward.

Paint was chipping. All the houses. Their paint was chipping even as he stood there watching it.

I began running. As I ran, birds fell from the sky. Airplanes crashed down nearby. Building crumbled. Disaster followed me wherever i went.

IS that what i want? For birds to fall from the sky just because i walked past? to be the bringer of death and decay? What was i becoming? Something evil i think? And i need it to go away.

That was my day.

Would you like to know what happened next. I Know youre curious diary so i'll tell you.

There was no way it could be as it looked. Nothing was that strange.

I saw Michael standing far at the distant corner, gaping in terror at the crashed plane. I rushed forward to him, "help me! Help me!"

Michael acknowledged me, running forward as well. "What happened here? Are you hurt?"

I shook my head. No, it was everything else on me that was shaking. "I don't know what's going on!"

Then the boils came. They appeared gradually on the michaels face and arms as he spoke. He looked uninterested at first, asking, "where are your parents? Has anyone called 911?" He rubbed at the one on his wrist, only a small bump, that for all he knew had always been there. Then he scratched absently at his neck, above the collar of his plain business suit. "Sorry, what was that?" he asked.

"You..." the I stammered as the bumps grew more prominent on the man's skin. "Your face. There's something... growing on you."

They grew white at the heads, large and pink in rashy red patches. "My... skin?" He scratched at his cheek. "What... what is this?" he muttered at the feel of them. He saw his hands then, now fully inflamed and covered. "Oh my god!" he shrieked. "Oh my god!" He looked frantically around, his eyes wide. "They really did it!? What is this?! Some kind of germ warfare!? Are we all contaminated! I gotta get to a hospital. You gotta help me."

I took several steps back instead. It didn't make any sense. I was delusional from the trauma, and I was misinterpreting everything I was seeing. I fled from the Michael, stricken with grief. I hadn't done anything wrong.

It was no coincidence, that my long days have become nightmares.

I dont think i can even tell the difference anymore.

Heavy.

The world was heavy and i had adopted the burden from michael as if I sacrificed myself for him to be fine. I didn't know I had iaken on the weight until it was already strapped over my back and pushing me down by the ton. Now i was spreading disease and chaos and people were dying because of me.

what did this represent?

Perhaps my guilty conscoius from wanting to kill Michael and tara so badly.

Death and decay.

Because I couldnt be strong. Because i wasn't careful enough to try and tell the man i loved how i felt about him.

Reject me Michael. Tell me you hate me. But dont tell me its because you met her first. Say its because i'm clumsy and lazy and not a good cook and worthless and not your type but please dont say its because you met her first. If i had met you first, would you have married me instead? I dont know. I dont know. I dont know.

There wasn't a single human being on Earth who would've believed it true. But even as everything fell apart around me, just as I happened to pass by, and as small crowds of people waiting at bus stops itched nonchalantly at their arms or shoulders when I ran by them, I still couldn't accept it as fact.

I had run for nearly an hour before I collapsed on the ground, this ground that died and gave way beneath me till I lay in crumbled stones and dirt, it was no sanctuary for me. My breath was tired. I was tired and confused, and still thinking it all a nightmare and maybe it was.

A nightmare.

I want to wake up Diary but i cant.

A woman approached me, young and pretty with blond hair. She looked like Tara.

"Tara?"

"That's right."

She clutched her pink purse as she stepped beside him. "Are you all right?" she asked. "Excuse me? I asked if you were all right?"

"Get away!" I shouted angrily. Everything was dying. Everything was falling apart. I tried to stand as he shouted.

She looked surprised at the response. "I was just worried." She reached out a hand. "Are you sure you're all right?"

"Just get away from me!" I swatted the hand away instinctively. The contact was made from the back of my knuckles to her fingers. She jumped in surprise. But the damage had been done. From index to pinky, each began to swell immediately to a violet color, and the boils that appeared on her arms and face came soon after. She began to die as she screamed out from terror.

i was terrified too as I stumbled to my feet, amd running away. There was a prolonged silence before the screaming started again, long and shrill and I imagined I was finally realizing what I had done to her.

I was a walking disease.

And I was spreading it.

251

CHAPTER 9

April 4thth 2010

I was captured on the second of April by the government. It was found by the military that regular confinement wouldn't hold me, peculiarly enough, only crosses made of silver were even the slightest bit useful in withstanding whatever bizarre disease it was that I was spreading, discovered purely by accident when a visiting priest asked to see the captive which was me.

A nation built on science and logic, they could hardly believe it themselves. My holding cell was now nothing more than a dirt basement, wall-to-wall in silver crosses that conveniently enough, couldn't be touched or removed by the subject without causing me injury. The cities I had inhabited in my madness had been immediately quarantined and the news barely spread further than that. It wasn't to be made public, this devil's child, I would not spread death or panic, I was to be hidden and studied, and nothing more. The plane crash was explained with terrorism, the quarantine, a new viral outbreak that had originated in South Africa and had reached the States by postal mail. Nothing could be simpler. And nothing could be further from the truth.

It wasn't just silver that was the key. As scientists tried to explain it, it had to be two sticks of silver tied or melted firmly and set across one another, not so much because it was a cross, which would've implied religion, and religion and science were two things that were never meant to mix, but rather because of the atomic stability the formation of the two sticks provided one another and therefore, provided stability to the subject in question.

I could only be approached with a cross attached firmly to the forehead, on the back, on the chest, and on each wrist and ankle, though it didn't stop the visitors from wearing particle masks and radiation suits over them, as was more traditional in preventive measures. I grew tired of them. I was normal. I had always been normal and healthy. The experiments, the tireless questions and ceaseless accusations, asking what government I was affiliated with, what my true intentions were, they did nothing for me. The room they kept me in was dark and cold. They found ways to shock me, to find out just how much I was capable of. They even shot bullets at me, made of silver, as they electrocuted me with cross tipped rods. Which hurt. But failed to kill me.

When I'm Leonard, I am a disease. When I'm Lace I'm insane and sad and know there's no Michael in my life, not now, not ever. To be honest, I'd rather be Leonard. It hurts a lot less. What the world probably looked like from far away was that I was in a mental institution for taking too much advil and trying to kill myself. which is what i did. Tried to kill myself. I called the police and they put me in the mental institution to recover. That's reality. Which i loathe by the way. So reality, I condemn you to an eternity of misunderstanding and abuse. I dont want. I never did and I never will.

Sometimes I wonder if I had been a selfish woman because I had chosen it in a past life. I could aruge I had been screwed over so many times and then reincarnated for it, that I hated life and wanted to get it back for hurting me so much, but something tells me that's not what happened.

Whatever was the issue, i didn't want to live anymore now that I knew Michael and Tara were getting married. I wanted to die.

D

I

E.

Die Tara die.

Die Michael die.

I can't live in a world without you MIchael.

Its heavy he cried t o me that night.

Well fuck you and the heavy world that mocks you. You claimed to live such life of burden you claim to be the king of suffering. Well you dont know a goddamned thing about suffering. You dont know a goddamned thing about what its like to hurt so bad you couldn't take it anymore. I know what that feels like and I'm not going to just sit here and listen to you complain to me any longer in my head.

The amount of suffocation was constant and terrible. I sat in the center of my dirt cell, curled tightly with my head down and my arms hugging my legs to my chest, and my face hidden in my knees.

Or maybe I'm in a mental institution or my trailer. I can't seem to tell the difference anymore.

The only place a camera couldn't see, I smiled to myself. The thin white pants and shirt offered by the doctors did little for the cold. But things had changed considerably since they had brought me to this facility exactly one year ago. I was different now. And not only that, but I was stronger.

A kind voice that whispered in my ear had been my only comfort. It granted me strength and promised of power far above and beyond anything I had ever imagined before my entire life. On this Halloween night, I would bring the world the scare of its life. What fun, what fun. How long had it been since I had been allowed any fun? I'm only thirteen and not allowed any fun.

"You're Lace," the voice reminded her. "Lace. You're thirty years old. You're not well Lace. You must reoover Lace. Pick up your clothes Lace. Take this pill Lace. Swallow this liquid Lace. Lace Lace Lace."

To be anyone in this world other than Lace.

"I know, I know, you're right," I agreed out loud. "I'm sorry."

"Then are you ready?"

"I suppose I don't have much choice, right?" I chuckled at my own reply. It was going to be fun. That was all I cared about. I missed having fun. "Just promise I'll be entertained?"

'It'll be an entertainment, for both you and I.'

There was a warmth inside me. It pulled at my flesh. Like a ball of heat born inside my belly and growing at exponential rate. The way it spread, from fingers to toes, I really couldn't wait, could I. It wasn't long before the warm was hot, burning hot. It was empowering. It was unbelievable. It was awesome. It was pulling me in, taking me whole. A burst of energy escaping the body that had been imprisoned for an entire year, nay, an entire life time, it was finally free. The ball of energy left me and all around me, like a crater made from falling stars, the dirt was pushed back and crosses bent, losing their mystical shape.

I broke out of my government prison, energy exploding out of my body.

Or to translate into real life, I broke out of the mental institution and ran way from life.

CHAPTER 10

April 6th.

Dear Diary

I'm at my parents house now. I dont usually go home but i thought now would be a good time to explain to mom why i had decided to go against her will and beciome a prostitute instead of doctor as she had insisted.

She screamed at me when I told her that i had escaped the mental institution and didn't want to go back. She threatened to take me back there. I had to explain to her how immoral she was being and that I'd never love her again if she did.

I went to the guest room and transformed into a child again. now that i was home, I knew that I was being grounded for being bad and should sit and think about what i had done.

i was now a young girl who had just turned eight. My birthday was today. I had never been very popular, My dark hair was usually pulled back and unkempt, wire-frame glasses sat on my pug nose, and I was deathly thin. That noon had been a dark one, with black clouds threatening heavy rain.

My name is Diana, not lace, but Diana and I sat alone in the noisy playground, curled under an old tree with a thick trunk, furthest away from the school building and just after the baseball field.

I watched as children played and called loudly to one another, a group of girls would snack on their brown-bagged lunches beneath the jungle gym. I wondered why I had never asked to join them. Turning away, I pulled out the book I had been reading, an adventure mystery with a boy and girl that were best friends. They had a whole series of books, and I had read every one of them.

A loud cry cut through the air, nothing unusual. The students always ended up screaming something or another in their games, false cries of 'help!',

'help!', the recess aides had long since learned to ignore them. The cry came again, louder than ever. I glanced up, hardly paying attention. I was surprised to see a Tara Jones, probably in junior high, her hair blond and loose and flowing, crossing the field from one side to the other, dressed in black pants and black trench coat, as she did, children fell to the floor, clutching their heads and screaming loudly as they writhed on the ground.

My eyes widened, even in the distance I could make out the faces contorted into expressions of pain, and without thinking, I darted behind the large trunk of the tree, shaking and frightened, my hand clasping around the tiny cross necklace my mother had given me for my birthday that morning. The screams continued, louder than ever, and I crouched lower, closing my eyes.

What was going on? What was happening? Then there was quiet. Quiet? Had I just imagined it all? I opened my eyes slowly, stepping slowly to the edge of the trunk and peeking around it. The shocking sight of the girl who should've been gone was still there in front of the building, standing tall and with dark stare, facing me completely, her eyes watching me carefully. I let out a gasp, falling backwards to the floor. The children were all laying in quiet heaps on the floor, unmoving and silent, and the once healthy tree was now peeled and chipped at the front, ruined grass in patches before her.

Tara Jones thin lips curled into a smile, her eyes laughing at me just before turning away and heading off the field. I was so frightened I could hardly take it. Why was everyone on the floor? The adults too? What had Tara done to them? And the way she had looked at me, like I was nothing, just an insect to be killed or swatted away.

Not long after the girl had disappeared, the forms on the floor had started to move. I looked up, my hands leaned against the tree bark as I watched the children and recess aides groaning and climbing to their feet. They were all right? The adults looked sick and weak, their skin looked odd as well, infected and red, but they were standing. I took a step out from behind the tree. They were okay. They'd tell me what had happened, and they'd tell me not to be scared. Everything was going to be all right.

And then, out of nowhere, the children were on their feet, screeching and animalistic in their movements. I bit my lip hard, my hands going to the metal cross around my neck as the children gathered in swarms and leapt on the adults, biting and scratching at them, knocking them to the ground. Their screams were earsplitting as they were ripped to shreds. Tears had gathered in my eyes as I shook uncontrollably at the sight. Several had noticed me, looking up from where they lay hunched before the fallen adults, and started running towards me, crazed red eyes, and what looked like blood dribbling from the corners of them, open sores covered their skin, and their mouths dripping with saliva and red slabs of torn flesh hanging from their jaws.

I screamed, turning around and running away from them. They chased after me, fast as ever, gibbering nonsense and spewing out flecks of spit as they ran.

As usual and to no surprise of my own, they had all turned into little zombie Tara Jones. Little monsters that wanted to ruin me. Little monsters that wanted to be the death of me. LIttle monsters that wanted me to hate myself and my life.

I ran faster, jumping onto the fence at the end of the field, and climbing over it to the other side. The crazed children tried to follow, tripping over one another in their attempts to climb the fence but falling to the ground in the end, grasping at the metal frame and shaking them angrily. "Lace," they hissed. "Lace...."

I cried out, sobbing loudly as I turned away from them and hurried off. I didn't know what to do. I ran home, beating my fists on the front door. When my grandmother opened the door, I fell into her arms, screaming uncontrollably, "they tried to kill me, Grandma! Everyone tried to kill me!"

The older woman was confused. "Lace, who tried to kill you? Why aren't you in school?"

"All the kids went crazy, Grandma! Tara Jones was there and she was the devil, Grandma! SHe made all the kids go crazy and they tried to kill me!" I shrieked out the last words, crying harder as I buried my face in the woman's stomach. "I'm so scared."

"Oh dear," the woman sighed. I knew she didn't believe me. I could tell she didn't. It wasn't fair. I hadn't lied at all, I never lied, and my grandma still didn't believe me. "Well," the woman comforted, "let's go to your room. I'm going to go call your father at work."

I nodded, making my way up the stairs and wiping at my wet eyes. It wasn't fair. She thought I was lying. And I wasn't. I wasn't making any of it up at all. My grandmother put me to bed, giving me a glass of milk and a peanut butter and jelly sandwich. I could barely swallow a bite. Even in the safety of my bedroom, with everything looking normal and the way it should, I couldn't erase the horrible images of Tara Jones from earlier. It didn't feel real. I drifted off to sleep sometime after that.

I woke to the sound of the doorbell. Rubbing at my eyes, I crawled out of bed, stepping into the hall and down the stairs. I stopped half-way down, finding my grandmother already at the door, and I watched in curiosity to see who it was.

"Well now," her grandmother doted, kneeling downward. "It's a little early in the year to be trick-or-treating now, isn't it? And what a scary costume you have on..."

I came down the stairs as if in slow motion, watching as my mother opened the door, and an assassin shot her dead. I screamed. He came shoving his way inside. "Lace," he demanded. "we've been looking for you."

Not a dream. Everything became very real from that moment on. I was running away now. Without thinking. I couldn't think. I was just running, and the assasin that chased after me, oozing flesh, and torn nails, was following me. He was a monster. I raced into my room, slamming the door shut behind her and locking the door, the unnerving sound of the two fists pounding on the door and scratching at it from the other side resonated through the wood, and I trembled. The sound grew louder.

The window above my bed was big enough to climb through. I ran to it, pushing up the heavy glass frame and locking my fingers onto the screen, pulling it out. It clattered to the floor and I pulled my head through it, just as the first sounds of splintering from the door sounded. The pounding from the hall was so loud now. I pushed myself through completely, pushing the glass window down behind me and watching in terror as the door broke open, and in came flooding in an army of the blood hungry assassins.

I tried to keep my footing as I climbed up the slanted roof, pulling myself up to the pointed top, and clinging with all my might to keep from falling off. I heard the window shattering, and watched as the assassins, one that she recognized, some whom she had never seen before, trying to climb through. One by one, they crawled onto the roof, stopping in front of her.

"Lace."

"What do you want from me?" She screamed at the zombie assassins.

"Why the hell didn't you kill Michael and Tara."

"I was going to. I was fucking going to. I promise."

A man exited a car on the road. I looked down. He wore a white suit and was in his early sixties. He brushed his thinning hair back with his hands and looked up at her.

"That's Andras," The assassin now sitting next to me explained. I blinked and realized there was only one of him. He's our boss.

"Boss. Of the H Group. He's our king. He pays us to kill."

"What do want from me."

"Come down."

"Okay." I cried, trembling.

We climb down the roof and climb back into the guest room of the house through a broken window. We head down the staircase and pass my mother's corpse, leaving the house. I'm pushed forward into the backseat of the car. The man that fetched me goes to the pasenger seat, riding shotgun to the driver, and Andras joins me in the back.

"Hello, there," he says to me, smiling casually. He lifts a hand and brushes a tangled strand of hair back from my face.

"Who are you?" i mumble.

"Andres of the H Group. We hired you to kill Michael and Tara. Youre a friend of his. We know that. We were watching you two. Why didn't you do it?" he; asked gently. "Why didn't you give them the poison."

"I.... I was going to," I stammered. "I was thinking about it."

"Well, I'll give you one more chance to kill him. He trusts you dear. I know that he would never suspect you were trying to kill him."

Love

Hate

Winning.

Defeat.

What the hell am i talking about anymore?

The drive was long and i zoned out throughout it.

Is anyone out there? I've wondered this constantly throughout the span of my existence in space. I think of things like God. A word that had I the ability to voice out loud, I'd want to hear it for myself. However it is a concept, an idea I can only dream and know. My creator. I had to come from somewhere. Who is he then? This God? Are there others like me? With logical thought of conscious self? There must be. To know yet not know. It's what pains me the most.

Is anyone out there? I can only wonder as I seek out my purpose. To only be. What a terrible thought. There has to be purpose. There has to be flow of continuity of one event leading from beginning to end, and likewise, all that is, being what it is, and in some way effecting the other. I need to be needed.

I need to be cared for. I need to be known. For if this were not so, then when I do cease to be, for whatever reason or the next, then it would not be known that I were gone. What tragedy. To come and go and the cosmos none the wiser. Tell me then, what is this cosmos? I sense you. I feel you. But who and what are you?

I see in the sense that I know where I am. I know my surroundings because I am me. If I am me, then the rest is everything that is not me. I am not quite warm, though not quite cold. If one were to go from neutral to negative, I wouln't say I was negative because I am energy. Because I exist, though I am not great, I am something. And that much more of something makes me that much more than nothing. So in that sense, I swing over to positive. I am a positive thing. Whatever it is I am. And I know that there are rocks that spin in cycles past me and tremendous pulls of magnetic forces that swing me as well.

Time is slow.

It feels as though I'm standing still.

They do not speak. These rocks. I am not a rock. What am I then? I am not the pull, nor the lack of something that makes this space as dark as dark can be. It's endless. Going on forever. I digress. Where do I belong? Is this my purpose then? To be pulled and dragged and swung in space like the rocks around me? But why? It doesn't make sense to me. There would have to be more. If there weren't then there'd be no reason to exist.

There's a dream I have. I've had it often. It's a dream of color. Something I've never experience personally but somehow know is real. I can't explain it to someone that's never known it. But I do know it's real. Just as I wonder and hope that someone I'm speaking to is as real as myself. I like to live under the assumption. I don't think of it as lying to myself. The dream, I can't stop or I'll start to forget. The colors are warm and cold and soft and hard. They're vibrant and dull and flat and bright and everything that is anything all at once. They fill me with emotions like passion and hate and fear. I feel it's important. To have these happen to me. They make me feel as though I'm headed somewhere, to a final cause.

This is the thing I need to explain. The point of my dreams, or what I've determined must be the point. I think they're a message, a way of preparing me for what's to come. As mentioned, I think of God, for as I determined what must be the point of my dreams, I also imagined God as the reason for this point. If he is my creator, then he must know why I'm here, and what I am meant to do. What I am and what I do now is nothing. I can't be considered whole with the way things are. But I dream of a future, a future of something more than all this. There's a reason for everything that happens in this place. There has to be. There's a reason for the rocks and for the spinning and the pulls that send me this way and that. There's a reason that there seems to be only me, when just as easily, there could be only them.

I am not them so I am me. I know that.

And though these are all just thoughts in my mind. I wonder again and again. Is anyone out there? I like to think so.

They take me back to their secret assassin hideout. It's an eleven hour drive. An elevator that looks like a tree, lost in a dark thick forest in the middle of nowhere, is where we are headed. i cough into my hand, feeling dizzy and sick and confused as they push me forward towards the elevator to the underground lair that looks like a fake tree.

The elevator doors opened. A clown stood there under the dim yellow lighting of a flickering light bulb, a handful of balloons hanging from white strings wrapped around his fingers. A clown. A very tall, very large clown. Lace and Andras step into the elevator immediately, and the doors closed shut behind us. Her meeting was on the twelfth floor of the hotel above them should be starting any minute now. As for the clown, I could only imagine what his purpose could be. The lights flickered more severely, shrouding them in darkness for nearly a full second before turning back on.

I Blink and snap back to reality. No clown. just her and two other assassins in a tree elevator headed to the underground lair.

"They should get those lights fixed," I joked.

The other two didn't reply, instead looking straight ahead with intense and focused eyes. Creepy. Their clown make-up was odd. A stark white and sharp red and purple designs around the eyes and mouth. Pointed angles and sharp contrasts, not at all the soft and fuzzy look I was more accustomed to seeing in a child's entertainer. I cleared my throat, taking a step back and leaning back against the wall and railing. The lights flickered again.

There was a jolt. And I felt myself fall forward, hands catching my fall on the tiled surface of the floor. A tiny yelp from my throat. I pulled myself up unsteadily, my eyes searching around frantically. The lights turned on and off crazily, engulfing them in dark then light then dark then light again. The yellow on the men's face was not flattering with their clown make-up job.

The shadows they cast on their faces made their features look contorted and demonic, as if they were a wild beast baring fangs through narrow slits of animal-like eyes. He turned to look at her and she jumped back, unable to help herself. The elevator went silent. The sound of fans and gears all completely stopped, the light had turned off completely, and had been replaced with a hazy red emergency light.

They were stuck, weren't they. The elevator had stopped completely. "Shame, huh," came a male's voice. Low and raspy. It terrified her. The clown was talking to her.

She nodded quickly. She squeaked, "yeah. What do you think we should do?"

He shrugged his shoulders, looking down at her shrunken form, bathed in blood red lighting. His eyes reflected the crimson color and she had to squeeze her own shut to keep from seeing them. Her entire body was shaking, alone and trapped with a man she didn't know, dressed like a psychotic killer with red eyes and fangs bared. I was terrified. I was terrified and I couldn't help it. He leaned down, the giant creature had to have been seven feet tall, with clashing colored clothes that looked as though they had once been bright and vibrant, but had dulled due to age and washing. He reached a large palm over to her, and she watched it as though it were coming in slow motion, a bear's paw coming toward her. She whimpered, shrinking down even smaller.

"We're stuck in here. Come get us out."

I froze, my eyes moving cautiously to the hand that had moved past mt shoulder. It pressed the red emergency button, activating a sort of intercom. The relief she felt was embarrassingly obvious. I was being cruel and paranoid, but surely under the circumstances he could understand.

"I was going to make a killing today," the clown commented. "I'm late."

"A killing?"

"Big gig. Kid's birthday party. They'll cut my pay if I don't show up soon."

"Oh." She didn't know what else to say. She didn't want to make conversation. She didn't want to be polite. She just didn't want to be here. She didn't want to be here with this... with this terrifying man.

"I hate kids."

Then he should get a new job. "Oh." She couldn't think. She wanted to get out. She wanted to get out. Where were the hotel workers? They should get to them faster. Why were they taking so long?

"I feel like strangling them, they get so bad."

She didn't care. Good god, she didn't care. She wanted out. She wanted out. Her meeting. She was late too. Her important meeting with her boss. She was supposed to get a raise. She wanted out. The red light. Blood light. Soaking them through with blood light. They'd be dripping wet by the time they were out. It would soak them to the bone.

He reached into his pocket, "sometimes when I get real mad, so mad at them I can't take it anymore, I take this out and use it on them." The slender object was pulled out carefully from his pocket, gleaming and shining under the blood light. Sharp too? Is that what it was? Something sharp? A knife?! The bastard! She wanted to laugh out loud hysterically she was so scared. A knife he used on the bad kids that made him mad. The object became fully visible and he put it to his lips, blowing gently on it, and a airy tune came to life, a low sad song. "See, I'm a musician too."

Just a flute? She did laugh, a little spurt of a laugh. She was being ridiculous. Completely ridiculous. It was good to laugh at herself for it. She edged a little further away from his large form, feeling entirely too close to him and Andras. The elevator was broken after all. It had gotten smaller when it broke. Broken things, they shrink sometimes. The walls were too close together because of it. And together and closer, like magnets of opposite charges, they'd pull toward one another, oblivious to her suffering till the second the hotel workers finally pried the doors open and got her out.

"You ever kill anyone before?"

"Excuse me?" Her voice caught in her throat. His sharp face of distorted nose and mouth and pointy things came closer to her own.

"I asked if you ever entertained anyone before. For whatever reason."

Was that really it? What he had really asked? Could she have been hearing things? "N... no, don't do that sort of thing," she stammered. "I... I'm in business."

"How would you like if I cut your throat?"

She cried out, "Wh... what?"

"I said you guys are real cut-throat. Business can get real tough."

"Oh... oh... Um... yeah. It's definitely competitive."

"I'll rip you into shreds." He smiled.

She whispered, "S...sir... I'm sorry, what did you just say?"

"I said I'll rip you into shreds." The smile didn't leave his face. He took a step closer to her.

The doors opened. Two men looked down on them from above, leaning their hands down and grabbing hold of her wrists pulling her up onto the floor. She glanced back down as they did, watching as the horrible clown below looked up at her, his eyes unwavering and bathed in blood light. He reached up a hand, a single white string pinched between two fingers, and he held out a balloon to her. She crawled the rest of the way onto the floor before breaking into a fit of sobs and pointing down to the elevator, and telling them about how he had threatened her.

They looked confused, and one man stated quite firmly. "Lace, I said follow me. We need to meet with Andras in his room."

"Okay," I squeaked.

We made our ways to his room. andras. What a strange man he was. He took me into his room, sat me down at a table and spoke me gently as if he were my father. "Listen Lace. I'm sorry about your mother. Seventeen is sorry too. We don't usually like to do things like that but i had to get my point out to you that you can't take on a job you dont plan on finishing."

"I understand."

I glance over at the taxidermied corpse sitting beside Andras at the dinner table. "And who's that?"

"That's Bee. My lover from a past life. She died. As you can see." He kissed her on the forehead. "I want To tell you about her."

"Okay."

He pulls out the chair and expects me to sit down. I do so soley because i barely know whats going on by this point. I ask for some water and he signals for a servant to bring us waters and wine. When the wine is set in front of me i guzzle it down in one gulp and ask for more,

"Don't let love destroy you is my point. Don't let it destroy in the way that it destroyed me. When Bee died, my world shattered. I could no longer live. I could no longer feel. I could no longer breathe. That was the pain I felt when Bee killed herself."

"Why did she kill herself?" I ask.

"Because I murdered her lover. She had tried to run away with him. I couldnt have that. And i hated Jon forty six. I really did. He was the worst one and she only ever chose him over me. I hated their love. It drove me crazy."

"What's crazy to you?" I ask, thinking that she found it hard to beilieve that this man hadn't been crazy to begin with in some way or form.

"It's when you see death and he says hi to you on your way to the bathroom. Now that's crazy. So whats your story anyway. Why do you want to kill Michael and Tara?"

"Michael I loved him."

"He was your favorite."

"Yes."

"He was very popular back when he worked here. We loved him dearly. I wish he had never decided to leave. This is the second time he has betrayed us."

"ANd then Tara. The bitch. She came back nto his life and stole him from me."

"And you thought to herself why couldn't that person be me that Michaal chose. Why won't he choose me?"

"And I kept wondering why wasn't I the girl that met michael met first. i couldn't i be the one that michael would die for?"

"Here, take this advice," Andras said. "Kill them. Be done with it. Dont think another thought about it. Then come back here and work for us. YOu can join us. We love you Lace. We're like a fmaily here. YOu belong with us. You dont have to do that petty prostituation. we'll treat you like a princess here. You wont regret it. choose us."

"I dont know."

"Please, have something to eat." He snapped his fingers, ordered some food from a servant and then continued talking. "We need more girls like you. YOu could be an undercover assassin. You could get close to the enemy and then kill them without them even realizing what hit them."

"Thank you. For the offer I mean," I said.

The food arrived and we ate in silence for few moments.

"You know equality is the answer. things should be even. There's no such thing as things not being perfectly even and equal no matter what. There's no difference between good and bad. There's no difference hate and love. There's no difference between pure good and pure evil. We're all just trying to get by. They're all just equal exchange to me. Look it up. Equality and even is a good thing. So the more the better right?"

"What are you trying to say."

"I'm saying revenge is the answer. You had a hard life Lace. Take it out on Michael and Tara. You deserve as much. Kill them and make it even. Get them back for what they did to you."

"Can I go now?"

"Yes you can go when I have finished speaking iwth you. Do you still have the poison."

"No. They confiscated it when i tried to commit suicide."

"You were put into a mental instituation from what i read."

"Yes."

'Then I'll have seventeen give you two new vials. Go ahead and get your revenge lace. Kill michael and Tara and be freed of your love. You can do it. Dont let love destroy you. Be rid of those two once and for all."

Love and hate.

And no real difference.

Maybe he was right.

To kill michael and get rid of her love for him. To be free of him. To not let love destroy her. That was all she wanted. To be happy.

"I'll do it," I agreed.

he calls for seventeen and seventeen gets me two new bottles of poison. I follow him out of the underground hallway, to the elevator full of clowns and out of the underground hideout. He drives me to my trailer.

I head inside my trailer, set the poison on the table and fall alseep on my couch.

April 7 2010

Dear Diary.

I have literally gone insane.

My insanity hurts.

The pain in my skull is ascending if that makes any sense. I am in pain.

I want you to save me.

For every pain i feel, i feel like i am pushing to a new level of crazy. It goes taller and taller and taller until i can go no taller in this world.

This is the seventh, the day of the wedding of Tara and michael.

And i have gone insane.

I write this knowing i attended the wedding several times.

The first time was the best one. I arrived toting a machine gun. I killed tara first. Then michael, then everyone else in the room. the room was splattered in blood. I carried it in buckets to a bathtub and took my clothes off and bathed in it.

I lay in the bathtub thinking about life.

If it was true that fairies brought love to us then maybe it was true that storks brought babies to expecting parents.

I knew that i could not cry any longer about Michael. The wedding had been a tragedy once i killed them. I knew I could go on no more with that.

The second time i attended their wedding went as so.

I arrived in a gorgeous pink dress.

"Outdoing the bride." one of the guests joked.

I smiled widely. "of course."

I approach and michael stared at me. I knew he wanted me. he asks tara if he can take a second to the say a few words to me and the two of us head somewhere in private.

We go to the bathroom and sneak inside. it isn't long before his hot mouth is over mine. He's kissing me. Im so happy. this is what it should look like. This is how it should've been.

I let him fondle my breasts and i stroke is big hard cock. We start fucking. We fuck so hard that our moans are heard from the hallway. Tara must be insane with jealousy. That's all i can thinking. I smile, biting his lip with my teeth. He cant take it he wants me so bad. Smiling wider, I pull a knife out from my dress and stab michael hard in the gut. I keep smiling. I stab him. I keep smiling. I stab him.

smile.

stab.

smile.

stab.

Death

Im crying over his corpse. He never saw it coming. He never thought i'd do it.

I collapse over him, and grab his face. "Speak to me Michael. Speak to me."

Death.

I Drop him and leave the bathroom, covered in his blood.

Tara screams at the sight of me.

I dash toward her knife still in hand and stab her hard in the chest.

Just die.

Please you two.

Just die.

The third time i attended the wedding, or the least favorite time, everything went perfectly for them.

They were married and there was cake and ice cream and some balloons. I didn't catch the bride's bouquet she threw because it was poisoned and i didn't want to die from Tara's bitch disease.

They were driven away in a limosine and never heard from again. I had a feeling they drove their car straight into the ocean and died then and there.

I dont remember that well.

Maybe i am crazy.

Or drunk.

Or high.

I cant tell the difference anymore.

All I know is that they're somewhere running around still alive and being happy in this alternate universe.

The fourth time i attended the wedding i did exactly what i always wanted to do. I poured the poison into their drinks right before the toast. I was disguised as a server and they never suspected differently.

THey smiled, kissed, drank and then they died.

Dead dead dead.

Just as they should be.

I can recall infinite other such examples of the wedding. I dont remember which one is real. All i know, is that if i called Michael and Tara right now, they'd pick up the phone and tell me they were fine and happy and on their way ot vegas or something for their honeymoon. Which leads me to believe that they are currently alive and well and that I am a lunatic for fantasizing their deaths so intriquately.

But i digress.

What i really want to see, is me, Lace, take the poison i have and put it into Michael and tara's food and kill them and be rid of them for once.

I want to know what i could've done to change this for me. I want to know where i couldve gone to take away this chaos in my mind. I want go away somewhere and make the entire thing disappear before my own eyes.

I picture myself at the wedding again.

I head in but this time I'm the bride. I walk up to Michael and we are married and we kiss and the whole thing is a dream come true. It's Tara that's in the audience that is crying and wishes she were dead.

Michael takes my hand and we head off to a vacation spot in the bahamas. I'm infatuated with him and he is infatuated with me.

A dream come true.

A real dream come true.

CHAPTER 11

I wake up from my dream and realize I am at the actual wedding even as I speak. Except in this reality, there is no sex with Michael in the bathroom, and no marrying Michael, and no vacation to the bahamas with Michael. Just Tara and Michael staring into each others eyes. I sit on the grooms side which has seven other people in it. I watch them kiss and they are married right in front of me.

I realize that Michael is unaware of the fact that I am even there. He only has eyes for tara and he doesnt seem to notice me.

During the reception aftewards, I grab two cups of punch. I think about pouring in the poison but lose all nerve so I dont. I Bring them to michael and tara and absently hand the drinks to them. "congratulations," I say smiling.

"Oh, Lace, I'm so glad you were able to make it," Michael says, his eyes lighting up. "I didn't realize you were here."

Didn't realize I was there. That sounded about right. Like the story of her life all over again. "I'm glad I made it."

They take the drinks and drink them and they are fine of course because there is no poison in them and the poison still remains in two blue vials in my purse. And I am disturbed that I did not kill them or could not kill them or would not kill them or whatever it was that kept me from doing what I had come to do. I feel like crying.

I want to kiss him. I want to tell him I love him. I want to cry out please, let me speak up against your marriage. Be with me instead michael. Be with me instead.

I leave the wedding reception about an hour later. I couldn't take it anymore. I leave and decide that this will be the last time i ever see Michael again. Goodbye michael. I loved you and lost you. I held you and then never held you again. I'm sorry it had to end this way. But forever is a long time and i love you forever.

CHAPTER 12

April 8 2010,
Dear Diary.
I decided today that I in fact will not become a murderer. In the game of life, I have lost and by losing, I feel like I have won forever.

I am instead going to kill myself and Andras too of the H GROUP. Dont ask how I got the courage, as I dont intend to explain myself much further, but this much is true, I loved Michael more than anyone else....

I've gone through many lives in my head. I've lived as both a woman and as a man and as a killer and as a saint. But I dont plan on living those lives anymore.

I plan to kill myself.

CHAPTER 13

Before I find assassin Seventeen, which wasn't hard to do seeing as I think he was following me around, I put on my favorite necklace, the one that Michael had bought me when we had met. "I lost the poison." I said quickly.

The necklace you bought for me hangs around my neck.

I'd give it back to you if it weren't for the fact that I never saw you again.

"You did?" Seventeen asks.

The smell of your cologne still clings to the back of my throat.

I'd wash it away if it weren't for the permenent stain it left on my memory.

"I'd like to see Andras again." I say.

The way it is. The way it'll be. Oh God. Why are we here and what can I do to make this world a less heavy place to live in?

"Of course."

In reality, the two vials of poison are tucked in my bra and go unnoticed by assassin Seventeen. We head to his car, climb inside, and drive for several hours until we reach H Group headquarters. Seventeen and I head through the woods to an elevator shaped like a tree, and go inside. Then we use the elevelator to go to the second floor and to Andras's room.

Seventeen knocks on Andras's door.

The door opens and Andras appears several moments later. "I'd like to speak with you for a little while."

"Of course."

"Just us two."

"Definitely."

I head inside and shut the door behind me. I grasp his thin shoulders and pull him closer to me. I kiss him deeply. I push him to the bed and we have sex.

I think about Michael, and our first time together. I think about all the times I had been with him and how much fun and how nice it had all been. I feel like I'm going to cry now. Because today is my last day on earth. Today is the day I die, and I feel very sad that I will no longer be able to look at his smiling face or think of him in the way that I have forever.

I keep my shirt and bra on so that Andras does not detect the poison i have hiding in beneath my breasts.

I stradle Andras, thinking of Michael and how much I loved him and how it felt to be a woman in love and how free I had felt for that moment when we were together.

I think of Michael and Tara's wedding and think that I am actually almost happy for them now. Yes. They were married. Yes, they would go off to some dream world and leave me behind and I would never see Michael again. But I was happy like that. I was happy knowing that he was happy.

Love had freed my soul.

My love had gone from an immature caterpillar to a beautiful butterfly. I had been in love with a dream. I had been irrational and immature my entire life and today I was a real woman that didn't need to dwell on a tragic past. I was happy. Finally, from deep within my soul I was happy for once.

Andras fell asleep and I pretended to sleep as well.

I was happy.

Today, I die a happy woman I thought. A happy woman free of pain and resentment and most of all, free of hate. Tara, I dont resent you for marrying Michael. I don't hate you or envy you any longer. As a matter of fact, I would even go so far as to say I love you. I love you and I love Michael and I love that you two are happy together. Happily ever after. That's what you looked like to me. Like a fairytale that reached happily ever after.

I crawl out of bed and go to the dining room table in the kitchen nook of the effiency dorm. I open a bottle of wine and pour two glasses. I fill each cup, take out the two vials of poison and pour them into the cups. Then I walk over to the bed, a glass in each hand, and sit down, naked from the waist down. I nudge andras and wake him up.

"Thirsty?" I ask.

"Yes, thank you."

He takes the glass and downs it with one gulp.

I drink from my own glass. The poison is surprisingly tasteless and I feel chills rushing up and down my spine as I drink it. I feel borderline excited to be drinking the poison myself. Finally, a chance to go to sleep. Finally, a chance to rest.

I lay down in bed, kiss Andras on the lips and pull the blankets high over us. I close my eyes, thinking of Michael and how handsome he had looked at the wedding. Tara had been absolutley dazzling in her white dress. They had been so happy. I was happy that they were happy. I fall asleep next to Andras. We sleep for a very long time before drifting quietly into death.

Andras and Lace, we slept away the rest of life until there was no more life at all and only death.

Andras and Lace.

Deceased.

And the universe smiled at Lace and told her she was a good girl for saving the planet from the H Group and its horrible leader. And as usual, the cosmos continued to turn.

Tara and Michael ALIVE and married.

END OF BOOK 4

BOOK 5

Underground Killers-
Seventeen and Anna's Story/
Jeffrey and Melissa's and
other prisoner"s stories

CHAPTER 1 prologue

"Angelic hands holding my own.

He touches my face and I drop to my knees.

I am his.

GOD.

Why are we here and what was I supposed to be doing this whole time?

If he were here right now, I'd ask him that."

-Anna Alice

CHAPTER 1

The universe turns. Slowly. The Microcasm. I feel connected to it. As if we are one. That's how I felt when I saw him for the first time. I knew what this was. I was in love.

The guy I like.... How do I describe him? He was tall, but not too tall, good looking but not too good looking, and charming, but not too charming. He had a good sense of humor and knew how to make people laugh.

I love him. I think. I don't know. I'm not sure.

He's a musician and he sings locally at the bars in our city. He comes to Tony's Bar and Grill every friday night to sing original songs and Beatle's covers. He's a true artist, who can play the guitar, the drums, and keyboard, as well as sing and write songs. He's talented and sweet and I adore him.

I think that life is all about making choices. In my life, I've spent an eternity of choosing from one thing or another. There's no going backwards in choice making. It starts off small like what do you want to do for a living and then escalates to who should you marry, should you have kids, if so how many, what are their names, what should they do for a living. Then you come to crossroads that look small but actually snowball into something much bigger, like should you tell someone you like that you like them, because the choice I decided to make was that I should, and the outcome was much bigger than I had anticipated.

"I like you," I admitted loudly after his show one night.

He smiled. "Bullshit."

"No really. I like you."

"You don't even know me." he said jokingly. "I could be a murderer for all you know."

"A murderer?" I laugh. "Good joke."

"No, really. What if I was an assassin or something."

"I wouldn't believe you if you said you were," I replied.

"Well, that's a good thing because I'm at something of a crossroads here."

"What do you mean?"

"Nothing. Don't worry about it. Well if you're worried I'm gonna hurt you or something I'm not. I kinda like you actually. You're cute. Very cute."

I felt self-conscious and brushed back my black hair and shifted uncomfortably in white strappy heals. I don't reply and he walks away. I leave as well, headed home and feeling detached from life as I think about him deep in my heart.

What was love?

And why did it have to hurt so much?

Did he think I was joking?

Maybe that was all I was to him. Some kind of joke.

I drop my purse into my car and drive home.

Why are we here and what could I do to make myself someone worth being here for once.

I have nightmares.

I don't tell anyone because I don't want them to think I've gone insane.

In them I am tied to a chair, and being threated. They threaten to murder me, to torture me, to devour me whole and I cry that I don't want to die. In them, I see monsters hovering over me, with scaly black skin and deep red eyes staring me down, promising to end my world and never let me come back.

I don't want to be the prisoner. Every so often I'm faced with the dilemma of wondering whether it'd be better to just commit suicide and be the one commiting the crimes instead of the one being the victim of such.

I want to hold on to my humanity. I want to hold on to my goodness and be a good person that doesn't do those things but motivation is waning.

I think of the nightmares and wonder if perhaps I'm becoming an evil person.

I want to believe that good is the answer no matter what. But who am I to say I know the answers.

On the roads of life,
I long for you.
I wonder why I'm here.
and I think if you'd stand by me no matter what
I could die a happy person.
I'm the kind of person that commits suicide.

If I thought that murder led to hell or nirvanna or eternal death I think I'd be first in line to murder someone. Not to hurt them but to hurt me.

If I thought that it were possible to live a good life as a dreamer and not a fighter I think I'd be in love with my own world of thought and not know what kind of life I was about to live.

I like not knowing. I like not knowing what the point of life is and why we're here. I think I would have chosen a world of not knowing and not living if I could start again. I never asked to be here and I don't want to be alive. I don't like being scared and I don't like feeling out of control of my life. I want to think that in terms of forever, if I could choose again, I'd be a falcon or a fish or something and never know love or what it felt like to hurt.

In my dreams.
He asks me with sympathy,
"Haven't you ever had that someone stand by you no matter what? You have no idea what that feels like, do you?"
In fact,
I do not have that someone that stands by me no matter what.
And the question haunts me.
As I feel I never will have that someone.
And know what it's like for someone to love me.

"All we do is fuck."
"I know. All we do is fuck."

Melissa and Jeffrey lay on the floor, huddled together, staring at each other intensely.

They had been kidnapped and brought there from two separate wealthy households. They hadn't known each other previously. They had been locked up together for nearly ten years already and they were getting bored and restless. And they had been brought there by Bee and Forty-Five back when they were among the living.

"All we do is fuck," Melissa said again.

"I know, you said that already," Jeffrey replied. They had just had sex. And the sex was a fine thing, of course, a fine thing, as sex normally is. But the circumstances had put them in a situation where sex was no longer the best thing and bordering on the worst one.

"I'm thinking about what I want to be in my next life," she continued.

I replied. "A princess?"

"No, a bunny rabbit," she said. "I'd love to be a bunny rabbit. What about you?"

"An alcoholic probably."

"Why's that?"

"So I can drink away my problems," I said. "I want to be poor and drunk and never have anything to lose. I feel like I had too much, appreciated too little, and lost all of it."

"Them's the breaks, huh."

"Yeah definitely." I smile at her, trying to keep her smiling too. "You're so pretty. When we get out of here I'd like ot take you out on a real date. I had lots of money you know. I'd buy you all the clothes and shoes and purses you wanted. I'd treat you like a real woman."

"You think we'll get out of here?"

"Definitely. I can tell. It wont be long before our parents pay the ransom and get us out of this fucking place."

"I hope so." she says to me.

Give a little

Take a lot.

That's how I used to be.

And then

to lose it all.

Life is like that sometimes.

And to give me one precious woman.

who I can't even protect.

though I would die for her.

she probably won't live to see thirty.

She kisses me and we have sex again. She sighs. "All we do is fuck."

"I'm starting to make that association too." I reply.

281

We gaze into each other's eyes and laugh.

I realize.

That even in dark times.

It's okay to think that this is what it feels like to be happy.

It's the next day since I spoke to the girl Anna.

I put the guitar away and say goodbye to my band. We usually play every Saturday at the Night Club. I head to my car and head to a woman named Lina Shine's house. I knock on the door quickly. She opens it and greets me kindly.

Quickly, I lift my gun and silencer, shoot her in the head. Then quietly pack up my gun and leave.

I'm Seventeen, an assassin for the dissolving H Group.

Andras is dead.

As far as we know, Michael and Tara are married and run off to some carrabean somewhere. I don't know and at this point I don't care. All I know is that I am leader now and it is up to me to figure out what to do with the H Group.

I could do one of two things.

I could dissove the group completely

or...

I could continue on this hellish lifestyle in the name of terror and never be free.

But without Andras why the hell are we doing this?

I could walk away.

Or I could stay.

Which one do I pick.

Pick your poison. That's what they say. Pick your poison. And I don't know what I want yet.

When I am done killing the woman, I head back to the bar for a drink.

I buy some liquor over ice and gulp it down. Anna swings up beside me, and I glance over at her. She is staring at me strangely and I smile at her.

Even in a simple dress

I think you look your best.

Your unrivaled pretty.

and my evil secrets.

I'm sorry I never told you sooner.

She says. "Where'd you go? You headed out for awhile."

"Did you watch us play?"

"Yes."

"What'd you think?"

"You were good. Like usual."

I order her a drink and hand it to her. "And to answer your question, just had to run an errand."

"I see."

"Is that all then?"

"No. I really wanted you to know," she began, stammering as she spoke. "I didn't mean to come on so strong the other night? I hope you weren't offended."

"I wasn't." I leaned forward and kissed her hard on the lips. Maybe I was drunk already. I don't know why but I really wanted to let her know that she was right to think she had a chance with me. I wasn't normally the type to think I could fall in love under such dangerous circumstances but I was thinking it sounded pretty good right about now.

I pull back and look at her. "What'd I say about watching out for guys like me. I could be a killer or something."

"Why do you keep saying that?"

"Just sayin'"

"No really, what do you mean by that?"

I finally tell her I'm an assassin. And the new leader of the H GROUP.

She gaped at me, pulling back. "You're joking."

"No joke. Just facts."

"Are you allowed to tell me something like that?"

"Depends, can I trust you?"

She stares at me for awhile before replying finally. "Yes, you can trust me."

"I thought so." I lean forward and kiss her again, more passionately this time and she kisses me back.

I take her back to my place and we have sex.

It's true.

I like her.

Just a little.

She's kinda cute and kinda my thing and kinda not. She's definitely worth thinking about. I feel glad that I met her.

And feel bad for the thing I'm about to do.

"All we do is fuck."

"I know I heard you before when you said it."

"No really. All we do is fuck. It's boring. You're boring me." she complained. "Don't we have something else to do."

"Not that I can think of."

"Then get awaaaaaay from me. I'm tired." She huffed, pushing him away and rolling to the other side of the cell. "You're so mean to me," she complained some more.

"Why are you in such a bad mood?"

"I just keep thinking that I did nothing wrong to deserve being stuck with you like this. It's boring. all we do is fuck and you're pissing me off."

"Maybe we should try killing ourselves."

"Even that sounds more appealing than being in this fucking room all fucking day long with fucking you."

"Sorry didn't realize I was pissing you off so much. Wanna fuck?"

"Fine. We can fuck. Just hurry up. Then I'm going to sleep."

I'm annoyed.

Why am I here?

There's such a thing as evading an apocolypse.

No happy ending.

and no hope here.

Hope does not sit well with me.

It hurts.

And if anything, the world could shatter and I'd still be the one at the bottom of the life pool.

So why am I here?

Did God put me here to suffer? Or to be sad? Or happy? Or what the fuck is going here.

I just want to go home, shower and sleep.

And instead. "All we do is fuck."

"So you've said."

I think about life and all I've come to regard as life.
And I wonder why the hell am I here? What the hell is the point?
WHY THE HELL ARE WE HERE?
I don't want it. I don't.
WHY?
WHY?
WHY?

CHAPTER 2 prolgue

"All we do is fuck."

~ Melissa

CHAPTER 2

Seventeen brought Anna to HQ. It was probably a stupid move but he had wanted to show her what he did for a living and what that looked like in real life.

I show her the prisoner's floor and try to explain to her what I do. "I'm something of a bad person. I know I look normal. But we do all this for money. Can you imagine that? An entire ring of suffering fueld by the almighty dollar. That's what money is. Fuel to us. I would do that. For just a little bit of money. I would do that to someone. That's pretty much how evil I am."

"I see," she replied, staring at the cell doors and pulling up toward him. He put an arm around her and pulled her closer.

"Does that bother you? That we do these things?"

"Yes."

"Well I'm thinking I might not continue on this group. The truth is, like Jon Forty-Five said, Andras wasn't a very good person. He wasn't that nice to anyone really and I'm not super motivated to continue on this place forever until I die just to flatter his ghost. I'd love to just run away. With you even? And never see this fucking place ever again. What do you think?"

"You would do that?"

'Yes. So what'll it be? Move on? Or move in? What do you want to do Anna. It's up to you."

"Move on?"

"I'm afraid it's not that easy. I can't just move on. I need to have some kind of ummmm..... motivation so to speak," I reply. "I need a reason to move on. "So... I'm going to ask you a very serious question. Will you marry me?"

"Marry you?"

"I would do that to you. I would take you to this fucking place. Drop this bombshell on you. Show you hell. Then ask you to marry me. You know that's possible, right? That someone would do that to you?"

"Can I think about it?"

"You have about three seconds."

"Then hold on a second." She pulled a quarter out from her pocket. "Flip for it. Heads or tails. Pick your poison."

I stared at her for a long time before replying. "Are you sure you want to do this?"

"Yes."

"Then tails. I pick tails. Because I'm a little backwards."

She flips the coin. And it lands on the back of her hand. When she moves her hands. They read what side it is on.

Angelic hands holding my own.

He touches my face and I drop to my knees.

I am his.

GOD.

Why are we here and what was I supposed to be doing this whole time?

If he were here right now, I'd ask him that.

The prisoners were annoyed.

All they could hear was the sound of sex in the next cell.

"All they do is fuck," the prisoner, Bill Paramon complained.

"Tell me about it. All they do is fuck," said Matthew Gist.

"I'm so sick of being here."

"Seventeen is thinking about letting us go."

"Yeah I heard. He's been playing around with his new girfrined trying to decide if we should live or die."

"Who the hell do these people think they are?"

"Bunch of lunatics. The whole lot of them."

Several assassins stalked the corridors. They opened the doors. "We're about to hang Jeffrey and Melissa."

"You can't," Bill cried out.

"I'm afraid so. Their parents never paid the ransom."

"That's so tragic," Matthew said.

"Common you guys. We're going to have a final meal together," the first assassin spoke.

They left their cells and followed the assassins to a dining hall where everyone sat down to eat.

They sat at their meals, surrounded by guards with rifles. An assassin sat with a machine gun at the table, speaking eloquently. "This is going to be the final night before we kill Jeffrey and Melissa. So let's all hold hands and pray."

They held hands and bowed their heads in silent prayer.

WHY ARE WE HERE?

W

h

y

?

I don't know why we're here. I don't pretend to know. No one does.

What the fuck is the fucking point?

All we do is fuck, she said.

That's all.

I'm Jeffrey.

Why is God angry. Maybe there's no such thing as god? Maybe, after all the chaos and lack for answers, there was never a god to begin with. Who knows. I definitely don't.

I'm sad.

I grab my fork and leap up from the table, stabbing the man with the machine gun in the eye.

He screams out, angrily, and fires the machine gun madly around the room. Bullets spray everywhere, killing almost everyone in the room and even wounding a couple of the guards and kill the third and fourth.

When he stops firing, he drops the gun, and yanks the fork from his eye. "What an idiot," he mutters.

Jeffrey laid on the floor dying, holding melissa in his arms. "Didn't I say it? I told you we'd get out of here," he says smiling at her.

"Freedom," she says, smiling before closing her eyes and passing away slowly.

I close my eyes and die too.
Why are we here?
I have no fucking idea.
And at this rate, I don't really want to know anymore.
And the universe, despite our tragic deaths, continues to turn.

Prisoners sect 234, deceased.
Prisoner 1 and 2 deceased.
Prisoner Melissa and Jefferey deceased.
Guards three and four deceased.

CHAPTER 3 prologue

"Why are we here?
I have no fucking idea."

~Jefferey

CHAPTER 3

The universe turns and turns and turns. It never stops. Good or bad. Love or hate. Fine or not. You can't stop time from going. And the universe, ever cold and present, turns and turns and turns.

"What do you know?"

They read the coin.

Seventeen smiles. "Tails. Guess that means you have to marry me."

"Guess that means you have to dissolve the H Group."

"Guess so."

"So we're going to let all the prisoners go."

"Yeah. We'll let them go. Let the kids go. Let the assassins go home. It'll be fine. Just fine."

"Thanks for a wild ride seventeen."

"You're welcome."

Seventeen and Anna.
ALIVE AND MARRIED.

END OF BOOK 5

BOOK 6

A killer's Instinct: Tara and Michael's story part two. Final

CHAPTER 1 prologue

"When you left, I was despaired.
A love that could not be repaired.
Your love is now far behind.
My darling, you are no longer mine."

~Tara jones

CHAPTER 1

One year later.

Michael and Tara sat sitting together at their home. Both of them were reading from books and drinking lemonade. It was hot and summer and they were relaxed on their own together.

There was a knock on the door and Tara went up to the door to answer it. I watched her as she walked to the door and opened it.

Wolf aka Assassin number ninety-eight stood at the door.

I jumped to my feet, feeling frightened by the sight of him. What the hell was he doing here?

"Some reading material maybe," he spoke, handing Tara a soft leather bound book. He smiled before tipping his cap and leaving.

She stared at it before handing it to Michael.

Michael frowned and took the book. It was labeled Lace's diary and he opened it to the first page.

The two of them stood there and began to read from the book.

Dear Diary, March 20, 2008

I met Michael today. A handsome tall man with no interest in me whatsoever.

Let's just say it was love at first sight. He used to say things to me like I was pretty and his type and nothing at all like any woman he ever met before. Do you think he was just saying that? Or do you think he could've liked me.

I skimmed the rest of the book and stopped on the last page.

Dear diary, April 1 2010.

I decided today that I in fact will not become a murderer. In the game of life, I have lost and by losing, I feel like I have won forever.

I am instead going to kill myself and Andras too of the H GROUP. Dont ask how I got the courage, as I dont intend to explain myself much further, but this much is true, I loved Michael more than anyone else....

I've gone through many lives in my head. I've lived as both a woman and as a man and as a killer and as a saint. But I dont plan on living those lives anymore.

I plan to kill myself.

I stop reading unable to continue. Kill herself? Lace? It wasn't true. Hadn't she just been at the wedding?

I think carefully before taking the book to the bedroom and locking the door. I read the entire thing. From beginning to end, thinking that if she were suffering so much she should've told me and I would've done something about it. I think about the last sentence that tells me she is going to kill herself.

I decide to go for a walk and leave the diary in the bedroom. I bring with me a carry on bag full of clothing and socks and my wallet.

"Where are you going?" Tara asks me, looking concerned.

"Nowhere, just going for a walk," Michael replied. He hurried out of the house and made his way outside. He was very unhappy that he had read what he had read and he decided that the only way in which he could ever feel better was to see the terrible truth for himself.

"Why are you bringing your suitcase with you?"

"I'll be right back," he lies. "Just going for a smoke."

He thought about love and loss and what it meant to be with someone forever.

Why hadn't he chosen Lace? And why had he let her get to the point that she was at?

I stuffed my hands into my pocket and walked for awhile. I finally decided to take a bus and took it to the city where Lace and I had met and where she had used to live.

As I rode the bus, I thought about God and the universe and what it meant to be a good person.

When I was younger I had wondered why I had been chosen to be kidnapped and raised to be a killer. Under normal circumstances, would I have been a good person? I would never know. And then as he had killed more and more, he had wondered if he had justified every crime against his soul with crimes against humanity.

My past.

it crawls up my spine and along my back.

I feel this way sometimes.

my shadow turned on me a long time ago.

and the glaring corpses.

laugh at me still.

The hanging corpses screamed and laughed. "Scared little MIchael!" they cried out. "Scared little Michael."

It wasn't on purpose. The betrayal had been so great, he had to kill him. It hadn't been on purpose that he had killed his good friend.

Michael remembered the past.

He had stepped on the belly of the overweight dead man. His gun hung from his hand. He had just finished his last assignment. He felt hollow as he gazed down at the man's blank stare from the floor. Another soul gone. Another ounce of blood to add to the flood. He looked away, reloading the gun in his hand and tucking it at his side. Lifting his foot off, he turned to Seven, and a mangled corpse dropped from his friend's hands.

"We get paid today," Seven smiled. "What do you say we get some drinks."

"Yeah, we could do that." Michael preferred saving his money. He watched the others as they blew it in hours on drugs and sex with women they had met on the road. He felt bad wasting it the way they did but one night wouldn't hurt. Besides, he didn't have to spend a lot if he didn't want to.

They went back to headquarters, joking and laughing about their last assignment. They did what they were told, and they were used to doing those things and never feeling the least bit bad for it.

Easy jobs.

Death.

Love and loss.

What was the difference anymore, anyway?

They entered the fake tree that served as an elevator. When they reached the halls of the undergournd lair, they took the stairs to the first floor. They found themselves before a large iron gate with lights on either side. They pulled it open and closed it shut behind them. There was a large main door in front of them. It was opened for them by two guards.

They stepped inside, finding a line had already formed in the narrow hallway. They took their place at the end of the line, watching as Andras smiled and placed a small envelope into each man's hand. Each envelope contained four crisp one hundred dollar blls. "Good job," They heard him say quietly to each person. "Keep it up." He approached Seven, smiling and setting the envelope in his hand. "Good job."

Andras stopped when he reached Michael. He paused, setting the envelope carefully into Michael's palm, Andras' hands stopping on Michael's skin. "Keep it up, Fifty-six," he said gently. "I'm very proud of you." Michael felt sick at the voice. Pulling his arm away, he tucked the envelope quickly into his back pocket. Andras continued to smile at him, lifting a hand and brushing it over Michael's cheek. "You don't have to be so cold."

"I didn't realize I was being cold." Michael said. As usual, he hated Andras with a passion.

"Did I ever tell you, you were my favorite."

Michael could hear snickers from the men further down the line. He felt frustrated, wanting to push the man off of him. "I think you mentioned it before," he replied.

"Good. Just don't forget that." He stepped back, turning his attention to the new men forming at the end of the line. He continued down the row, handing out the small pay.

Seven nudged him. "Let's go," he whispered.

Nodding, Michael followed him around the men and through the front door again. He needed a drink. They squeezed through the crowd, heading out of the hall and out through the iron gate. Hurrying up the stairs, they pushed the door open and climbed outside again.

"Payday only comes once a month," Seven said loudly, clapping an arm around Michael's shoulder. "We should enjoy ourselves, right? Fifty-six?"

Michael nodded. It was hard to be as enthusiastic as Seven was all the time. He felt better now but his skin had crawled to no end where Andras had touched him. It pissed him off inside.

"Somethin' wrong?" Seven asked.

"No. Why?"

Seven shook his head, pulling his arm away and fiddling with the envelope in his hand and glancing inside at the contents. "Don't let Andras get to you. He's just a big psycho anyway. We all know it. It's only because you let him get to you that he does that."

"I'm not worried about it." Michael replied.

They headed out of the woods. There was a bar, a nightclub they all went to frequently when they got paid. They walked down the road, the sky above them dark and cloudy.

It was a twenty minute walk to get there. They talked about guns as they hiked. Ones they wanted. Ones they had used and not cared for. Ones they would like to use when they got the chance.

The nightclub came into sight. Parked cars and motorcycles lined the front and men and women stood in groups along the wall. Michael and Seven headed inside, finding many of the other H Group members already there. Jon Forty-Five sat on a musty couch with several other hitmen, downing a bottle of beer. One hundred was seated at the bar next to a young woman, chatting casually with her. Seventeen's handsome form was stuffing something into his mouth and chewing thoughtfully from his seat. George, aka Assassin thirteen was chatting with Seventeen.

Bee ran up to Michael as they stepped inside. "Fifty-six!" she exclaimed. She tugged on his arm. "Wanna dance?"

"That's okay," Michael said. She was Andras' woman, or Jon Forty-Five's. He never really understood the concept. Either way, he didn't find her that attractive.

"Go dance with her," Seven said loudly slapping him loudly on the back. "Why not?"

Jon Forty-five appeared behind her then, grabbing Bee by the arm and dragging her away. "I wasn't going to do anything," She complained to him as they walked.

"I think Jon's claimed her already," Michael stated matter-of-factly. "Besides, she's not my type."

Seven made a face, scratching at his dark hair. Michael noticed there was a spot of dried blood still stuck to the side of his face.

"I forgot. You've never been with a woman before."

"You shut up." he gestured to the bar. "Common. Let's just drink."

They made their way to the bar, pulling up stools and sitting down. In the distance, they could make out Aiden and Wolf seated at the end of the counter. Aiden held an empty glass in his hand and Wolf was chatting with the bartender.

Michael ordered a beer. He watched as Seven did the same. He drank from the tall plastic cup. He wasn't enjoying himself. Andras had upset him more than he realized.

"*She looks pretty hot there, doesn't she,*" Seven commented, lifting his empty cup towards Bee dancing with Jon Forty-five.

"*I told you she's not my type*"

"*That doesn't mean she's not mine. Ass.*" Seven smiled, ordering another beer. "*I think she's gorgeous as hell.*"

"*Don't let Andras hear you say that.*"

"*Big fucking deal,*" Seven snorted. "*He doesn't scare me.*"

Michael shrugged. "*Just saying.*"

"*Maybe you like 'em dumb and blond, but not me.*" Seven continued. "*Give me a skinny little brunette any day and I'm set.*" he turned to Michael, frowning at the cup in his hand. "*you still on that same one.*"

"*Yep.*"

Seven slugged back the second cup, setting it down in front of him. "*We should get some hookers. What do you think?*"

"*Nah. I'm not in the mood.*"

"*You're the only guy I know that's never in the mood for hookers. That's fine. When your penis shrivels up and falls off, don't say I didn't warn you.*"

Michael ignored him, guzzling down the rest of his beer. He couldn't help that he hated wasting money so he usually saved it, hiding it in his pillowcase and inside his mattress in their room. It wasn't that he saved it for anything in particular. He just wanted to have it in case he did need it one day. Not that he could say that out loud. They weren't allowed to save their money technically. If Andras ever found out, they'd take it away from them. That was years of money saved up that he wasn't about to lose.

He watched as Seven was pulled away to the dance floor by a young woman in her twenties. She was hot, tan and blond, and despite his complaining earlier, it didn't stop him from going with her.

Michael sat alone at the bar until Aiden stood up and came over to him. The oldest in the group, his gray hair was slicked back for the night and the stubble on his chin shaved. "*Hey Fifty-six,*" he said," taking a seat in Seven's empty seat. "*What're you doing here by yourself.*"

"*I came here with Seven,*" Michael said. "*He's over there right now.*"

"*Ah, I see.*" He lifted a glass, taking a large gulp. "*It's a good night to be out. Good night to be alive. If you know what I mean. I'm glad to see everyone here Every day's like that for me, you know?*"

"*Like what?*"

Aiden shrugged. "Wondering who's going to come back. You start noticing more when you get to be my age. Eventually you look around and no one's the same age as you anymore. They're all young and new at this stuff. Everyone older than that is dead."

Michael wasn't sure how to reply. He decided one more beer would be fine with his budget. He ordered a second cup. "Well, I've seen people die too," he said finally. Feeling bad he didn't think of a better reply.

"Nah, it's not the same," Aiden sighed. "Everyone I trained with in class is gone now. I'm the last one left. It's not easy being the last. It makes you feel lonely."

Lonely. Michael felt that way now. It was a lonely life to be in the H group. "I'm sorry."

The man smiled. "Don't let me ruin your night. I just need to complain once in awhile. That's another thing that happens when you get too old. You start to talk too much."

Michael took a sip of the new drink that had been placed in front of him. He felt a tug on his shoulder and turned around, catching sight of Seven with two girls in his arms, the tall one he had danced with earlier and a new girl with light hair and eyes. "I finally found someone that'll dance with you. She thinks you're cute," Seven beamed loudly.

"Come on," the woman urged, grasping his shirt with painted nails. "Let's go."

Nodding, Michael let them lead him to the floor. He wasn't much of a dancer. They usually made fun of him for it, but it wasn't like he had anything better to do.

It wasn't on purpose.

The betrayal was too great. My best friend Seven had to die.

A couple days went by.

Michael had been sent to kill the Johnson family. Then Tara. But he had let Tara go. He wasn't sure why but he hadn't been able to do it.

Seven lay in the bunk beneath him, punching the top bunk and annoying Mihcael for no other reason than to be a dick.

"What're you doing?' Michael asked finally.

"Just trying to get your attention," he said.

"Why's that?"

He could hear Seven's reply from beneath him. "You haven't been yourself. I was wondering what's up."

Michael folded his arms behind his head, laying flat on his back as he looked up at the ceiling. It wasn't something he felt like talking about. "She looks a lot like her, her friend Stella Johnson. Did you know that?"

"Who looks like Stella?"

"Tara Jones. The one I'm supposed to go back and kill again. She looks just like Stella."

"The saint woman, right?"

"Yeah."

"I didn't really notice." Seven commented. "Is that what's bothering you?"

"It's not just that," Michael said. He lowered his voice, not wanting to wake up the rest of the men. "It's just, I let her go thinking I couldn't do it. I just couldn't kill her. I thought of Stella and her family and how terrible I felt for killing them and I couldn't do it. I couldn't kill their friend Tara too. So I let her go. Now Andras wants me to go back and get her for good. I have to relive that stupid night all over again."

"Deja vu, huh."

"Pretty much. They have the exact same face. You think something like that's a coincidence?"

"Oh, I don't know," Seven replied, letting out a breath. "I really have no idea about stuff like that. Just try not to let it get to you. We got enough going on, you know?"

"I guess you're right."

The corpses hung from wire and moved in circles around Micheael. They spun and danced. They laughed and screamed at him, crying out, "Scared little Michael! Scared Little Michael!"

The betrayal had been so great, he didn't have any choice but to kill Seven. He hadn't any choice but to let him die.

Seven stood outside of Tara's apartment building, the night before she took the flight to Germany. Michael had just left Tara's apartment and given her the envelope of money, to find Seven standing outside of the apartment building. Michael watched him, his own gun raised in front of him. They faced one another in a standoff, neither moving nor breaking their stare.

"Andras sent you?" Michael asked even though it was obvious. The rage was impossible to suppress. Seven had betrayed him. He was here to kill Michael for not finishing the job, and then probably to go and kill Tara right afterwards. Michael knew what that meant. It meant he couldn't lose.

"You know I don't have any choice, Fifty-six," Seven said, sounding angry and frustrated. "You never should've failed. You should've just killed the stupid bitch."

"Fuck you, Seven."

They fired, moving quickly in opposite directions. There was no turning back. It could never be the same again. He wasn't welcome there anymore. The H Group was his enemy, along with everyone in it. Michael dodged behind a bush and Seven did the same at the opposite end of the lawn. They were all enemies now. He didn't have any choice but to fight them.

Michael made a dash forward toward Seven, narrowly missing a shot to the throat, and fired at Seven once more. Seven jumped back, falling when the bullet entered his leg and he fell to the ground. Michael regained his balance and they were aiming at each other again. Michael aimed downward and Seven's gun raised from his place on the floor.

Seven hesitated, as if regretting their battle, and Michael fired mercilessly. The bullet entered Seven's chest. Narrowing his eyes, Michael fired again and again until the sound of empty clicking sounded only. The devastated body lay in a heap on the floor, blood pouring out from the open wounds. Michael watched him for a moment, watching as the life poured from his companion's body.

It was over.

Seven was dead.

It hadn't been on purpose. It wasn't his fault.

He cried. Seven was dead.

It hadn't been on purpose that he killed Seven,

but the betrayal had been too great.

Michael woke suddenly.

Awakening from the nightmare.

He wiped at his face, feeling uncomfortable as he did so, still riding on the bus.

Not his fault, he thought.

It wasn't his fault that he killed Seven. The betrayal had been so great, that he hadn't any choice but to finish him off. He put his hands over his face and began to cry.

I realized finally what I had done. I had murdered my best friend. Eleven years later and my friend's death still haunted me. I had never told

Tara what I had done. Depsite the fact that i had done the deed to save her life and potentially my own.

Why did I do that?

Just to save a woman I barely knew?

Yes I loved her now but could I love her forever.

What did it mean to be in love.

Why did I do these things for a woman who could never return the favor.

My life.

My entire life had been full of sacrifice. I had sacrificed my very existence to save Tara. I had sacrficed ally after ally, friend after friend, and even my best friend Seven.

Why had I done those things

and what could I do to make my past hurt less.

I lowered myself in the chair on the bus.

To Hell I'll fall.

I sing quietly to myself.

for murder and theft and deceit

and I may never see you again

my love.

for you are not a killer like me.

What does it mean to kill.

and who am I to say I know.

I was a murderer once

and I was no saint.

Saints.

Like you sisters and father and mother that I killed.

Why did I do the things I did.

and if there is forgiveness.

why does it hurt so much.

As death claimed the lives of all my colleagues.

I am alone.

I have survived.

and I am alone.

who am I to survive?

To kill and kill and kill and be the last one left.

Who is to say that love and life are worth such violence.

Tara. If I killed for your sake.
Does that mean our love is official? Eternal? More real?
Why did I do those things and what can I do to heal the pain.
I give up.
Tara. I can't hold you any longer.
After reading Lace's journal.
I can no longer be with you, Tara,
the only woman I ever truly loved,
for I have betrayed you in my heart for a dead woman.

Assassin number Seven, deceased.

CHAPTER 2 prologue

"I cry.
I love you.
Don't disappear forever.
You promised you wouldn't.
I love you Michael.
You'll come back won't you?"

Tara Jones

CHAPTER 2

It's not normal that I cry. I always thought tears were for children and I was no longer a bright eyed child that dreamed of becoming a unicorn one day.

I read Lace's diary and I understood something.

Both she and I had been in love with the same man.

And Michael had left and may never come back now that he knew that Lace had killed herself over Michael and Tara's wedding. Tears spilled down my face as I read the diary, realizing that Lace had gone through so much and kept the entire thing to herself.

Michael, when you walked out, I was despaired.

A love that could not be repaired.

Your love is now far behind.

My darling, you are no longer mine.

I put the diary down and realize that without Michael. I am no longer angelic and evolved and truly a person.

Instead I am petty and evil and jealous and angry at Michael for leaving and God only knew if he'd come back or not.

Even when he's in your arms.

Love is not eternal.

It leads to loss.

Why do we do these things. Knowing it will end someday.

Why do we start something, knowing it will only go away when we need it the most.

CHEMICALS.

"Your sisters and father and mother are dead. What is there to live for? What good does it do to be the only surviving member of the family."

Michael had said this to me years ago. Why hadn't I listened to him. Because right now I wanted to die. My life. Why had I begged him so intensely to spare it. Maybe he had been right when he said there was nothing worth it to live for.

RUNNING ON PURE CHEMICAL.

HUMAN.

ROBOT.

THE HUMAN MACHINE.

WHY DO I FEAR DEATH.

BECAUSE I AM CHEMICALLY INCLINED TO DO SO.

Those are the thoughts I had thought.

I was becoming human again.

A human robot

a petty and simple machine that sat there and did nothing until it was told to.

I think of my jealousy and petty anger and I cry harder. Why did I have fall in love with someone so deeply that it broke my heart when he left. It hurt. It hurt so much.

CHEMICALS.

RUNNING ON PURE CHEMICALS.

I'm jealous and angry.

My body is no longer my own.

I feel controlled.

and I feel fake.

I have gone backwards and become what I hate the most.

The most pathetic person in the universe.

The assassins.

Guns.

My broken television that I shot in a fit of rage that night that Michael had visited me.

My shattered reality.

I hope things get better?

Right?

RIght???

God.

Why are we here and what are we supposed to be doing?

Once I said I would rather die than walk alone. If a spiritual journey is what I must go on then at least let there be love in my life and someone to keep me company. But there was no love and no hope and no good and no angelic evolution and only a backwards progress from the place I had begun.

There are words for my feelings for you Michael. You are my twilight. My starry sky. You are the world to me and I need you. My heart needs you and so does my mind and body. When you aren't here. I die a little bit.

I cry.

I love you.

Don't disappear forever.

You promised you wouldn't.

I love you Michael.

You'll come back won't you?

CHAPTER 3 prologue

"You never came back
And I think that it's like poison to think it.
but poison is good and strong and potent
and I think I would like to take some.
Someday. I'll tell you my story Michael.
And you will fall into my arms and tell me that you love
me still."

~ Tara Jones

CHAPTER 3

I drop the bag I had brought with me and gaze around Lace's empty trailer. The door had been unlocked and it appeared that the place had been unoccupied all year.

I lay down on the dusty unmade bed and think about Lace and what it had felt like for her to be with me. The nights we had spent together had been entrancing. I missed her. It wasn't long before I fancied she'd walk in just as I am about to give up and tell me she loved me and everything would be okay, just like she used to when I was being held hostage by H GROUP.

But she didn't show up.

Instead, her friends show up at the door and let themselves in. "She's still not here," he hears them whisper. "I don't think she's coming back."

"Michael!" Amanda says in surprise, pushing back dark hair behind her ear. "What are you doing here?"

"Just waiting for Lace to get here," I mumbled.

"She's been missing for a year, scum," Witherspoon spat. "This is your fault, you know. You never should've sent her that wedding invitation. She loved you, you know. She loved you so much and you rub salt into the wound and rub it in by making her watch you guys get married. What are you? Some kind of idiot?????"

Amanda slaps Witherspoon lightly over the shoulder. "Stop it. He doesn't need to hear this. She's gone. Screaming at him isn't going to bring her back."

"Did she do it? Kill herself? Where's she buried."

"We don't know. She never came home and she left behind a diary saying she was going to commit suicide."

"I read the diary."

"So you know what you meant to her, jerk," Witherspoon muttered.

"Where did you see her last?"

"Don't ask us," Penelope replied. "She could be anywhere. Or dead like it says in the diary. How are we supposed to know. We don't know any more than you do. She never used to tell us anything, if you know what I mean. She was a very private person."

Michael sighs and gets off the bed, headed out of the trailer without another word. He pulls out his cell phone and calls Wolf, the assassin that had brought him the diary the day before.

"Hello?"

"It's me Fifty-six."

"I know who this is."

"Listen. Where's Lace. You brought the diary. Where's the body?"

"Don't know. I ran away very shortly after you did. You'd have to talk to Seventeen. He was heir after you. Ask him and he'll tell you."

"Thanks."

I hang up and call Seventeen and ask Seventeen to meet me at the bar we all used to hang out at when we were assassins.

When I get there, Seventeen is already seated on the couch, a chick seated next to him.

"Fifty -six," he smiles.

"Hey."

"Meet Anna," Seventeen says. "My lovely wife."

"Nice to meet you."

"Where's Tara? Didn't think to bring her along. It would've been fine if you did. We don't bite."

"I'm not quite following. Why aren't you threatening me?"

"Such harsh words in the presence of a lady," Seveteen reprimanded.

"Look, I didn't come to chit chat. Where's Lace?"

"Probably in the pile of rubbish at H Group."

"Which he dissolved," Anna spoke up. "We dissolved it together, right honey?"

"Thats right doll," Seventeen smiled, rubbing his nose against hers.

"I'm leaving," Fifty-six said.

"No stay stay we'd love to chat with you a little longer."

"No thank you. I'm leaving." Fifty-Six turned around and left, and began walking the mile to H Headquarters.

313

He found the artifical tree elevator and dialed the password. When nothing happened. He frowned.

He went behind it and pushed away piles of leaves to the emergency exit and entrance and opened the trap door in the dirt open, revealing a dark staircase. Pulling out a flashlight, he made his way down the dark staircase and followed it about a mile underground. The flashlight grew dim and he shook it, wishing he had brought batteries.

He made his way down a narrow passage until he reached his old room. The room was empty save for some candle light.

"Fifty six!" a voice shouted. "Good to see ya good to see ya. It's me. Assassin four-hundred."

"Four-hundred," I mumble, blinking in surprise. I turn off the flashlight and head inside. Giving the man a hug. "What are you doing here?"

"Now that we're all broken up, just thought I'd hang around. This place is as good as any when it comes to finding a place to sleep at night. Hardly any rats at all if you know what I mean."

"I see."

"So what'cha here for. Here to visit me or something?"

"Not quite."

"What is it then?"

"Do you know where Lace's body is."

"Probably still in Andras room with Andras. They died in bed together, Funniest thing. Looked like murder, but then again, what is there other than murder, if you know what I mean."

"I see. I'd like to check it out myself if you don't mind."

"Hell, do whatever you like. Take a candle with you if you need some light. It gets really dark since the generator stopped running a couple months back."

"Thank you, my friend." I say. I take the candle holder and lit candle and head out of the room. I head slowly down the metal corridor, blood on the walls and floors replaced with corrosion and rust.

The place is dead, empty, silent, and dark.

I realize there are no terrified screams echoing from beneath the floors. No smell of congealed blood and guts. I feel sick at the memory of such and have to hold back from throwing up.

I get Andras's room and push open the ajar door. When I get inside, I stare in wonder at the room, dusty but in almost exact state it had been in the year before when he had decided to try to assassinate the boss himself and attempt to run away.

I think of Tara, remembering the sacrifices once more that I had made just to be with her. If I thought about it too deeply, I could leave forever now and nothing bad would happen to her. She would be just fine.

Love.

Love and loss.

Loss.

Loss and love.

What was the difference anymore when one thing just led to the other. And I am sad to think that I had spent ten years of agonizing time as a hostage and assassin just to realize later that maybe I was at a time of loss and not love.

What I'm trying to say is that I no longer wish to be with Tara. I wish to be alone. I am probably the worst person in the world for saying this but love is not an eternal contract. I don't have to be with her anymore to keep her safe so maybe I won't.

That's all I can think.

If she'll be fine on her own, why wouldn't I wander the world my own man and make a life for myself, by myself.

How ironic.

How sad.

I loved you so hard.

It drove me mad.

My heart it breaks.

That's right it broke.

When I realized.

Our contract broke.

That the love that binds.

in fact is not forever.

And our love was finite.

the time we spent together.

So I will sit and think awhile.

to figure out if you are the one.

and when it's over

and when it's all done.

I'll fly right back

as birds they do.

When the time is right.

I'll be with you.

I find Lace on the bed with Andras, blankets cover their naked bodies and I can tell that they have been dead for several months now. I see the dried dark bodies, their faces withered like prunes and their jaws hanging open. I recognize Lace by her lovely hair and the pendant around her neck being the one I gave her back when we were friends.

My fingers go to the necklace and unclasp it. I sigh, holding it up and staring at the pendant. On the back are the carvings of me and her initials.

Lace.

My heart it aches.

I can't take it.

She's gone

And there's nothing I can do to bring her back.

I put the pendant necklace on around my own neck and clasp it.

Then I lean forward and kiss Lace on the forehead.

Goodbye Lace.

You're gone

and there are no tears. No funeral. No getting married or running away from the truth. I hadn't been there for you and you have died.

I'm sorry I hurt you so badly.

And I hope you aren't mad.

It's been a year since the wedding.

and I'm terribly sad

to think you suffered.

forgive me for never coming home.

and expecting you to love me as a friend only.

You're gone now

and I regret hurting you.

Good bye lace.

I never meant to make you cry.

and in the end.

lose your life.

I leave the room, candle in hand. Tears begin to fall and I wipe them away frantically.

Tara. How could I possible be with you now that Lace is gone and died for my sake.

Tara I'm so sorry.

I may have to lose you too.

CHAPTER 4 prologue

"I'm dying without you.
Come home soon.
And I'll be waiting for you.
For you see.
You ruin me."

Tara Jones

CHAPTER 4

I sit before the fireplace, lit cigarette in hand and I smoke it, thinking that I wished they were menthol. Without hesitaton, I lean forward and take Lace's diary and toss it into the flames.

I sit back again and smoke from the cigarette, inhaling deeply. I watch as the diary burns up in flames.

Lace.

I hated her.

And I hated that Michael had loved her once.

It has been three weeks since Michael had disappeared. If he planned to come home, he hadn't told her, and where he was, she had no idea. She could only hope she'd see him again someday. And that they would be together once more.

I'm dying without you.

Come home soon.

And I'll be waiting for you.

For you see.

You ruin me.

Three weeks later and

You never came back

And I think that it's like poison to think it.

but poison is good and strong and potent

and I think I would like to take some.

Someday. I'll tell you my story Michael.

And you will fall into my arms and tell me that you love me still.

And I stare at a bottle of painkillers on the coffee table and consider taking the whole bottle. I would do that you know. Kill myself. And if you never came home, you'd never know I was gone. Never even notice I had disappeared from this world.

I sigh.

The world was full of this or that. This one told me that life was hard, but that told me that living without love was even harder.

I miss him.

And with every breath I take.

I fear I'm closer to death.

I don't want to live without you.

And if you don't come back.

In the name of love and loss.

I would do that you know.

Die instead of waiting for you.

I'm the kind of stupid person that does things like that.

without you.

I may not want to live at all.

I fall asleep. In my dreams I picture myself on a beach laying on a folding chair and beside me, laying in chairs as well are Bee, Lace and Snow white the maid, who I had never met but could understand somehow was a real person and important to me somehow.

I am beyond myself as for some reason in this dream I know exactly who they all are and why they are here.

"Have you guys come to take me too?" I ask. "To the land of the dead." It wasn't that I feared death, but I was afraid of missing Michael too much.

"Yes, dear," Bee replies, pulling off a pair of sunglasses.

It is bright out and the sky is a clear blue, the waters crystal clear.

"I hope you're okay with that."

"Even in my dreams, and in death, your ghosts haunt me," I smile. There are tears in my eyes as I say. "You've come for me still, even now that I am saved from Hell itself. Even as the hit is taken off of me and I am free, you've come to steal my soul from me. Why is that? Did you hate me so?"

"Yes. As we have all died in the name of love and loss, so shall you die too. Dearest Tara." the maid replies.

"Love and loss." Bee says.

"And the way it'll be," says Lace.

"Don't forget me, even when I'm gone." Bee finishes.

"It's people like you, he told me," says Tara, "that make life worth nothing to me. Do you think it could be worth something. Even now. Even now that I am going to die."

"Yes. Life could be worth something. It could be worth the dark times and be filled with LIGHT," Bee replied.

"LIGHT," Lace repeats. "Are you ready Tara?"

"Not only am I ready, I'm already there," I laugh. I wake up and find myself already in the process of swallowing the entire bottle of painkillers.

Poison for the body.

Without you here.

I think I should like to take some.

CHAPTER 5 prologue

"In the name of love and loss.
I would do that you know.
Die instead of waiting for you.
I'm the kind of stupid person that does things like that."

~Tara Jones.

CHAPTER 5

I do not decide to go home to Tara right away. I sit in a bar and think to myself first about why I'm here and what I had meant when I rejected Lace and married Tara instead.

I think about never going home and what it would feel like to be alone forever.

I think about my loves and my losses and if I should even consider being a friend or foe to the world.

I think of Tara again.

Chemically. I loved her like a doll. She was my present for all the work I had done in my life to be free of the H GROUP and to protect her life had meant more to me than anything else in the world.

Chemically, I loved her as my wife.

Chemically I loved her like my friend.

But chemicals are trite and minor and petty and not necessarily the answer. I don't want to be a human machine. And if a human machine is what I was, then by all means, let the machine die and let the human version of me be born.

I want to evolve.

Like Tara did.

I want to become something I never was before, a thinking, feeling, happy human that could harbor love for another without regret.

Now, I felt like the chemicals were waning.

I pull out a picture of Tara from my wallet. My face is ragged with beard and my clothes are dirty and I haven't showered. I stare at the picture and think of her.

Chemicals are waning.

Waning.

Waning.

I feel like I have grown up a little bit. I have evolved into a man that can truly forgive, truly move on, and truly love someone. I feel as though I have finally let go of my past and embraced my future.

Chemicals drove me to fight and to love. Now I was no longer a machine, as Tara had put it but a true person capable of feelings.

If I had to live one life, I wanted to live that life with Tara from now on.

I wanted her to be there too.

I feel sad and I feel glad and happy all at the same time.

In the past.

I broke your heart

made of glass

it broke apart.

and now I'm sorry

for what I've done.

I did not think

I could go on.

I feel as though I could forgive Lace now for dying and even go so far as to say that I forgive Tara for marrying me despite my being a terrible person. I think that I love Tara once more. Not in the way that a man loves a woman, but in the way two souls can communicate with one another on a higher spiritual level. On a transcendent level, she was my everything.

Tara was my soulmate.

I had no doubt.

And I didn't want to live without her.

Why are we here had always bothered me when I was younger. Were we here to suffer or be glad? Were we here to love or to lose and why do the first when it led to the last?

WHY ARE WE HERE?

It's always bothered me.

And I think that I knew then that Tara was the reason I existed and the reason I continue to exist. I believe in her. In her love for me and in my love for her.

Love is real.

Damn it.

It is.

And I know I love her now.

I can feel my love for her coursing throughout my heart and soul and radiating out towards the heavens. I love her and I will never abandon her. Never leave her.

Just love her forever no matter what.

That was how I felt at that moment.

I drink the rest of my beer and head home, taking a bus the rest of the way home.

Your heart.

My heart.

I watch them beat.

Throughout a life

of intense blood and heat.

And when we met, our chemicals declined.

I don't know how. I don't know why.

And we evolved into beings

that knew.

That love was real.

and our love true.

Together we conquer the world.

Apart we die slowly.

If I ever I thought you were going to hurt yourself love, I never would've left you alone for three weeks.

But you'll forgive me, won't you?

When I get home, Tara is laying on the floor, unconscious, with an empty bottle of painkillers at her side.

CHAPTER 6

I awaken and youre here by me.

My love, forgive me for scaring you.

In God, I believe. I do. I believe in him now.

I believe in his goodness, in his righteousness, and in his hand that gives.

The world is good Michael and we are here because it is good and God is good and so are people.

I'm grateful, Michael, for everything.

~ Tara Jones.

I wake up and I am in a hospital bed. Michael is beside me. I smile. I am relieved to see him. The woman were unable to take me and the prophetic dream proved false.

Once again, throughout hardship and strife, I find I am still alive and I am in fact not alone.

"You came back," I mumble quietly.

He kisses me and tells me he is sorry for leaving and will never leave again. He tells me he loves me and I tell him that I love him back.

I think about God and cosmos and realize that maybe things aren't as bad as they seemed. For every tear was a smile and for every take there was a give.

TO GIVE.

I feel it now.

Hope in my heart.

Why are we here made sense when I was younger but now I knew it was not about why we were here. It was actually for me to tell God the answer of why. And everyone's answer would be different and beautiful in their own way. For me, to live, was to be with Michael. And that meant more to me than anything else in the universe.

I think about the people that had passed away and feel sorry but know that heaven is real and someday we would all see each other again. That was what made life worth living. The fact that we had each other forever.

In this world.

In this life.

We could be evolved and transcendent and live in the name of love and not loss. We would never live in loss again. Someday, forever even, we could live in a world where we lose less and less forever.

There was such a thing as second chances.

I believed this was my second chance to be happy.

Because happiness, perhaps, was all I really was looking for this whole time.

It wasn't so much about the question anymore.

It wasn't so much about the answer anymore.

It was more about the way the question and answer presented itself to me fully instead.

Happiness.

Where was it?

Maybe it had been here all along.

I used to say to Michael that we'd be happy someday.

And I'd like to think that perhaps he was right when he told me we already were.

I hold his hand and think that I am glad we are fine.

I think I am glad that everything is better now and that life can go on as it always had but with a better perspective.

I awaken and you're here by me.

My love, forgive me for scaring you.

In God, I believe. I do. I believe in him now.

I believe in his goodness, in his righteousness, and in his hand that gives.

The world is good Michael and we are here because it is good and God is good and so are people.

I'm grateful, Michael, for everything.

EVERYTHING.

The universe continued to turn, from beginning to end, everlasting, ever growing, it never stops. Today was no exception. The universe turned and LIFE CONTINUES FOREVER.

Tara and Michael alive and married

Printed in the United States
By Bookmasters